"There, 'tis done," said the vicar.

"So it is." The Honourable Gideon Albury smiled down at his new wife. "I think we can dispense with this now."

He reached for her veil, but she quickly put her gloved hand over his.

"Not yet," she whispered.

He laughed. "Be careful, my love, I shall begin to think I have married a little prude!"

He expected to hear her delicious throaty laugh but she was silent, merely putting her fingers on his arm as he escorted her to the door.

After the darkness of the stone building the spring sunshine was almost blinding when they stepped outside. He stopped and turned to her again.

"Now, Miss Propriety, let me kiss you... Good God!" He stepped back, his eyes widening with horror as he looked down into the face of a stranger.

* * *

Lady Beneath the Veil
Harlequin® Historical #1174—February 2014

Author Note

The very first page in *Lady Beneath the Veil* is, in fact, the very first idea I had for this story. I wanted to explore what would happen if a man suddenly found himself married to a woman he had never seen before. Of course this is not a new idea—throughout British history many sons and daughters of the aristocracy have been married off for political or economic reasons to virtual strangers—but this was to be no reasoned alliance: it was to be a cruel hoax.

You might think that no one would play such a trick.... Well, one only has to look into history to see that life in Georgian England could be cruel and brutally short and, as if in response, the Georgians could be tough, crude and boisterous. There are the much-recorded practical jokes of Sir Francis Blake Delaval, of Seaton Delaval in Northumberland, who played the most outrageous practical jokes upon visitors.

Mechanical hoists were installed so that when unsuspecting guests were undressing the bedroom walls would suddenly be lifted up, exposing them. In one bedroom the bed could be lowered into a tank of cold water, and in another guests would wake to find everything upside down—the whole room inverted—with furniture suspended from the "floor" and a chandelier rising up from the middle of the "ceiling." It must have been a most unnerving experience. One elderly (but rich) widow was even persuaded to marry Sir Francis after a charade involving a fortune-teller and an "accidental" meeting.

So I thought the marriage of Gideon and Dominique might well have happened—but what about the happy-ever-after? Could such a marriage work when it was not the fairy-tale wedding that either of them had wanted? Well, they struggle, of course, but I think I have found a way for them to resolve their differences and find happiness together. I hope you agree. Please feel you can contact me at www.sarahmallory.com.

Do look out for *At the Highwayman's Pleasure,* coming March 2014. This is linked to *Lady Beneath the Veil.*

Lady Beneath the Veil

Sarah Mallory

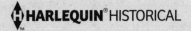

Recycling programs
for this product may
not exist in your area.

ISBN-13: 978-0-373-29774-0

LADY BENEATH THE VEIL

Copyright © 2014 by Sarah Mallory

Printed in U.S.A.

HARLEQUIN®

™ www.Harlequin.com

***Available from Harlequin® Historical and
SARAH MALLORY***

Look for

At the Highwayman's Pleasure
Coming March 2014

**Other works include
Harlequin Historical Undone! ebooks**

ΔThe Tantalizing Miss Coale

*linked by character
ΔThe Notorious Coale Brothers
§part of the Castonbury Park Regency miniseries

**Did you know that these novels are also
available as ebooks? Visit www.Harlequin.com.**

To Sally,
my best friend through good times and bad.

SARAH MALLORY

was born in Bristol, and now lives in an old farmhouse
on the edge of the Pennines with her husband and
family. She left grammar school at sixteen to work in
companies as varied as stockbrokers, marine engi-
neers, insurance brokers, biscuit manufacturers and
even a quarrying company. Her first book was published shortly after the birth of her daughter. She has
published more than a dozen books under the pen
name of Melinda Hammond, winning the Reviewers'
Choice Award from www.singletitles.com for *Dance
for a Diamond* and the Historical Novel Society's
Editors' Choice for *Gentlemen in Question*. As Sarah
Mallory she is the winner of the Romantic Novelists'
Association's RONA Rose® Award for 2012 and 2013
for *The Dangerous Lord Darrington* and *Beneath
the Major's Scars*.

Chapter One

'*Those whom God has joined together let no one put asunder!'*

The words boomed around the small church, echoing off the walls. The Honourable Gideon Albury grinned down at the heavily veiled figure at his side. Bless her, she was taking maidenly modesty to new heights!

Perhaps she thought it would inflame him, but she did that perfectly well without dressing as a nun. With her voluptuous body, golden curls and cornflower-blue eyes, she was a rare beauty. And that little trick she had of peeping up at him from under her lashes, those blue eyes promising the lush delights to come—his body hardened with anticipation. At last he would be able to enjoy those ample curves to the full!

Not that the little darling had flaunted her charms. She was, after all, a lady—the Earl of Martlesham's cousin, in fact. He would not else have contemplated marriage without his father's approval. Depraved as Lord Rotham might think him, he had not sunk so low that he would marry out of his sphere. But 'fore Gad, Gideon had never before seen such perfection in a gently bred young lady. She had allowed Gideon a glimpse of her pretty ankles, his hands had spanned that tiny waist and her plump, snow-white breast had been just crying out to be kissed. By heaven, just the thought of it made it difficult to concentrate on the marriage service. The register was produced. Gideon scrawled his own name carelessly and watched as his bride added her name to his. He guessed that damned veil was making it difficult for her to see because her hand shook a little as she held the pen. As a witness, Martlesham signed with a flourish and grinned.

'There—'tis done.'

'So it is.' Gideon smiled down at his new wife. 'I think we can dispense with this now.'

He reached for her veil, but she quickly put her gloved hand over his.

'Not yet,' she whispered.

He laughed.

'Be careful, my love, I shall begin to think I have married a little prude!'

He expected to hear her delicious, throaty laugh, but she was silent, merely putting her fingers on his arm as he escorted her to the door.

After the darkness of the stone building the spring sunshine was almost blinding when they stepped outside. He stopped and turned to her again.

'Now, Miss Propriety, let me kiss you… Good God!' He stepped back, his eyes widening with horror as he looked down into the face of a complete stranger.

Chapter Two

Dominique stood very still, staring up into the shocked face of her new husband. It was all there, everything she had expected: horror, revulsion, disgust. She had known how it must seem to him once the trick was revealed. He pushed his fingers through his auburn hair, disturbing the carefully arranged disorder, while behind them Max's cruel laugh rang out.

'Caught you there, Albury!'

'But I don't understand. Your cousin—'

'This *is* my cousin.'

Max chortled and Dominique's heart went out to the man standing before her. He looked stunned.

As well he might. Instead of the beautiful, voluptuous blonde he had courted for the past two months he was married to a diminutive brunette whom he had never seen before in his life.

'Is something amiss?' The vicar looked from one to the other before directing a vaguely worried look towards Max. 'Lord Martlesham?'

'No, no, nothing's wrong,' declared Max, still chuckling. 'The groom is struck dumb by the enormity of the occasion, that's all.' He began shepherding the guests away from the church. 'Come along, everyone, the carriages are waiting!'

'Just a moment!' The man beside her did not move, except to shake her hand from his arm. 'Where is Dominique?'

'Lord, Albury, have you not understood it yet? You have married her!' Max gave him a push. 'Come along, man, don't stand there gawping. Let us return to the Abbey.'

'Please.' Dominique forced her vocal cords to work. 'Come back to the Abbey and all this can be explained.'

Frowning, he grabbed her arm and set off for the gate with Dominique almost running to keep up with him. As was usual with weddings, the path was lined with well-wishers who showered them with rice as they hurried to the carriage. It was decorated with ribbons for the occasion, the Martlesham coat of arms displayed prominently on the door. Without ceremony her escort bundled Dominique into the carriage, climbed in after her and the door was slammed upon them. Max's grinning face appeared in the window.

'Now then, Gideon, try to contain your lust until after the wedding breakfast. The journey from here to the Abbey ain't long enough to tup a woman properly. I know, I've tried it!'

Dominique closed her eyes in mortification. The carriage began to move and the raucous laughter was left behind them.

'So, this was one of Max's little tricks.'

Dominique looked at Gideon. His voice was calm, but there was a dangerous glitter in his hazel eyes that made her think he might be about to commit murder. She swallowed.

'Yes.'

'And everyone at the Abbey was privy to the joke, except me.'

'You and…my mother.'

'Max told me she was too unwell to attend the ceremony.'

Dominique bowed her head.

'She does not know. *Maman* would never have agreed to such a scheme.'

'I take it the female I knew as Dominique was hired for the part?'

She nodded.

'An actress. Agnes Bennet.'

'And a damned good one. She fooled me into thinking she was a lady. Whereas you—' His lip curled. 'You may be Max's cousin, but no true lady would lend herself to this, this *joke*.'

His contempt flayed her. Given time, she could explain to him why she had agreed to Max's outrageous scheme, but they had already arrived at the Abbey. She waited in silence for the carriage to stop and a liveried footman to leap forwards and open the door. Her companion jumped out first and with exaggerated courtesy put out his hand to her.

'Well, madam, shall we go in to the wedding breakfast?'

Miserably, Dominique accompanied him into the house.

'Now, perhaps you will explain to me what the hell is going on.'

Gideon looked about him at the company assembled in the dining room. The servants had been dismissed and it was only the twenty or so guests who had comprised Lord Martlesham's house party for the past two months—with the exception of the blonde beauty, of course. The woman he had believed was Martlesham's cousin. She had been replaced by the poor little dab of a girl who was now his wife.

Everyone stood around, ignoring the festive elegance of the dining table, all gleaming silver and sparkling glass, set out in readiness for the wedding breakfast. His eyes raked the crowd, but no one would meet his gaze.

'It's a practical joke, old boy,' said Max, who was helping himself to a glass of brandy from the decanter on the sideboard.

'Not one that I appreciate!' Gideon retorted.

Max turned to him, still smiling.

'No? Strange, I thought you would, given what happened at Covent Garden last year.'

'Ah…' Gideon nodded slowly '…so that is it. You are paying me back for stealing the divine Diana from under your nose!'

The scene came back to him. He had been one of a dozen rowdy, drunken bucks crowding into the dressing rooms after the performance. Max was paying court to a pretty little opera dancer, but Gideon knew from her meaningful smiles and the invitation in her kohl-lined eyes that she would happily give herself to the highest bidder.

'Confound it, Albury, I had been working on that prime article for weeks, then just when I thought she was going to fall into my lap you offer her a *carte blanche*!'

Gideon felt his temper rising. There was a world of difference between competing for the favours of a light-skirt and trapping him into marriage!

'And because I bested you on that occasion you concocted this elaborate charade?'

'Why, yes, and I thought it rather neat, actually,' returned Max, sipping his brandy. 'I hired Agnes Bennet to play my cousin and you fell for her—quite besotted, in fact. All I had to do then was persuade you to propose. Of course, it helped that you were still smarting from the roasting your father gave you at Christmas and ripe for any mischief that would pay him back.'

Gideon could not deny it. He recalled that last, fraught meeting with his father. They had rowed royally. If he was honest, Gideon had already been a little tired of Max and his constant tricks and stratagems, but he did not like his father criticising his friends. He had lost his temper, declaring that he would do what he wanted with his life. He remembered storming out of the house, declaring, 'I will make friends with whom I like, do what I like, marry whom I like!'

How unwise he had been to relay the whole incident to Martlesham.

The earl continued, 'You knew that marrying any cousin of mine would anger your father. It helped, of course, that she was such a little beauty. A typical English rose.'

'Couldn't wait to get her into bed, eh?' cried one of Max's cronies, a buck-toothed fop called Williams.

Dear heaven, Gideon wondered why he had never noticed before just what a hideous smirk the fellow had! Max filled a second glass with brandy and handed it to him.

'Then, of course, you said you could never marry a Frenchie.'

'Well, what of that?' said Gideon, stiffening.

Max's smile grew.

'It so happens that my dear cousin here is most definitely French. Ain't that so, m'dear?'

The girl made no answer, save for a slight nod of the head. Gideon's eyes narrowed.

'Reynolds is an English name. And you told me Dominique was an old family tradition...'

'Now there I admit I misled you, my boy. The name *is* a family tradition, but it belongs to her French ancestors, not mine.' Max's hateful smile widened. 'My dear Gideon, you should have looked more closely at the register before you signed it. You would have seen then that her father's name was *Rainault*, not Reynolds. Jerome Rainault, a wine merchant from Montpellier. A full-blooded Frenchman, Albury, and a paid-up Girondin to boot.'

'What!'

Gideon was surprised out of the dispassionate hauteur he had assumed. Max's pale blue eyes gleamed with malicious triumph.

'Oh, yes,' he said softly. 'You swore that the French were all your enemies, did you not? It seemed poetic justice to marry you off to a Frenchwoman.'

More of Gideon's last, heated exchange with his father flashed into his head.

'Martlesham is a bad lot,' the viscount had said. 'You should choose your friends more carefully.'

He had been angered by his father's words, but now the truth of them stung him even more.

Williams guffawed loudly. 'What a good joke. You have been well and truly duped, Albury! You fell head over heels for Max's actress, didn't you? He made the switch this morning. He even had shoes made with a heel so that you didn't see that your new bride was shorter than the lovely Agnes.'

Williams pushed his silver-topped cane under the bridal skirts, but the girl whipped herself away from him, her cheeks aflame with embarrassment. The others sniggered and Gideon cursed silently. How had he ever found their childish humour amusing?

He said furiously, 'This goes beyond a joke, Martlesham. This time you are meddling with peoples' lives.'

Max shrugged.

'We all found it devilishly amusin', old fellow.' He held out the glass. 'Here. Admit we caught you fair and square. Then let us enjoy the wedding *déjeuner* and afterwards I'll summon the vicar and my lawyer from the village and we can arrange to have the marriage annulled. After all, there's witnesses enough to the fact that you have been tricked.'

Gideon took the brandy and sipped it. Everyone around him was grinning, save the bride. The heat had left her cheeks and she now stood beside him, pale and silent. This slight, dark figure could not be less like the bride he had been expecting. The enormity of his folly hit him. He had not consulted his father about the marriage—a petty revenge against his parent for daring to ring such a peal over him at that last meeting. He had not even notified his lawyer, knowing that Rogers would demand settlements should be drawn up. In his eagerness to secure his bride he had accepted Max's assurances that they could deal with all the usual formalities later. Now he knew why and a cold fury seized him.

He said slowly, 'Admit I was tricked and become a laughing stock? No, I don't think so.'

It gave him some satisfaction to see the smiles falter. Max frowned. His bride turned to stare at him. Gideon forced a smile to his lips.

'No,' he drawled. 'I have to marry sometime. Your cousin will do as well as anyone, Martlesham. The marriage stands.'

* * *

'No!'

Dominique gasped out the word. This was not the way it was meant to be. She looked imploringly to her cousin, but the earl's face was a mask.

'Come.' Gideon was holding his hand out to her. 'Let us sit down and enjoy our first meal as man and wife.'

His tone brooked no argument. Reluctantly she accompanied the stranger who was now her husband to the table. Only he was not a stranger to her. For the past two months she had watched him from the shadows as he laughed and danced and flirted with the woman chosen to impersonate her. How Dominique wished that she was more like the beautiful Agnes, with her deep, throaty laugh and bewitching smile. She had watched Gideon fall in love with the actress and realised that she would willingly exchange her dusky locks and green eyes for blonde curls and cornflower-blue eyes if Gideon would give her just one admiring glance. Max had not objected when he discovered Dominique had dressed herself as a servant so that she could watch the courtship. Indeed, he had enjoyed the added piquancy her masquerade gave to the proceedings and gradually she had found herself being drawn ever closer to Gideon Albury. He was different from the others, more thoughtful, and lacking the cruel humour that characterised so many of Max's friends. She had thought at first that his lean face was a little austere, but she had seen the way his smile warmed his eyes and she had learned to listen out for his voice, deep and rich as chocolate.

And she had fallen in love.

If someone had told her she would lose her heart to a man who didn't even know she existed she would have said it was impossible, but somehow, over the weeks of watching and listening she had come to believe there was more to this handsome young buck than his devil-may-care attitude. She had seen the brooding look that would steal into his countenance when he thought no one was attending and had caught the fleeting sadness that occasionally clouded his eyes. In her disguise it had been difficult to avoid the leering glances and wandering hands of Max's other guests, but Gideon had not ogled her, and if he noticed her at all it was with a careless kindness, a word of thanks when she presented him with his drink or a quiet rebuke when one of his friends tried to importune her.

He was a true gentleman, even if today there was only anger in his tone and a touch of steel in his hazel eyes when they rested on her. He despised her and, knowing the part she had played in this charade, she could not blame him. She knew how she would feel if someone played such a trick upon her, so why should she be disappointed that the bridegroom should now look at her with such contempt? She felt sick at heart, but it would do no good to repine. She had made a bargain with Max, and if he kept it then all this charade would have been worth it.

Dominique partook very little of the food served at her wedding breakfast and even less of the wine. On the surface Gideon appeared to be at his ease, smiling and joking with his companions, the perfect bridegroom. But when he called for a toast and turned to salute her his eyes were cold and hard, and a little frisson of fear shivered down her spine.

At last the meal was over, but not her torment. People

were getting up, congregating in little groups. Gideon tapped his glass and brought a hush to the assembly.

'Carstairs, I cannot tell you how grateful I am to you for putting Elmwood Lodge at our disposal.' He rose and put his hands on the back of Dominique's chair. 'Now, *wife*, it is time you changed into your travelling dress and we will be away.'

She cast another startled glance at Max, who merely shrugged. Silently she rose, but as she passed her cousin she hesitated. Surely he would intervene now. She said quietly, 'The joke is played, my lord. I have done my part, pray you, call an end to it.'

To her dismay Max merely took her hand and raised it to his lips.

'Let me be the first to congratulate you, *Mrs Albury*.'

She gripped his hand, angered and frightened by his mocking smile.

'And my mother? You promised.'

Those haughty eyebrows lifted a fraction higher.

'I gave you my word, did I not?' He leaned a little closer and murmured, 'Go along, my dear, do not keep your husband waiting.'

Her lip curled and she wanted to retort, but Gideon was approaching, so she whisked herself out of the room.

Dominique went up to her bedchamber, seething with anger and not only for Max. She had lent herself to this and could hardly complain now if things did not go as she had expected. It had seemed so simple when the earl had explained it to her: the trick would be played and upon discovery the lawyers would be summoned, the sham marriage annulled and everything would be put right. Only Gideon was not playing by the same rules as her cousin. He wanted to continue the farce a little longer, to save face, to turn the joke on to her cousin and probably to punish her for her impudence in duping him. She glanced in the mirror, her spirits falling even further. It was inconceivable that he would really want to keep her as his wife, but for now she had no choice but to prepare to drive away with him.

The only gown she had with her was the olive-green walking dress she had arrived in. It was not new, but the colour suited her, and with its mannish cut and the gold frogging it looked well enough for an earl's cousin. The embroidered lace veil would fill in the low neckline and keep the cold March wind at bay. She squared her shoulders. If Gideon Albury wanted to continue with this charade it would have to do.

To her consternation everyone was gathered in the hall, waiting for her. They all seemed determined to pretend that this was any normal going-away ceremony. Max ran up the final few stairs and gave her his arm as though he was about to give her away all over again.

'I have had the maids fill a trunk for you,' he murmured. 'Can't have you going off without a rag to your back.'

He led her up to Gideon, who stood rigid and implacable. Dominique glanced once at his face—it could have been chiselled from stone, so cold and impassive did he look. Concealing a shudder, she dropped her eyes to his exquisitely embroidered waistcoat. Perhaps he had ordered it especially for the wedding, to impress his bride. She felt even more ashamed of allowing herself to be a part of Max's cruel scheme.

With much cheering they were escorted to the waiting travelling carriage, where her trunk was being strapped on the roof. She felt a light touch on her shoulder as the carriage pulled away.

'Well, madam, are you not going to smile for your guests?'

She shrugged off his hand.

'How far do you intend to carry this joke, sir?'

'Joke?' His voice was icy. 'I do not know what you mean, madam. It was Martlesham who played the joke.'

'And you have repaid him. He was quite shocked when you said the marriage would stand.'

'Yes, his reaction was delightfully amusing.'

'You have had your fun, sir,' she said coolly. 'Now I pray you will abandon this charade.'

'Oh, it is no charade, madam. I am in deadly earnest.'

She stared at him, a cold hand clutching at her heart when she saw his implacable look.

'But—but you never meant to marry me. You cannot *want* me for your bride.'

'Why not? As I told Max, I have to marry sometime, and you are as good as any other wife.' His eyes swept over her, as if stripping her naked and she felt a hot blush spreading up through her body. She realised for the first time how fully she had put herself in this man's power. She summoned up every ounce of indignation to respond.

'That is outrageous!'

'Outrageous or not, madam, you should have considered every possibility before you gave yourself to this plan. You married me, for better or worse. There is no way back.'

Unsettled by the look of horror on his companion's face, Gideon closed his eyes and feigned sleep. He was still furious at being duped into marriage, but he had some sympathy with his bride. Knowing Max, he suspected that pressure had been put on the chit to comply. But she could have declared herself in church, if she had really objected to the whole thing. No, he would punish her just a little more.

He wondered what they would find when they eventually reached Elmwood Lodge. Carstairs had almost choked on his wine when Gideon had reminded him that he had offered it—obviously no one had expected the marriage to go beyond the wedding ceremony, so no arrangements had been made. While everyone had waited for the bride to change her gown a rider had been despatched to Elmwood on a fast horse to notify the servants that a bride and groom were on their way.

How soon after they arrived he would call a halt to this masquerade Gideon had not yet decided.

When the carriage turned into the gates of Elmwood Lodge sometime later it was immediately apparent that the news of their arrival had been received with enthusiasm. The open gates were decorated with ribbons and as they bowled up to the entrance an elderly couple appeared, the man hurriedly buttoning his livery. Gideon recognised Chiswick, the butler and man of all work, and the woman following him in her snowy apron and cap was his wife and housekeeper of the lodge.

'Oh, lord,' Gideon muttered as the door was wrenched open. 'We are properly for it now.'

'Welcome, sir, madam! We are delighted you have come to Elmwood Lodge.' Mrs Chiswick almost hustled her husband out of the way as she greeted them with an effusion of smiles. 'If you would care to come into the parlour, you will find cakes and wine set out there, and a roaring fire. If we'd had more notice then the rest of the rooms would be ready for you, too, but they may take a while yet, although I have sent for Alice from the village to come and help me.'

Gideon jumped down and turned back to help his bride to alight. She did so silently, looking pale and dazed. He pulled her hand on to his sleeve and followed the still-chattering housekeeper into the house. The large, panelled hall had been hastily decorated with boughs of evergreens and spring flowers. Gideon's heart sank: the couple were clearly overjoyed to be entertaining a pair of newlyweds. He felt the fingers on his arm tremble and absently put his hand up to give them a reassuring squeeze.

More early spring flowers adorned the wainscotted parlour where a cheerful fire burned in the hearth and refreshments were set out on the table. Gideon waited until his garrulous hostess paused for breath, then said firmly, 'Thank you, Mrs Chiswick. We will serve ourselves.'

'Very well, sir. And...' She turned to look out of the window. 'Do your servants follow you?'

'No, we are quite alone.'

'Ah, of course.'

Her understanding smile brought a flush to Gideon's cheek and he dared not look at his companion to see the effect upon her, but as soon as they were alone he said, 'I beg your pardon. When Max told me your servant was remaining at Martlesham to look after your mother I thought it best to leave my man behind, too. Now I see that it has given rise to the very worst sort of speculation.'

'Very natural speculation, given the circumstances.'

Her calm response relieved his mind of one worry: she was not going to fall into hysterics. Yet he should not have been surprised. She could have no proper feeling to have lent herself to this madness in the first place.

He retorted coldly, 'These *circumstances*, as you describe them, are very much your own fault.'

'I am well aware of that.'

She took off her hat and gloves and untied the strings of her cloak. When he put his hands on her shoulders to take it from her she tensed, but did not shrug him off. He was standing so close behind her that he could smell her perfume, a subtle hint of lily of the valley that made him want to drop his head closer still, perhaps even to bend and place a kiss upon the slender white neck exposed to his view.

Shocked at his reaction, he drew back. This woman was nothing to him—how could he even contemplate making love to her? But the idea lingered and it disturbed him.

Gideon threw her cloak over a chair with his own greatcoat, placing his hat and gloves next to hers on the small side table. His temper was cooling and he was all too aware of their predicament. Perhaps it was not too late to remedy that. He dashed out of the room. He found the butler crossing the hallway and called to him as he ran to the main door.

'Has the coach gone? Quickly, man!'

'Y-yes, sir! As soon as you was set down. We took off the baggage and they was away, wanting to get somewhere near home before nightfall, there being no moon tonight.'

Gideon yanked open the door and looked out at the empty drive.

'But that was only minutes ago. We must fetch it back. There must be a horse in the stables you can send after it.'

Startled, the butler shook his head.

'I'm afraid not, sir. There's only Bessie, the cob, but she pulls the carts and has never worn a saddle in her life. I suppose old Adam could harness her up to the gig…'

Staring into the gathering darkness, Gideon realised it would be impossible for them to call back the carriage now.

'How far is it to the nearest town, or even the nearest inn?'

The butler looked at him with astonishment and Gideon thought grimly how it must look, the bridegroom wanting to run away before his wedding night! However, the truth would be even more unpalatable, so he remained silent while the man pondered his question.

'There ain't an inn, sir,' he said at last. 'Not one as would suit you, at any rate. And it's all of seven miles to Swaffham, but you wouldn't be wanting to set out tonight, not without a moon.'

'No, of course not.' With a shake of his head Gideon stepped back from the entrance, leaving Chiswick to close the door while he made his way back to the parlour. He could hardly complain. After all, he himself had hired the post-chaise and his instructions had been quite clear: it would not be required again for two weeks. He had fully intended to enjoy his honeymoon with his bewitching bride. Now he was stranded in the middle of nowhere with a young woman he had never met before today. And a respectable young woman at that, despite her part in this charade. Damn Max and his practical jokes!

Chapter Three

Gideon returned to find the lady in question pacing up and down the parlour. He said as calmly as he could, 'It seems we are stuck here, at least until the morning.'

'Was that not your intention?'

Her glance scorched him and he frowned.

'No, I had not thought it out. I was angry.'

'And now?'

'Now I realise that it would have been better if we had remained at the Abbey.' He paused. 'We are in the devil of a coil.'

She sighed. 'I know.'

His eyes fell on the table.

'Shall we sit down?' He held a chair for her, thinking that they were like two cats, warily circling each other. When they were both seated he filled two glasses and pushed one towards her. 'Why did you agree to Max's outlandish scheme? You do not look like the sort to indulge in practical jokes of your own accord.'

'No.' She put a small cake on to her plate and broke it into little pieces.

'Did he offer you money?'

'Something of that sort.'

'But you are his cousin.'

'An impoverished cousin. My mother brought me to England ten years ago, seeking refuge with her brother, the earl—Max's father. When Max inherited Martlesham he also inherited us. We have been living off charity ever since. A few months ago Max set us up in a cottage in Martlesham village.' Her fingers played with the crumbs on her plate. 'He promised... If I agreed to take part in his scheme, he would sign the property over to my mother and give her a pension for the rest of her life.'

'And for this you would marry a stranger.'

Her head came up at that. She said angrily, 'Do you know what it is like to be someone's pensioner? To know that everything you have, every penny you spend, comes from someone else?'

'As a matter of fact I do, since I am a younger son. For many years I was dependent upon an allowance from my father.'

Their eyes clashed for a moment, then her glance slid away and she continued quietly, 'Max promised it would only mean going through the ceremony. He said that once the trick was uncovered the marriage would be annulled.'

'The devil he did!' Gideon pushed back his chair and went to the window. The darkness outside showed only his scowling reflection. 'The servants must have known what was going on—that the woman I thought was Martlesham's cousin was an impostor.'

'Yes. Max threatened instant dismissal to anyone who did not go along with his deception.'

He turned back to face her.

'And your mother? Will Max explain everything to her?'

'I doubt it.' She bit her lip. 'Max tends to think only of those things that affect him.'

'But won't she worry about you?'

She looked down at her hands clasped in her lap.

'I wrote a note for her, telling her that I would be remaining at the Abbey for a few days.'

'And she will be content with that?'

Her head dipped even lower.

'*Maman* has her own concerns and will think nothing amiss.'

Gideon finished his wine and poured himself another glass. Dominique—he almost winced. He must get used to calling her that. The girl had hardly touched her wine and the cake lay crumbled on her plate. A tiny spark of sympathy touched him.

'Do not despair,' he told her. 'In the morning we will return to Martlesham and I will arrange for an annulment.'

'And until then?'

Her gaze was sceptical.

'We are not alone here. Mrs Chiswick is a respectable woman and, when we tell her there has been a mistake she will look after you until we can get you back to Martlesham.' He tried a reassuring smile. 'I think she can be relied upon to protect your honour.'

Dominique forced herself to meet his eyes, wondering at the change in tone. It was the first time Gideon Albury had done anything other than glower at her. Oh, he had smiled in the church, but then he had thought her someone else. Now he was smiling at *her*, plain little Dominique Rainault, and her heart began to thud with a breathless irregularity. Often in the preceding weeks she had dreamed of such a moment, but had never expected it, not after the scene outside the church that morning.

The revulsion she had seen in his face had quite chilled her and since then he had regarded her with nothing but repugnance. She was not prepared for the sudden charm, or the way it made her want to smile right back at him. Common sense urged her to be cautious. Despite the attraction she felt for him he was, after all, one of Max's cronies, one of that crowd of irresponsible young bucks who were more than happy to play cruel jokes upon one another. Just because he was the victim of this particular jape did not mean she could trust him.

There was a light scratching on the door, and the housekeeper peeped in.

'Beggin' your pardon sir, madam, but I was wondering if you would be wishing to change before dinner? The bedchamber's not prepared yet, but your trunks have been taken up to the dressing room and there is a good fire burning in there…'

Gideon shook his head.

'I will not change, but perhaps Mrs Albury would like to make use of it?'

'Yes, thank you, I would like to wash my face and hands.' Dominique made for the door, thankful for the opportunity to gather her thoughts. Unfortunately, the housekeeper was eager to talk as she escorted her up the stairs.

'I haven't had a chance to make up the bed, ma'am, for Alice hasn't come yet so I've only got Hannah, the scullery maid, to help me and I can't trust her to look after the kitchen, but I shall get around to that just as soon as I have finished cooking dinner. If only we'd had more notice, we would have been able to give you a welcome more suited to a new bride, but there, Mr

Carstairs has never been one to give us much warning.'
The woman gave a wheezy laugh as she opened the door
to the dressing room. 'I've no doubt he'll descend upon
us one day with a bride of his own, and never a bit o'
notice of that, either!'

Dominique knew this was her opportunity.

'Mrs Chiswick, could you have another bed made up
for me, if you please, in a separate chamber?'

The housekeeper gave a fat chuckle as she went
around the room lighting the candles.

'Lord bless you, dearie, you won't be needing that
tonight.'

'But I shall. You see, this is all a mistake, I never
intended—'

Dominique found her hands caught in a warm clasp.

'Now, now, my love, you ain't the first young bride
to have last-minute nerves. Do you not know what to
expect on your wedding night?'

'Well, yes, but that's not it…'

'Now don't you be worrying yourself, my dear, I've
been with Mr Chiswick for nigh on thirty years and I
can tell you that you have nought to worry about, especially with a kind young man like Mr Albury. He's
always been a favourite here at Elmfield, more so than
many of Mr Carstairs's friends, I can tell you. But there,
it's not for me to criticise the master. Anyway I'm sure
Mr Albury will take very good care of you. You just
go and enjoy your dinner, and I've no doubt that once
you and your man are tucked up warm and cosy in the
bedroom next door you will enjoy yourself there, too!'

Dominique looked into that kindly, smiling face and
knew she would have to tell the housekeeper that she
and Mr Albury were not really man and wife and must
have separate rooms. She took a deep breath.

'Thank you.'

The explanation withered before it even reached her tongue. The idea of confessing the truth—and her own collusion in the deception—even to this kind-hearted soul, was beyond her. She shrivelled at the very thought of it and allowed the housekeeper to withdraw without uttering another word.

Dominique berated herself soundly. She should have insisted Mrs Chiswick make up another bed for her and put a second bed in the room for herself. She removed the lace fichu and poured water into the basin to wash her face. Did she really expect Gideon Albury to keep away from her if she did not take such measures? She might think him charming, but what did she really know of him? Should one not judge a man by his company? He was friends with her cousin and Max was a cruel bully.

The heavy gold band on her finger touched her cheek, reminding her of her perilous situation. She was married. The register had been signed and she now belonged to the man sitting downstairs in that snug little parlour. The law of the land was quite specific: she was his property, to do with as he wished. A shiver ran through her.

The distant chiming of a clock caught her attention. She had dallied as long as she dared, but she could not remain in the dressing room forever. Picking up the bedroom candle, she snuffed the other lights and made her way out through the adjoining bedchamber. The large canopied bed loomed dark and menacing in the centre of the room, the hangings casting ominous shadows over the bare mattress. Dominique averted her gaze, looking instead around the room. A large linen press stood against one wall next to a bow-fronted chest of drawers, while under the window was a pretty little writing desk, still adorned with its accessories. As she passed the light glinted on the silver inkstand with its cut-glass inkwell, silver nib box and a fine ivory-handled letter opener.

Dominique stopped and set down the candlestick. She picked up the letter opener and slid it into her sleeve. The ivory handle pressed against the soft skin on the inside of her wrist, but the buttoned cuff disguised its slight bulge. She dropped her arm. The letter opener did not move, her tight-fitting sleeve holding it fast. Satisfied, she picked up her candle and continued on her way downstairs.

Gideon was waiting for her in the parlour, a fresh bottle of wine open on the table. He had loosened his neckcloth and was lounging in a chair by the table, one booted ankle resting on the other, but she thought he looked incredibly handsome, the candlelight accentuating the smooth planes of his face. Her eyes were drawn to the sensual curve of his lips and Dominique found herself wondering what he would taste like. The thought shocked her so much that she stopped just inside the door.

Perhaps he thought she was offended by his negligent attitude, for he rose to his feet and pulled out a chair for her. Silently she sank down on to it, aware of his hands on the chair back, his presence towering over her. She took a deep breath to steady herself, but instead found her senses filled with the sharp tang of soap and a musky scent. She had a strong desire to lean back against his fingers, to turn her head and press a kiss against them, inviting him to—

No! Good heavens, where did such wicked thoughts

come from? She sank her teeth into her lip, forcing herself to sit still.

'Well…' he refilled her glass and held it out to her '…did you explain our situation to Mrs Chiswick?'

'No.' His surprised stare would have made Dominique flush, if her cheeks had not already been burning with her own wayward thoughts. 'I thought perhaps you should do so.'

'Me?'

'Yes.' She took the glass, resisting the urge to slide her fingers over his. 'I thought if I broached the subject she might think you had coerced me into this marriage.'

'Instead of you tricking *me*.'

'I did not!' she retorted hotly. 'I was as much a victim as you. Well, almost.'

His lips tightened.

'Let us agree to blame Max for this sorry mess, shall we? He knew that someone with French blood would be the worst possible match for me.'

'Of course.' She recalled his reaction when Max had explained her parentage. 'Will you tell me why that should be?'

'Because—' He broke off as they were interrupted again, saying impatiently, 'Yes, Chiswick, what is it now?'

'Dinner is ready now, sir, if you is amenable.'

'Very well, we will be over directly.' As the butler withdrew he turned back to Dominique, 'We will continue this discussion later.'

He spoke harshly, but she detected a note of relief in his tone. Silently she rose and took his proffered arm as they crossed the hall to the dining room. Beneath her fingers she could feel his strength through the sleeve. He was tense, his anger barely contained. This courtesy was a veneer, a sham, and she felt as if she were walking beside a wild animal—one wrong word and he would pounce on her.

Chiswick served them, passing on his wife's apologies for the lack of dishes upon the table. Dominique was quick to reassure him that there was more than sufficient. Indeed, by the time she had tried the white soup, followed by the neck of mutton with turnips and carrots, a little of the carp and the macaroni pie she had no room for the fricassee of chicken or any of the small sweet tarts and the plum pudding that followed. Mrs Chiswick proved to be a good cook and the wines her husband provided to accompany the dishes were excellent. Dominique drank several glasses, partly to calm her nerves. She had never before dined alone with any man and she was all too conscious of the taciturn gentleman sitting at the far end of the table. She shivered, regretting that she had left her lace fichu in the dressing room. Not that she was really cold, just…nervous.

Conversation had been necessarily stilted and she was relieved when the meal was over and she could return to the parlour. She hesitated when Gideon followed her out of the room.

'Are you not remaining to drink your port, sir?'

'Chiswick shall bring me some brandy in the parlour. I do not like to drink alone.'

'I admit I have always thought it an odd custom, to remain in solitary state when there are no guests in the house. My cousin insists upon it at the Abbey, although he is rarely there without company.'

Dominique babbled on as Gideon escorted her back across the dark and echoing hall, but she could not help herself. It was nerves, she knew, but there was something else, an undercurrent of excitement at being alone with Gideon. It was a situation she had thought about—dreamed of—for weeks, only in her dreams he had been in her company out of choice, not necessity. She continued to chatter until they were both seated in the parlour. Chiswick deposited a little dish of sweetmeats at her elbow and placed a tray bearing decanters and glasses on the sideboard.

'Shall I send in the tea tray in an hour, madam?'

'No, let Mrs Chiswick bring it in now,' Gideon answered for her. He added, once they were alone, 'You can tell her when she comes in that you will require another bed to be made up.'

'Will not you—?'

He shook his head

'The running of a household is a woman's business, madam. 'Tis for you to order the staff.'

He got up to pour himself a glass of brandy while Dominique stared miserably into the fire. No matter how embarrassing, she must do this. The alternative was too dreadful to contemplate.

Gideon was still standing by the sideboard moments later when Mrs Chiswick bustled in.

'The tea tray, madam, as you requested. You must be very tired from your journey, ma'am, and you won't be wanting to prolong your evening.'

'Actually, Mrs Chiswick, I—'

'Alice and I are going upstairs to make the bed now. I've taken the liberty of heating a couple of bricks for the bed, too, seeing as how it hasn't been used for a while, but I don't suppose you will be wanting me or Chiswick to remove them, now will you?' The housekeeper gave a conspiratorial smile that made Dominique's face burn, which only made Mrs Chiswick smile more broadly. 'Bless you, my dear, no need to colour up so. You are on your honeymoon, after all! Now, the bedchamber should be all ready for you in two shakes of a lamb's tail. Chiswick will leave your bedroom candles in the hall for you and we'll say goodnight now, so we don't bother you again. And we won't disturb you in the morning, either, 'til you ring for us. I doubt you'll be wanting to be up with the lark.'

With another knowing smile and a broad wink the housekeeper departed, leaving Dominique to stare at the closed door.

A strained silence enveloped them.

'By heaven, what a gabster,' remarked Gideon at last. 'Difficult to get a word in, I admit.' He sat down beside her on the sofa. 'I suppose I can always sleep here.' She turned to look at him, surprised. His lips twitched. 'We were neither of us brave enough to stem the flow, were we?'

Dominique's hands flew to her mouth, but could not stifle a nervous giggle. Gideon began to laugh, too, and soon they were both convulsed in mirth. It was several minutes before either of them could speak again.

'It is very like a farce one would see in Drury Lane,' Dominique hiccupped, searching for a handkerchief to mop her streaming eyes.

Gideon pulled out his own and, cupping her chin in one hand, turned her face towards him and gently wiped her cheeks.

'But if such a story was presented, one would say it was too far-fetched and could never happen.'

He was still grinning, but Dominique's urge to laugh died away. Carefully she disengaged herself.

'But it has happened.' His touch on her face had

been as gentle as a kiss and yet the skin still tingled. He was leaning back now against the sofa, relaxed and smiling. She thought again how handsome he was, with those finely chiselled features, the thick, auburn hair gleaming in the candlelight. If they had met in other circumstances... She stopped the thought immediately. He hated the French and there could be no denying her parentage, nor did she want to do so. She was proud of her father.

Gideon was on his feet, going back to the sideboard.

'You shouldn't be maudling your insides with tea. Let me get you some port.'

She looked towards the tea tray. He was right, she did not feel up to the careful ritual of making tea this evening. She was so nervous she feared she would drop one of the beautiful porcelain cups. When he held out a glass of dark, ruby-red liquid she accepted it with a murmur of thanks, holding it carefully between her hands. Perhaps it would put some spirit into her. She took a large gulp, swallowing half the contents in one go but thankfully Gideon did not see it, for he was busy pouring himself more brandy.

'We are in a pickle, my dear.' He sat down beside her again. 'I lost my temper and I apologise for it. If we had remained at Martlesham everything would have been so much simpler.'

'You were very angry, I understand that, and I beg your pardon for my part in it.'

The corners of his mouth lifted a little. He said ruefully, 'It is the red hair. When the angry mist descends I am not responsible for my actions.'

A smile of understanding tugged at her own mouth.

'My hair is not red, but I have a temper, too, at times.'

'Your Latin temperament, perhaps.'
'Yes.'

There was a shy smile in her green eyes, and Gideon was pleased to note the anxious frown no longer creased her brow. She looked so much better when her countenance was not strained and pinched with worry. A soft blush was mantling her cheek as she went to the sideboard to put down her empty glass. Gideon noted the way the walking dress clung to her figure, accentuating the slender waist, the sway of her hips. As she returned he could appreciate the curve and swell of her breasts rising from the bodice of her gown. She was no ripe beauty, but he would wager that beneath that mannish outfit was a rather delectable body. He remembered standing behind her earlier, breathing in her fragrance and felt a flicker of interest—of desire—stir his blood.

As if aware of his thoughts she chose to sit in the armchair beside the fire. Gideon cleared his throat.

'I believe there is a gig in the stables. When it is light I shall drive you to Swaffham, and from there we will hire a post-chaise to take us back to Martlesham.'

'Not the Abbey,' she said quickly. 'Will you please set me down in the village, at my mother's cottage?'

He shrugged. 'If you wish.' A sudden thud on the ceiling made them both look up. 'But first we have to get through this evening.'

The port had had its effect. Dominique knew now what she must do.

'I shall remain down here,' she announced, sitting very straight and upright in her chair. 'You may have the bedroom.'

'Nonsense. I have already said I shall sleep on the sofa.'

She put up her chin. 'I have made up my mind.'

'Then unmake it.'

His autocratic tone only strengthened her resolve.

'I will not.'

'I am not so unchivalrous as to condemn you to such discomfort.'

'I shall be perfectly comfortable. Besides, there are bolts on the parlour door, while the bedchamber boasted not even the flimsiest lock.'

Gideon sat up, frowning.

'Are you saying you do not trust me?'

'Yes, I am.'

He jumped up.

'Damn it all, when have I given you occasion to doubt me?'

Her brows went up.

'When you insisted we come here.'

The truth of her statement caught him on the raw and he swung away, striding over to the window.

'Do not be so damned obstinate, woman! I have said I will sleep on the sofa and I shall.'

His words appeared to have no effect.

'Impossible. It is far too short for you. Why, you must be six foot at least.'

'Six foot two,' he said absently. 'But that is not the point.'

'It is very much the point.' He heard the quiet rustle of skirts. 'You see, it is the perfect length for me.'

When he looked around she had stretched herself out on the sofa. Her gown fell in soft folds around her, accentuating the contours of her body, the swell of her breast and curve of her hip that only served to emphasise the tiny waist. And how had he failed to notice the length of her legs? She stretched luxuriously and he had a glimpse of dainty ankles peeping from beneath the hem of her skirts. In any other situation he would have found the view enchanting, but—hell and confound it, she was mocking him!

'The bedroom has been prepared, madam and you *will* sleep in it.'

'And I tell you I shall not.'

He almost ground his teeth in frustration.

'I admit it was a mistake to come here.' He spoke carefully, reining in his anger. 'I was at fault, but you will agree the provocation was great.'

'Of course.'

'However, when all is said and done, I am a gentleman. I will not have it said that I enjoyed the comfort of a feather bed while you spent the night on a sofa!'

Dominique felt an unexpected frisson of excitement at his rough tone. He was rattled and clearly no longer in control of the situation. An exulting feeling of power swept through her. She put her hands behind her head and gazed up at him defiantly.

'But I am already in possession, so I do not see that you can do anything about it. I suggest you admit yourself beaten and retire in good order.'

She closed her eyes and forced herself to keep very still, feigning indifference. He would see she was not to be moved and would go away and leave her in peace. She expected to hear a hasty footstep and the door snapping closed behind him. Instead she heard something between a snarl and a growl and the next moment she was being hoisted none too gently off the sofa. Her eyes flew open and she gave a little scream as she experienced the novel sensation of being helpless in a man's arms. But not just any man, and along with her natural indignation she was aware of the urgent desire curl-

ing through her body. It frightened her, but she would
fight it. She would show him she was no milk-and-water
maid, to be treated so abominably.

'You said you were a gentleman,' she protested,
struggling against his hold. In response his grip tightened, one arm pressing her against his chest while the
other supported her knees, so that her frustrated kicks
met nothing but air.

'I am, but you have tried my patience too far!'

'Put me down this instant!'

She tried to free her arms, but at that very moment he
loosened his grip around her shoulders. Instinctively her
hands went around his neck to save herself from falling.
He looked down at her, a wicked glint in his hazel eyes.

'I thought you wanted me to let go?'

She was feeling extremely breathless and her heart
was thudding so painfully against her ribs that he must
feel it, since she was pressed against his hard chest, but
she replied with as much dignity as she could muster.

'I do *not* wish to be dropped on my head.'

With a little grunt of satisfaction he settled her more
comfortably before him. Her arms were still around his
neck and she could not for the life of her release him.
Dominique told herself this was solely for the purpose
of supporting herself, should he drop her, but she could
not deny the sensual pleasure of feeling the silk of his
hair, where it curled between her fingers and the back
of his collar. Shocked by the idea that part of her was
enjoying Gideon's masterful behaviour, she gave a half-
hearted kick. His arms tightened and her breathing became even more constricted.

'You are suffocating me,' she protested.

'Keep still, then.'

He crossed the room in three strides and somehow managed to open the door.

'Put me down!' she hissed at him as they crossed the empty hall. 'I can walk perfectly well.'

'And give you the opportunity to run straight back into the parlour? I think not.'

Silenced, Dominique marvelled at his strength as he took the stairs two at a time. He held her firmly with his arm around her back and his hand clasped about her ribs and she was achingly aware of how close his fingers were to her breast. She was filled with outrage—at herself, for her wanton feelings, but even more so at Gideon for his cavalier behaviour. How dare he manhandle her in this way!

As they reached the landing Chiswick appeared in the corridor. He stopped, his eyes almost popping out of his head.

'Don't just stand there gawping, man,' barked Gideon. 'Open the door for me!'

Speechless with anger and shock, Dominique watched the servant throw open the door to the bedchamber. The golden light of the fire and several candles greeted them. Gideon sailed through with his burden and the butler reached in to close the door behind them. As it clicked shut there was the unmistakable sound of a throaty chuckle. It was all that was needed to fan the spark of her anger into full flame. She began to kick and struggle violently.

'How dare you treat me like this!'

'If you behave like a fishwife, then I will treat you as one.'

'Fishwife! I merely asked you to leave me alone.'

With an oath he set her on her feet, but kept hold of her wrists.

'By Gad, woman, you are beyond reason! Do you not *want* to sleep in a comfortable bed tonight?'

'No! I was quite happy to sleep downstairs.'

'Well I was not! Damnation, madam, you are here now and here you will stay, whether you like it or not.'

'Oh, and who is going to make me?'

'I am, even if it means I have to stand guard outside your door all night.'

'Much good that will do you, since there is a door from the dressing room on to the landing.'

'Then I had best stay here where I can see you.'

He released her, but there was a challenging look in his eye. Dominique knew that if she made a bolt for the dressing-room door he would catch her. She threw up her head.

'I demand you let me go back downstairs.'

'Ho, demand, do you? What about those wifely vows you took, to honour and obey?'

'Worthless. Now will you let me go?'

'Never.'

He towered over her, sparking a tiny frisson of unease as she realised she was now in the very situation she had been trying to avoid. However, her temper was up and she was not daunted by his superior height and strength.

'I refuse to sleep in that bed.'

'That may be so, but you are not leaving this room again tonight.'

She took a step back, glaring up at him as she folded her arms across her chest. As she did so she felt the solid line of the letter opener against her left forearm. She pulled it out with a triumphant flourish.

'What the devil are you going to do with that?'

'Stab you with it, if you don't get out of my way.'

* * *

Gideon stared at her.

'Good God, madam, anyone would think I intended to ravish you, instead of offering you the most comfortable bed in the house.'

He wished he hadn't used the word *ravish*, it brought all sorts of unhelpful connotations to his mind as she stood before him, breasts heaving and eyes flashing fire. Her hair had come loose in the struggle and now fell in a dusky cloud to her shoulders. The desire he had felt earlier stirred again, only stronger. He reminded himself he was a gentleman and should retire now, before it was too late. But she was still defying him, brandishing the letter opener like a sword, and that was a challenge he could not resist.

'Step aside,' she ordered him. 'Let me return to the parlour.'

'The devil I will.'

'I—I will stab you if you get in my way.'

He threw his arms wide.

'Stab away.'

His taunt brought a blaze of anger to her eyes again and with a shriek she launched herself at him. He grabbed her wrist. The letter opener was not that sharp and he doubted it would do much damage, but she seemed intent upon attacking him and he was damned if he was going to allow that. She was surprisingly strong. He twisted her wrist and she dropped the weapon, but immediately she sank her teeth into his hand.

'Ouch! You little termagant!' He wrestled her backwards on to the bed, pinning her wrists above her head. '*Will* you stop fighting like a wildcat?'

She continued to struggle and he was obliged to use

the weight of his body to hold her down and prevent her flailing legs from kicking him.

'Let me go!'

'Not if you are going to scratch my eyes out. *Stop it!*' She ceased struggling and glared up at him, the gold braid on her bodice glinting with the rise and fall of her breast. 'That's better.'

He, too, was breathing heavily, but he recognised it was not just exertion. The feel of her body beneath him was exciting him almost beyond reason. He smiled and earned for his troubles a smouldering look that sent the blood pounding faster through his body. He was lying between her legs, crushing her skirts against the bed, and for one searing moment he imagined what it would be like if her thighs were pressed against his, skin on skin rather than separated by numerous layers of cloth.

'That reminds me.' His voice seemed very distant and slightly unsteady. 'I have not yet kissed the bride.'

He told himself he was teasing her, punishing her just a little more. She watched him from those huge eyes. Large and dark, unfathomable pools, dragging him down. His gaze moved to her mouth.

Better stop this now, before it gets out of hand.

Too late. The pink tip of her tongue flickered nervously across her lips and he could not resist lowering his head to capture her mouth. It was a swift, hard kiss and she trembled beneath him. Immediately he drew back.

Dominique took a quick, shuddering breath. That was the last straw. Her blood was up, she had been aware of a sharp exultation when she had flown at him with the paperknife in her hand and her heart was still pounding from the ensuing tussle. He had overpowered her, of course, but she was not beaten. She told herself she would never give in, even with his body pressing down upon hers she felt herself stronger, not weaker, as sensations she could not explain took control of her body. She felt alive, buzzing with energy, ready to fight him again. Then he had closed the distance between them, his mouth finding her parted lips and taking possession. Her body responded with a shudder of desire that shocked and startled her. A longing, a need she could not control was unleashed—she wanted him as she had never wanted anyone, or anything, before.

It was a shock to realise she would sell her soul to the devil for one night with Gideon Albury, and what did it matter? Her reputation was ruined, whatever happened, so why should she not have one glorious night to remember? He was easing himself away. In another moment he would be lost to her forever.

'I beg your pardon,' he muttered, releasing her hands. 'I should not—'

Gideon broke off in surprise as she reached up and clutched at his neckcloth. She pulled him close and began to kiss him, a little inexpertly, but with such eagerness that desire lanced through him. He was lost. It was as if someone had opened the floodgates and a torrent of passion poured forth, carrying all before it.

Clothes were hurriedly discarded, buttons torn off in their haste to disrobe and all the while they strove to continue those heady, desperate kisses that kept all coherent thought at bay. Gideon lifted her easily on to the cool silk covers of the bed and measured his naked length against her. She clung to him, eager for his touch, returning his embraces with a fervour that more than matched his own. She cried out as he entered her, but when he hesitated she pulled him to her, claiming his mouth, tangling her tongue with his and leaving him in no doubt that she wanted to continue the hot, passionate coupling that carried them on to a heady, exhilarating climax and left them both panting and exhausted.

Dominique woke up when the fire was dying down and the night air cooling her skin. She lifted one hand to her head, trying to make sense of where she was and what had happened. She remembered dining with Gideon, then arguing with him and finally, when he had laid hands on her—understandably, since she was trying to stab him—she had wanted nothing more than to cling on to him forever. It was as if she had been possessed, filled with desire that must be satisfied. She ran a hand over her body. It felt no different, yet everything had changed. She was no longer a virgin.

She tried to examine her feelings about that and about the naked man sleeping beside her. She felt numb. It was as if there was some great unhappy void ahead of her that she dare not face just yet. Perhaps in the morning she would be able to make sense of it all. For now her main concern was to get warm. She slid between the covers. The hot bricks so thoughtfully supplied were gone. They had fallen out on to the floor at some point, unnoticed, and the sheets were cold.

Her movements disturbed Gideon and he followed her under the covers, silently pulling her close. She could not deny the comfort of his warm limbs wrapped around her. Nothing mattered when she was in his arms. Tomorrow. She would think about it all tomorrow. She closed her eyes and, as she was drifting away into sleep, she felt his breath against her cheek, heard him whisper one word.

'*Dominique.*'

Chapter Four

The early morning sunshine was just peeping into the bedchamber when Dominique opened her eyes again. She was alone in the canopied bed. Soon she would have to get up and face the day—and Gideon—but for now she lay very still and allowed the memories to flood back. Perhaps she had been wrong to agree to her cousin's plan, but if it had secured her mother's independence then she could not regret it.

And her night of passion with Gideon? She would regret that, she was sure, but it had been inevitable. From the first moment she had peered through the thick wedding veil and seen him standing at the altar, tall and athletic, with the bars of sunlight from the windows striking red-gold sparks from his auburn hair, she was lost. Her heart had turned over and, oh, how she had wished that his smiles had really been for her and not for the person he thought her to be.

His anger, when he discovered the deception, had been monumental, but she could forgive that—as she would have forgiven him if he had taken her in anger, forced himself upon her. After all, what rights did she have now, as his wife? But she truly believed he had planned to protect her. If she had not been so obstinate, they might well have spent their wedding night in separate rooms, emerging chaste and unsullied this morning. But his autocratic behaviour had angered her and she had a temper equal to his own. Over the years she had learned to keep it in check, except in the most trying circumstances, and there could be no denying that yesterday had been extremely trying.

Once she had lost her temper there had been no way of regaining it again and when Gideon had kissed her she had reacted instinctively, taking her opportunity to possess him, if only for one night. She had given in to pure, wanton lust and now she must pay for it.

Dressing took some time. Clothing was scattered across the room—one stocking was dangling from the handle of the linen press and her garters had disappeared completely. She rummaged through the trunk that Max had supplied, but soon realised that her cousin's cruel sense of humour was present even here. The diaphanous nightwear and flimsy muslin gowns were more suited to a courtesan and had probably been left at Martlesham by one of Max's numerous lovers. She would have to wear her walking dress again.

However, she found in the trunk a clean chemise of the very finest snow-white linen and a pair of silk garters to replace her own embroidered ones. She considered cutting off the gold tassels from the garters, but in the end decided to leave them. After all, no one would see them under her skirts—unless Gideon wished to repeat last night's passionate encounter.

Oh, if only he would! A delicious curl of desire clenched her stomach and left an ache between her thighs as she remembered how it had felt to be in his arms, to have him love her.

Love. How could it be love? Gideon had no reason to think well of her. And for herself, she had watched him courting the actress, but had never spoken to him before yesterday. It could only be a savage, primitive animal attraction, acceptable in a man, but not at all the sort of thing that a respectable young lady would admit.

Dominique made her way downstairs. She found the housekeeper in the parlour, spreading a cloth over the little table.

'Good morning, Mrs Albury. I'm setting up breakfast for you here. Mr Albury thought you would prefer that to eating in the dining room, which can be draughty when the wind is in the east, as it is today.'

Dominique nodded absently and asked if she had seen Mr Albury.

'Aye, madam, he took himself off for a walk about an hour ago, it being such a fine morning. Would you like to break your fast now, madam, or will you wait for your husband to come back?'

'A little coffee now, if you please. I will take breakfast when my…husband returns.' She stumbled over the words, but she was glad to have a little longer to compose herself before meeting Gideon again.

She did not have long to wait. The thud of the front door, footsteps and the rumble of voices in the hall warned her of his arrival. She remained at the table, trying to look calm. He strode into the room, his greatcoat swinging open, his face alight with the effects of fresh air and exercise. He greeted her civilly, but she saw the sparkle fade from his eyes, replaced by a closed and shuttered look. She glanced away, trying not to feel hurt. She gestured to the table.

'There is coffee here, sir, and it is still warm, if you wish for it.'

'Thank you, yes. Mrs Chiswick is bringing in a fresh pot, but that might be some time.'

He threw his greatcoat over a chair and came to sit down. Dominique poured coffee into a cup and Gideon accepted it in silence. She wondered if she should say something and was relieved when the bustling entrance of Mrs Chiswick made speech unnecessary, at least for a while. They managed to get through breakfast with mere courtesies, but when the table had been cleared and they were alone again, the silence hung heavily between them.

'We need to talk,' Gideon said at last.

Dominique looked around her, seeking an escape from the suddenly oppressive room.

'It—it is such a lovely morning and I have not yet seen the gardens. Would you mind if we walked outside?'

'Not at all.'

She picked up her cloak and they made their way to the shrubbery, where the high walls sheltered them from the biting east wind. They walked side by side, taking care they did not brush against each other. So different from last night, thought Dominique, when they could not touch each other enough. It had to be mentioned. She launched into speech.

'About what happened—'

'A mistake,' he interrupted her. 'And one I deeply regret. I apologise, madam, most humbly.'

She answered him firmly, 'I am as much to blame as you.'

'Perhaps, but the consequences for both of us are disastrous.' He paused. 'You realise the marriage cannot be annulled now.'

'Surely, if we return to Martlesham—'

He silenced her with an impatient wave of his hand.

'Do you think anyone would believe the marriage was not consummated? The servants would be questioned. Mrs Chiswick prepared the bridal chamber for us, her husband saw me carrying you up the stairs and I'd wager any money the maid will check the sheets!' He kicked a stone off the path. 'No, last night's folly is our undoing.'

Folly! That was how he saw the most wonderful experience of her life. Hot tears prickled at the back of Dominique's eyes, but she would not let them fall. She swallowed and clenched her jaw so that her voice did not tremble.

'What do you suggest?'

He looked up at the sky, the breath escaping between his teeth in a hiss.

'Divorce will be my father's suggestion. He abhors the French as much as I and will strongly oppose the connection. I believe he would even bear the ignominy of our family name being dragged through the courts.'

Dominique shivered. Was this to be her punishment, to have her wantonness publicly paraded?

'He could arrange the whole,' Gideon continued thoughtfully. 'But that would mean your taking a lover and I would have to sue him. A humiliating business for both of us, enduring shame for you. I will not countenance that.'

'Then what?' she asked. 'Separation? I can go back to Martlesham and live with my mother—'

He shook his head.

'No. Too many people know the circumstances of our marriage. It is unthinkable that they will all remain silent.'

'That is true,' she agreed, bitterly. 'Max has always delighted in bragging about his jokes.'

'And the chance to make me a laughing stock will prove irresistible.'

Dominique stopped.

'What shall we do, then?'

'Brazen it out.' He turned and looked down at her. 'We will continue with the marriage.'

She stared at him, her world tilting alarmingly.

'But…' She swallowed, struggling to push out the words. 'It will be a sham. You love someone else.'

That an actress would be even more unacceptable as the wife for the future Viscount Rotham did not concern Dominique, only that he loved the beautiful blonde. Gideon waved aside her objections.

'There are many such marriages in our world. It does not follow that it must be unhappy. We need only present a united front for a few months, perhaps a year or so, until the gossip has died down.'

'I have no dowry.'

He laughed, but there was no humour in it.

'Money is one thing the Alburys have in abundance.'

'Then your father will say we are even more ill matched.'

He shrugged. 'Father will come about, especially once you have provided a grandson to carry on the family name. And after that—if you want a lover you will not find me unreasonable, as long as you are discreet. That should not be a problem for you, since you grew up in France. These arrangements are understood there.'

Not in her world. Dominique thought of her mother,

still so very much in love with one man, after all these years.

'Well, madam, what say you?' Gideon asked her. 'Are you prepared to continue with this marriage?'

After the slightest hesitation she nodded.

'Yes. Yes, I am.'

After all, what choice did she have?

It was early evening by the time the post-chaise bowled into Martlesham village and drew up at a line of cottages. Gideon handed out his wife, then followed her through the nearest door. He was too tall to enter without stooping, but he was relieved when he entered the small sitting room off the narrow passage to find that the ceiling was considerably higher. The serving maid who had admitted them retired to the nether regions of the little house to fetch refreshments, bidding Dominique to go in and greet her mother. The maid had subjected Gideon to a frowning, silent stare before disappearing. He was well aware that she had been a party to the hoax and he had no doubt that she was agog to know how matters stood now. He gave a mental shrug. If his wife wanted to tell her, then he had no objection. In fact, it concerned him very little: he was about to make the acquaintance of his mama-in-law.

The little sitting room was comfortably if sparsely furnished. A couple of armchairs flanked the hearth, where a cheerful fire blazed and a small table stood by the window, its surface littered with papers. A silver inkstand rose from the centre of the chaos, like an island amid a turbulent sea and to one side sat a lady in a dark woollen gown with a tight-fitting jacket. She was hunched over the table, writing furiously, and did not appear to notice their entrance.

'*Maman?*'

Madame Rainault looked up. Gideon detected some likeness to his wife, but the lady's fair complexion and light eyes reminded him more of Martlesham, save that she had none of the earl's blustering arrogance. She wore a muslin cap over curls which were sprinkled with grey, and her eyes held a distracted look, as if her thoughts were elsewhere. She seemed to struggle to focus as she put down her pen and smiled.

'Dominique, my child. Are you back from the Abbey so soon? I had thought to have all these letters done before you returned.'

'*Maman*, I have something to tell you.' Gideon found himself pulled forwards by a small but insistent hand. 'This is Mr Albury, *Maman*. He—we…'

As the words tailed away he stepped forwards and picked up Madame Rainault's hand.

'*Enchanté, madame.*' As he bowed over the thin fingers he realised how long it was since he had spoken in French and he had to fight down the painful associations before he could summon up a smile. 'What your daughter is trying to say is that she has done me the honour of becoming my wife.'

Madame Rainault withdrew her hand and regarded him, bewildered.

'Your wife? But when, how?'

He felt a touch on his sleeve.

'Perhaps, sir, I should talk to my mother alone.'

'Yes, of course. I will go on to the Abbey. I need to arrange to have the rest of my luggage packed up and sent on to me.' He hesitated. 'Unless you wish to see your cousin?' He received a darkling look in answer and gave a wry smile. 'I thought not. I will be back as soon as I can.'

* * *

His arrival at Martlesham caused no little consternation. It was the dinner hour and Gideon told the butler not to disturb his master, but to send Runcorn up to his room immediately. It took very little time to explain the situation to his valet and give him his instructions.

Half an hour later he was ready to leave. He found Max waiting for him in the hall.

'Albury. Back from your honeymoon already? Is my cousin not with you?'

'I left her with her mother,' said Gideon, pulling on his gloves.

The doors to the dining room were open and the guests were beginning to wander out.

'Ah, tired of her already?' The earl grimaced. 'Can't say I'm surprised, she's too tight-laced and proper to please a man.'

Gideon was already furious with Max for the way he had cheated him. Now, when he heard the earl's insulting description of his young relative, Gideon was aware of a burning desire to knock the fellow's teeth out. But he had decided he would beat Max at his own game, so he concealed all signs of anger and merely raised his brows a fraction.

'Really? Are we talking about the same woman, Martlesham?' He noted the look of uncertainty in Max's face and smiled. 'We are going to London. I need to buy my wife a new wardrobe before I take her into Buckinghamshire.'

The uncertainty was replaced by amazement.

'You are taking her to Rotham?'

'Of course, that is her due.'

'B-but the viscount hates the French. He will refuse to acknowledge her.'

The thought had occurred to Gideon, but Max's shocked tones angered him and he responded with more than a touch of hauteur.

'He will be obliged to do so, since she is the wife of his heir.'

Williams came mincing forwards, quizzing glass raised.

'Now look here, Albury, we all know the marriage is a farce, it was never intended to go this far. Bring the gel back here and let Martlesham sort it all out—'

'But there is nothing to sort out,' replied Gideon, smiling again. 'I am exceedingly happy and I have you to thank for it, Max.' He patted the earl on the shoulder as he passed him. 'Now, if you will excuse me, I have to collect my wife. I have booked rooms at the Globe and we have an early start for town in the morning.'

'The Globe!' Williams dropped his quizzing glass. 'But that's devilishly…'

'Expensive, yes.' Gideon smiled. 'Only the best for Mrs Albury!'

He walked out, leaving them gaping and speechless behind him.

When he arrived back at the cottage, Lucy, the maid, accorded him a grudging curtsy and a slightly less-hostile look, from which he guessed that she had been apprised of the current situation. His wife he found in the sitting room with her mother. They were side by side in the armchairs, which had been drawn together. As Gideon entered the room Madame Rainault rose.

'Dominique has explained it all to me, Mr Albury, including my nephew's part in your marriage. It was a very wicked trick, sir, but I understand you intend to stand by my daughter. However, if you cannot be kind to her, then I pray you will leave her here with me.'

'*Maman*, you know that is impossible!'

'*Madame*, I give you my word that your daughter will receive all the kindness and consideration I can give her. As my wife she shall want for nothing.'

Madame Rainault's anxious eyes searched his face and at last, satisfied, she held out her hands.

'I believe you will do your best for her, sir, and I commend her to your care. Put on your cloak, Dominique, it is only a few miles to the Globe, but it is growing dark and there is no moon tonight.'

Mother and daughter exchanged kisses.

'*Maman*, I wish...'

'Go along, my love, I shall do very well here with Lucy to look after me. Besides, I have work to do. Now the new treaty with France is signed I am hopeful I shall begin to make progress. I have at last had word from one of my old friends and I am writing to him now, for news of your father. Lucy shall take it to the post office. She takes all my letters there now, instead of asking my nephew to frank them for me. I was never sure that he sent them on, you know...'

Madame Rainault was still talking as she waved them off. As his bride settled herself in the carriage, Gideon thought he saw the gleam of a tear on her cheek. He said, to distract her thoughts, 'What news of your father? I thought he was dead.'

She shook her head.

'He disappeared, soon after he sent us to England in ninety-three. He wanted to protect the king and queen, but the revolution had gone too far. Many moderate Girondins were executed, or imprisoned at that time.

When we lost touch, *Maman* began writing to everyone
she could think of in France, trying to find out what had
happened. She has been doing so ever since.'

'Ten years and you have heard nothing?'

'No. Max thinks Papa is dead, but my mother does
not believe that.'

'And you?'

Her face was no more than a pale oval in the fading
light, but he saw her chin go up.

'I never give up hope, sir.'

The Globe was a prestigious hostelry and the couple
were made to feel their lack of servants and baggage,
until Gideon's haughty manner and generous purse convinced the landlord that this wealthy viscount's son
was merely eccentric. Gideon had sent a runner ahead
of him to bespeak a suite of rooms, which included, as
Dominique discovered as she explored their apartment,
two bedrooms.

'It is de rigueur for married couples, so no one will
think anything amiss,' explained Gideon. 'And I did
not want to impose upon you.'

'You are very kind, sir.'

'Gideon,' he corrected her gently.

'Gideon.'

The lackeys had withdrawn and they were alone
again, a situation that Dominique found disconcert-
ing, despite their intimacy the previous night. Gideon
came closer. His hand came up, as if to touch her cheek,
then dropped away again.

'I want you to be comfortable,' he told her. 'Is there
anything I can do, madam, that will help?'

She clasped her hands together.

'There is one thing, sir.'

'Yes?'

She raised her eyes to his.

'If—if you could call me Dominique.' Silence met her words and she hurried on, 'You never use my name—well, only once.' She blushed furiously at the memory. 'I do not think we can be c-comfortable if you continue to call me madam.'

She was looking down, and saw his hands clench into fists.

'That is one request I am afraid I cannot fulfil, my dear.'

'Oh.' She blinked to clear the tears that had suddenly sprung up. 'N-no doubt you think of Dominique as that b-beautiful actress.'

He did not contradict her. After a moment's tense silence he said, 'It is not only that. It is a French name.'

'And—and is that so very bad?' she asked him.

He hesitated, no longer than a heartbeat, but she noticed it.

'Yes, my dear. I'm afraid it is.'

He turned towards her, his face polite, smiling, but that shuttered look was in his eyes, telling her he was unreachable.

They retired to their separate rooms that night. Dominique did not sleep, but lay tense and still in the middle of the bed, listening. She convinced herself that she was dreading a soft knock at the door, but when it never came she realised just how disappointed she was. Yet what could she expect? Gideon had never wanted to marry her; he was in love with the actress who had taken her place. So much in love that now he could not even bring himself to use her name.

At breakfast the following morning Gideon was all consideration. He escorted her to her chair, poured her

coffee and helped her to the freshest of the toasted muf-
fins before sitting down to his own meal.

'You are right,' he declared. 'I cannot continue without a name for you.'

She bridled instantly.

'I have a perfectly good name, thank you.'

'You have indeed.' He smiled at her and she found
her anger melting away. 'I have been thinking about it.'

'You have?'

Had he stayed awake to relive their night together,
as she had done? The little flare of hope quickly died.

'Yes,' he continued. 'We could shorten it to Nicky.
A pet name, if you like.'

'My grandfather, the old earl, used to call me that.'

'There we have it, then. I shall call you Nicky—but
only with your permission, of course.'

She gave him a shy smile.

'I should like that, si—' She noted his sudden frown
and corrected herself. 'I should like that, *Gideon.*'

By the time they reached London Dominique thought
they were getting on famously. They laughed at the
same things, shared a love of music and poetry, talked
for hours, like true friends. But not lovers. Gideon was
polite and considerate, but nothing more, and Dominique, afraid to risk the fragile bond between them, lay
awake in her lonely bed and ached for him to come to
her. It would not do, however, to admit such a longing,
so she hid it behind a smile and accepted as much companionship as her husband was willing to give.

Chapter Five

Her new home was a neat house in Brook Street, which Gideon informed her belonged to his father.

'I do have a house of my own I inherited from my godmother, Lady Telford,' he told Dominique as he helped her out of the chaise. 'But it is a few miles out of town and so run down that I have never used it.'

'I think this would be more convenient for you,' remarked Dominique, looking up at the elegant facade. At that moment the door was thrown open and a liveried servant came out, beaming at them.

'Master Gideon, welcome home, sir!'

'Thank you. My dear, this is Judd, who has known me since I was a babe, which means he takes the greatest liberties.'

The old man chuckled in a fatherly way.

'Now then, Master Gideon, you don't want to be telling Mrs Albury such tales. Welcome to you, mistress. Mrs Wilkins is waiting inside and will show you over the house.'

'Perhaps she will begin by showing Mrs Albury to her bedchamber,' suggested Gideon, taking her arm and leading her into the narrow hall. 'We have had a long journey and I am sure my wife would like to rest before dinner.'

'Aye, of course, I will do that, Master Gideon.' A plump, rosy-cheeked woman in a black-stuff gown and snowy apron bustled forwards and dropped a curtsy. 'If Mrs Albury would like to come with me, there is hot water already on the washstands and I will send Kitty up to help you dress. She is only the second housemaid, but she's a good girl and has ambition to be a lady's maid, but if she don't suit we will send to the registry office for someone else.'

'I shall be delighted to see how she goes on,' said Dominique quickly.

'Very good, madam. Now, which of these trunks is yours, and we'll have them taken up immediately.'

'Only one.' They had brought only the trunk Max had sent with her to Elmwood and now Dominique met Gideon's eyes in a mute appeal.

'My wife is to have everything new, as befits a future viscountess,' he said coolly. 'She will manage with what is in the trunk and tomorrow we will set about replenishing her wardrobe.'

The housekeeper looked a little shocked.

'Very well, sir. If you would care to come with me, ma'am, I'll show you to your room and we'll unpack that single trunk of yours and see what there is for you to wear tonight…'

Taking a mental review of the items she had seen in the trunk, Dominique hastily declined the offer.

'You have more than enough to do, Mrs Wilkins,' she said. 'I am sure the maid you have found for me will be able to help.'

* * *

When Dominique came downstairs for dinner she was wearing one of the muslin gowns from the trunk Max had provided. The previous owner of the gown had been somewhat taller than Dominique, but Kitty had proved to be very useful with a needle and had soon taken up the hem. The unknown woman had also been more generously endowed and Dominique had had to cover the extremely low and rather loose décolletage by draping a fine muslin handkerchief across her shoulders, crossing the ends over her bosom and tying them behind her.

When she joined Gideon in the drawing room he raised his brows and she felt obliged to explain.

'I was delighted to leave off my travelling dress, but the trunk my cousin packed up for me was sadly lacking in suitable clothes. This is the most respectable of the gowns and even this required several petticoats beneath it before I was fit to be seen.'

Gideon raised his quizzing glass and surveyed her. His lips curved into a grin.

'Yes, I can see that.'

She fingered the skirts, chuckling.

'It is the finest quality, as is everything in the trunk, but most of it is highly improper. I think it must have been left behind by one of Max's less-respectable guests. He is forever filling the house with lightskirts and actresses— Oh!' She stopped, colouring painfully. 'I—I beg your pardon, I d-did not think…'

The cheerful camaraderie disappeared in an instant. Gideon's grin was replaced by a polite smile. He waved one hand, as if to dismiss her words, but Dominique knew she had erred.

* * *

Gideon saw her stricken look and wished he could say something to comfort her, but the words would not come. He had never been one for dissimulation. How could he tell her it did not matter that he had married the wrong bride when it *did* matter, when he regretted it so bitterly? The woman he had courted, the bride he had expected, was tall and fair and buxom, with blue, blue eyes and a smoky laugh full of sexual promise. Instead he found himself married to a diminutive brunette with a damnably obstinate streak. She was pretty enough, perhaps, if you liked thin women.

Here he stopped himself. She was petite, yes—the top of her head barely reached his chin—but she was not thin. He remembered their wedding night, when they had both allowed their pent-up emotions to run away with them. He recalled how well her small breast fitted into his hand, how her tiny waist contrasted with the full, rounded softness of her hips. Their lovemaking had been as hot and passionate as anything he had ever experienced and her untutored ardour had fuelled his desire. He hoped he had not hurt her. He had always expected to take his virgin bride gently, to go slowly and teach her the pleasures of the flesh.

Instead they had tumbled into a hedonistic, lust-filled coupling and he had risen at dawn bemused and mortified by his lack of control. He remembered glancing down at his sleeping bride, seeing her hair arrayed over the pillows in a dark cloud and feeling an unexpected tenderness for the innocent, fragile girl he had married. He had wanted to protect her—from the world, from himself. He had made a vow then, that he would conduct himself with proper restraint in future.

And there could be no going back. Having consummated their marriage, he must now commit himself to it and put aside all thoughts of the actress—what had Max called her? Agnes Bennet. Gideon doubted he had truly loved her, but he had been captivated by her beauty and she had shown him a flattering attention that had put all sensible thought to flight. No, it had not been love. Gideon recognised that it was his pride that was hurt most and the woman now sharing his life had colluded in the shameful trick. For that he could never forgive her. Of course, there was no reason why they should not be happy enough and have a comfortable, civilised existence together. Many couples entered into arranged marriages and rubbed along well enough, but it wasn't only her deceit—he could not ignore her French blood.

It was twelve years since his brother James had died at the hands of the French mob and the pain of that loss had never left Gideon. His father had trained him to take his place, to become his heir, but James had been everything Gideon was not, quiet and studious, but with a charm of manner that made him universally loved—not for him the rakehell existence of a young man on the town—and Gideon knew how unworthy he was to fill James's shoes.

Dinner was a strained affair. They were achingly polite to each other and by the time the covers were removed Dominique was glad to leave Gideon to enjoy his port in solitary state. She realised sadly that, however friendly he might seem, Gideon could not forgive her for her duplicitous actions. It had been a cruel trick and she should never have taken part, but when she had agreed to it she had been in turmoil. Blackmailed by her cousin and half in love with the man behind whose eyes she glimpsed a sadness that set him apart from the others, while at the same time detesting the man who would run with Max and his self-seeking, hedonistic crowd. However, standing beside him while Max gloatingly explained the deceit, the hurt and humiliation Gideon had suffered was quite clear to her, if to no one else.

Sitting alone now in the drawing room, she felt thoroughly ashamed and knew she should be grateful that he treated her with any kindness at all. Thoughts of their wedding night returned and she wrapped her arms about her, as if to hold the memory close. Desire had made her reckless and she had given in quite freely to the passion that had swept them up, but she knew—from what she had overheard from the gossiping servants and her own observations at Martlesham Abbey—that it was different for a man. Gideon's taking her that night had been no act of love, it had been simply lust, easily roused and as easily forgotten. She was not the woman he loved, merely a substitute.

Dominique wondered if she dared go to bed, but decided the proprieties must be observed and asked Mrs Wilkins to bring in the tea tray when the master joined her in the drawing room.

When Gideon came in she was relieved to see that the shuttered look was gone and he addressed her in a cheerful, friendly tone.

'I have been thinking, Nicky, I have not yet given you a wedding present. I shall take you to Rundell's and you shall choose something for yourself, but in the meantime I found this—my godmother's jewel case.' He held out a small leather box. 'Most of Godmama's jewellery is at the bank, but you might like these trinkets to be going on with.'

Dominique set the case on her lap and pushed up the clasp, her eyes widening as she opened the lid. The contents glittered in the candlelight. A profusion of gold and silver and coloured stones winked up at her.

'Th-thank you,' she murmured, bemused. She pushed her fingers gently into the tangle and lifted out a handful of the jewels, letting them fall back into the box in a sparkling cascade. 'They are beautiful, Gideon, *thank* you.'

'Some of the stones—perhaps all—will be paste,' Gideon explained, watching her. 'I noticed that you wear no jewellery, but I thought these trinkets might amuse you.'

'Amuse!' She gave a little laugh. 'They are much more than amusing. We brought very little to England, Papa disposed of everything to pay for the journey, including most of Mama's jewels.'

'No doubt she kept her most precious pieces to pass on to you?'

'They have all been sold now. The attempts to find information about Papa have cost her a great deal.'

'But surely Martlesham...?'

Dominique shook her head.

'While my uncle lived we were very comfortable, but once Max became earl he said he could no longer afford to fund Mama's search for my father. She sold her jewels, gave him everything she had to pay the bribes the French officials demanded for information, but it all came to nought. Max thinks Papa is dead and would do nothing more than frank Mama's letters.' She bit her lip. 'You have a penniless bride, Gideon.'

'Martlesham told me as much before the banns were called.'

Colour stained her cheeks, but she refused to look at him.

'But then you thought you were marrying someone else...'

An uncomfortable silence fell. Gideon felt a tug of sympathy and a keen desire to distract her from her unhappy thoughts.

'May I?' He reached down and pulled out a necklace gleaming with green fire. 'This would suit you, the stones are the colour of your eyes. I remember Godmama wearing it and there should be some ear-drops in there, too...'

'Yes, here they are.' She looked up. 'May I put them on now?'

'Of course.' He watched her, smiling at her enthusiasm as she carefully put the box down and went over to the mirror to fix the ear-drops in place. He followed her across the room. 'I was right, the colour does suit you. Let us add the necklace.'

She laughed. 'First I must remove the kerchief.' She reached around and began to fumble with the knot at the back.

'Here, let me.' Gideon untied the lacy ends and pulled it carefully away from her shoulders.

Without the concealing fichu it was apparent just how badly the dress fitted. Its original owner had obviously been of much more generous proportions than the waiflike creature who stood before him. Even with the drawstrings pulled tight the décolletage was extremely low, exposing the gentle swell of her bosom and more flesh than was becoming. Even as the thought entered his head he knew he was being unfair. Many ladies wore dresses as revealing as this, possibly even more so.

A glance in the mirror showed him that his wife was uncomfortable. One hand had come up to her breast, as if to protect herself from prying eyes and a faint blush

mantled her cheeks. He smiled, wanting to reassure her
as he carefully put the necklace around her throat. She
tilted her head, lengthening the back of her neck, and
as he brushed aside the dark curls his fingers grazed the
delicate ridge of her spine. He wanted to place his lips
there, then to trail a line of kisses across the soft whiteness of her shoulder, where the candlelight played upon
the exposed skin. But she had trembled as he struggled
with the catch. She was clearly frightened of him—
why should she not be, since he had taken advantage
of her innocence in such a way? Besides, to kiss her
now would be the action of a lover and he could never
be that.

He removed his hands and stepped back.

'There. You have a beautiful neck and the emeralds
enhance it.'

She seemed to stand taller at his compliment and
his breath caught in his throat when he met her eyes
in the mirror. They twinkled with a shy smile that far
surpassed the gleaming emeralds.

How long they would have remained there he did
not know, for at that moment the housekeeper bustled
in with the tea tray and the mood was broken. Nicky
reached for her kerchief, but he held it away.

'No, you look very well like that, so there is no need
to cover up again. Unless you are cold?'

'Not in the least, sir. There is a good fire in here,
you see.'

'Indeed there is,' agreed Mrs Wilkins, setting the
tray down on a small table. 'The mistress used to say
this was the cosiest room in the house when the fire was
burning.' She glanced back at the nervous housemaid
following her into the room.' That's right, Jane, put that
down here—it's the spirit kettle,' she explained as the

maid set down the shining silver pot and its burner on a small square wooden stand beside the tea table. 'It hasn't been used since the mistress died, but I thought it should come out again, now we have a new mistress in the house.'

'How thoughtful of you, Mrs Wilkins.' As the servants bustled away Dominique returned to the table, throwing Gideon a look that was brim-full with mischief. 'Since Mrs Wilkins has gone to so much trouble you will have to take tea with me this evening, sir, even if you do consider it to be maudling your insides.'

He grinned, pleased to have their previous easy companionship restored. He took a seat on the opposite side of the hearth, where he could watch her. It was very restful, he thought, to be sitting at one's own fireplace with no need to go out for company or entertainment.

Dominique took great trouble brewing the tea. Gideon must have seen his mother do this a hundred times and she did not want to fall short of his expectations. And when she at last held out a cup to him, she had to try hard not to feel self-conscious in her low-cut gown. The emeralds, be they paste or real, rested heavily upon her neck and gave her a certain amount of reassurance. Gideon had given them to her and he was smiling now, so she was confident she was not offending him. She recalled the touch of his hands on her skin when he had fastened the necklace. It had caused such a leap of desire that she had found it difficult to keep still. If they had been sweethearts, she thought she would have turned and kissed him to thank him for his thoughtfulness, but they were strangers, thrown into marriage, so she must be careful not to put herself forwards.

* * *

'My sister Gwendoline is in town,' he said, settling back in his chair. 'I shall visit her tomorrow to explain our situation and ask her to take you shopping.'

Dominique almost dropped her cup.

'You—you will tell her about our marriage?'

'Of course. There is no point in hiding it. As soon as Max and his cronies return it will be all over town anyway.'

'I suppose you are right. But will she want to help me?'

'She is my sister and will want to dispel any gossip.'

Gideon replied with calm certainty, but Dominique was not so sure.

It was in a mood of trepidation that Dominique went downstairs to greet her visitor two days later.

She was immediately struck by the likeness between brother and sister, the same auburn hair and hazel eyes, but although Lady Ribblestone was tall she could not be described as lean. A gown of the finest cream displayed her ample figure beneath the holly-green pelisse that hung open from her shoulders, while a matching bonnet of the same dark green silk sat jauntily on her burnished curls.

'So you are Gideon's bride by mistake,' she said bluntly.

'Yes, Lady Ribblestone, I—'

'Oh, no formality, please, you must call me Gwen.' The lady came forwards and hugged her. 'And what shall I call you?'

'Dominique—that is, G-Gideon prefers to call me Nicky,' she said, emerging, startled, from the scented embrace.

'Now, why should he do that, when Dominique is such a pretty name?'

'I—it is French…'

'Ah, of course.' A shadow crossed Gwen's countenance, but she recovered quickly and gave another blinding smile. 'Gideon tells me you are seriously in need of clothes.' Dominique found herself being scrutinised from head to toe. 'Well, perhaps it is a little out of fashion, but it is not that bad.'

Dominique glanced down at her walking dress and gave a rueful smile.

'Perhaps not, but it is the *only* thing I have.'

'What? My dear girl, you must explain everything.'

And suddenly Dominique found herself on the sofa beside Lady Ribblestone, telling her about her sudden departure from Martlesham and the trunk Max had sent with her, full of improper garments. Immediately Gwendoline demanded to see them.

'I am sorry to say it, my dear,' she said as they made their way to Dominique's bedchamber, 'but I cannot like your cousin. If this whole sorry business has given Gideon a dislike of the earl's company then some good has come of it. And Gideon's marrying you, of course.'

'I am not sure he thinks of it that way,' replied Dominique, a little wistfully. She led Gwendoline into her room and pointed at the trunk. 'Everything is in there, save the muslin dress I wear in the evenings, which my maid has put in the linen press.'

Her sadness gave way to amusement as Lady Ribblestone began to pull out quantities of silk and lace, holding up the items for inspection before throwing them on to the bed. Gwen was not shocked or outraged by the see-through muslins, lacy undergarments or diaphanous nightgowns, she merely chuckled.

'Perhaps not *quite* suitable for you to wear in public,' she remarked, holding up a particularly sheer gown, 'but the lace negligee might be just the sort of thing Gideon would like.'

Dominique's face flamed.

'I d-don't think so.' She slumped against the edge of the bed, thinking of the chaste peck on the cheek he had given her the previous two evenings, before marching off to his own bedroom. 'Besides, all these clothes are far too big for me. They might even have been bought for the—the lady Gideon thought he would marry—'

'He told me she was an actress.'

'Yes.'

'Then you need not call her a lady,' Gwendoline corrected her, coming to sit beside her. 'Did you see her?'

'Yes, she is… She has a—a fuller figure.'

'And no doubt will run to fat as she gets older.'

Dominique giggled. 'Perhaps. But she is much taller than I am. She is very beautiful, too, and fair.'

'A big, blowsy woman, then,' said Gwendoline. 'Not at all the sort to suit Gideon. He is very chivalrous, you know, and will much prefer a wife he can cherish and protect. Once we have bought you a few gowns that are more becoming to your size and figure, I have no doubt he will find you irresistible.'

Dominique sighed.

'I doubt it. But it is not only that she was so very beautiful. He thought she—that is, he thought *I*—was English, but I am not. I am half French and I cannot alter that.'

'Ah.'

Dominique looked uncertainly at her new friend. 'Why does Gideon dislike the French so much?'

Gwendoline's smile disappeared.

'You do not know?'

'No. Will you tell me?'

Gwendoline hesitated, saying at last, 'Very well, but not until we have been shopping. My carriage has been standing at the door for far too long. We must leave now, if we are to get anything done today.' She jumped up. 'Come along, my dear, put on your bonnet, we are going out.'

To one who had lived very retired for the past ten years, a shopping trip with Lady Ribblestone was a revelation. Dominique soon lost count of the modistes, milliners, bazaars and warehouses they visited. Gwendoline sailed through the establishments, setting everyone running to do her bidding.

By the time they returned to Brook Street an alarming number of orders had been placed and an even more alarming number of packages and bandboxes filled the carriage.

'I think we have done very well for the first day,' remarked Gwendoline, reviewing their purchases.

'First day!' Dominique laughed. 'I do not think I have ever had so many new things in my life.'

'Well, you came to town with nothing,' reasoned Gwendoline. 'Tomorrow we shall order you a riding habit. I shall take you to Ribblestone's tailor, he makes all my habits. Unless you think Gideon would prefer you to use his own tailor…?'

'I think Gideon will say I have spent more than enough,' declared Dominique. 'Heaven knows how much all this will cost.'

Gwendoline shrugged.

'Gideon can afford it. Old Lady Telford left him everything, you know, and until now he has frittered it away on larks and sprees. It will be good for him to have some responsibilities.'

The word threw a cloud over Dominique's spirits.

'And I am a responsibility.' She sighed. 'Will you tell me now why Gideon did not want to marry a French-woman?'

'The war, my dear, surely that is reason enough.'

'No, it is more than that,' said Dominique, a tiny crease furrowing her brow. 'He looked very shocked when he found out my father is French. He seemed quite, quite repulsed.' She fixed her eyes upon Gwendoline. 'Please tell me, then perhaps I can do something to alleviate the situation.' She added quickly, 'What is it, why do you look at me like that, as if you pity me? What is it I should know?'

Gwendoline hesitated.

'I think Gideon should tell you himself.'

'Please, Gwen.'

Her pleading look and the hand placed so insistently upon Lady Ribbleston's arm had its affect. She sighed and nodded.

'Very well. You see, our aunt—Papa's sister—married a Frenchman, the Duc du Chailly. They were guillotined during the Terror.'

'Oh, I am so very sorry!'

'She was also my godmother and I am named after her. We knew her as Tante Gwendoline and when we were children we spent many happy times with them in France, until the Revolution. It was quite devastating for the family when they died.'

'Oh, that is so very sad. And Max knows this?'

'Martlesham? Yes, of course. It was no secret and the executions were much talked of in town at the time.'

'Then how cruel of him to trick Gideon into marrying me!' declared Dominique angrily. She frowned. 'Max thought that as soon as the deceit was known Gideon would seek an annulment.'

'Yes, Gideon mentioned that.' Gwendoline added quietly, 'He also told me why that is not possible.'

Dominique bowed her head, her cheeks crimson.

'He could still divorce me.'

'Not Gideon,' said his sister decidedly. 'He is far too honourable to drag any woman through that.'

'Then we are man and wife, until death.' Dominique sighed. 'That sounds so bleak, but perhaps, given time…'

Lady Ribblestone reached out and covered her hands, saying quickly, 'You must not hope for too much, my dear.' She hesitated. 'I think it best if you know everything. Our older brother, James, died in France, too. At the hands of the Girondins.'

'And Papa was a Girondin.'

If there had been any light at the end of the long tunnel Dominique saw stretching before her, it was shut off in an instant. Beneath Gwendoline's warm clasp she gripped her hands together very tightly, hoping that small pain would stop her from crying.

'Tell me,' she said, her throat constricted.

'It was the winter of ninety-one. The Legislative Assembly had been appointed—young, fanatical antiroyalists hell-bent on destroying the old order. James went to France to try to help *tante* and the *duc*. Father had friends there, you see, contacts opposed to the new administration. He had arranged a meeting, but on that very night they were attacked and James was killed.'

'And the Legislative Assembly was Girondiste,' Dominique said in a whisper. 'Papa was against the violence. He wanted to end it, but who will believe that now?' She looked up, all hope gone. 'How can your brother bear to be married to me? Is it for revenge?'

'No, no. Gideon is an honourable man and he will take his marriage vows seriously.'

Dominique looked around her at the packages littering the carriage.

'What is the point of buying me all this? He can never love me.'

'Very few of us marry for love, my dear.'

'But I represent all that he abhors. And you are Gideon's sister—you have just as much cause to hate me—'

'Gideon does not hate you, my dear, I am sure of that, and nor do I. *You* are not responsible for what happened in the Terror. My godmother married the Duc du Chailly because he was a good, kind man, and before the war we met many such people in France.' Gwen turned and put her hands on Dominique's shoulders. 'You must look upon this as an arranged marriage. Not perhaps what you would have chosen, but you must make the best of it. Gideon has already decided to do so, that is why he asked me to take you under my wing.' She gave Dominique a little shake. 'You have to make a life for yourself, my dear. You are not an antidote, there is no reason why you and Gideon should not be happy together. With the right clothes and a little confidence I think we can pass you off quite creditably in society, and when Gideon sees other people taking notice of you, he will do so, too.'

Dominique looked at her. 'Do you really think so, Gwen?'

'I am certain of it. We will make you into such a beautiful, stylish wife that he cannot fail to be proud of you!'

Chapter Six

Dominique was not convinced by Gwendoline's brave talk, but they had reached their destination and there was no time to discuss anything more. Judd informed them the master was in the morning room and they went to find him.

'My dear Gideon,' declared Gwen, greeting him with a kiss. 'Have you been waiting in for us? How sweet of you. We are quite exhausted.'

'And is my credit similarly exhausted?' he asked, smiling slightly.

He invited Dominique to sit on the sofa and sat down beside her, once Gwen had dropped elegantly into an armchair.

'Lord, no. I had everything put to Ribblestone's account and he will sort it all out with you later.' Gwendoline paused while the wine and cakes were served. 'Now, Gideon,' she said at last, selecting a dainty confection from the selection on her plate. 'We have made a start in setting your wife up with clothes for the Season. I have been promised that the first of the gowns will be delivered here tomorrow. What about Court Dress? Are you presenting her at a drawing room?'

'Oh, I would rather not,' murmured Dominique in some alarm.

'Nonsense, your husband will be the next Viscount Rotham. You must be presented.'

'But not yet,' said Gideon. 'I think my father should meet Nicky first. This visit to town is merely an—er— informal one.'

'And when do you intend to go to Rotham?'

'All in good time.'

Gwen frowned. 'You cannot put off the meeting forever, Brother. Whatever was said in the heat of the moment Papa will not hold it against you, you know that. Your tempers are too similar for him not to understand. He is lonely, Gideon, and however harsh his words he does care for you, very much.'

'I do know that.' He rubbed a hand across his eyes. 'I shall go, but not yet, not yet.'

Dominique sipped her wine and listened to the conversation, aware of a tension between the brother and sister.

'Is it because of me?' she ventured. 'Will Lord Rotham be angry with you for marrying me?'

'Of course not—!'

Gideon put up his hand to stem his sister's denial.

'He will not be happy about it, but his wrath will be on my head, Nicky, not yours. I shall not take you to Rotham without his assurance that you will be received with the respect that is due to you.'

Respect! That sounded very bleak indeed. Dominique was relieved Gideon had no immediate plans to take her to Rotham. Perhaps once she had her own clothes she would feel more courageous. From all Gwen had told her she knew she would be a fool to cling on to any hope that Gideon would ever feel more for her

than a mild friendship, but perhaps she could gain *his*
respect. She resolved there and then never to embar-
rass him by any show of affection that he would have
to rebuff. No, she would show him—and his father—
that despite her French heritage she could be a model
wife, a fitting consort for an English lord.

Dominique was soon on good terms with Mrs
Wilkins and slipped naturally into her role as mistress
of the house. She began to make little changes, such as
ordering a fire to be kept burning in the morning room,
and she asked Judd to remove some of the heavy silver from the dining table, so that she could at least see
her husband when they dined together each evening. If
Gideon noticed he said nothing, but she was heartened
when he suggested a place should be laid for her at his
right hand for dinner, rather than sitting so far apart,
and she was quietly pleased when he began to seek her
out for a glass of wine when he came in each afternoon,
before going upstairs to change for dinner. For the first
week she remained in the house, going out only with
Lady Ribblestone on shopping trips, but by the end of
Dominique's second week in Brook Street, Gwendoline
declared that her sister-in-law was at last fit to be seen.

They were having breakfast and Lady Ribblestone
suggested they should drive through the park at the
fashionable hour.

'I should like to go out,' Dominique admitted, 'but
Hyde Park—will it not be very crowded?'

'Oh, excessively,' replied Gwendoline cheerfully.
'The world and his wife will be there.'

'So many people?' exclaimed Dominique, dismayed.
'I am not sure I am ready—'

She broke off as Gideon came in.

'Now, what are you two plotting?' he said, smiling. 'Are you off to spend more money today?'

'Not at all,' retorted Gwen. 'I want Dominique to accompany me to the park. It promises to be a very fine afternoon and we could drive out in the barouche.'

He sat down at the table and poured himself a cup of coffee. Gwen watched him in surprise.

'This is a change, Brother,' she said, momentarily diverted. 'I thought you only drank ale at breakfast.'

He grinned. 'Bachelor fare, Sis. I am a married man now.'

'Then help me to persuade your wife to drive out with me. She has been cooped up in this house long enough.'

'I agree,' said Gideon, 'but I am not sure if riding with you in a stuffy barouche is how she should make her entrance into polite society.'

'There is nothing stuffy about Ribblestone's barouche,' retorted his sister, offended.

'Perhaps not, but I would rather drive Nicky in my curricle.'

It was the first time he had suggested they go out together and Dominique felt her cheeks going pink with pleasure.

'I cannot compete with that.' Gwen laughed and wagged her finger at Dominique. 'Accept immediately, my dear. I have never known my brother to take up a female in his curricle before!'

'Quite true, Gwen.' Gideon turned to Dominique, smiling. 'Well, madam, will you give me the honour of driving you out for your first introduction to the *ton*?'

Dominique was in a panic. What to wear to drive out with Gideon? Her new riding habit had not yet arrived,

and although her new promenade dress was beautiful it
had been bought for the warmer months. She even ran
out into the street to test the weather. The sun was shining, but there was a chill wind blowing and she did not
want to make her first public appearance wrapped up in
a shawl. After much deliberation she decided she would
wear her new pelisse of crimson silk, with a matching
cap. Gwendoline had persuaded her to have it trimmed
with fur and frogged *à la hussar*, prophesying correctly
that the chilly days of spring were not yet at an end.
She had also added that not everyone could wear such
a strong colour, especially not a blowsy blonde.

At the appointed hour Dominique made her way
downstairs to find Gideon waiting for her in the hall.
He glanced up as he heard her step on the stairs, then
turned for a second, longer look. She saw the surprise
in his eyes, but there was admiration, too, and her heart
gave a little skip. She was emboldened to ask him if
she would do.

'You will do very well,' he said slowly. 'The colour
suits you admirably.'

She was relieved and said with a smile, 'Remind me,
then, to thank your sister for persuading me to buy it.'

A gleaming curricle waited at the door, two beautiful grey horses in harness and his groom at their heads.

'This is Sam, my tiger,' said Gideon, a laugh in his
voice. 'And the reason he is looking so deuced savage
is that we are not in the habit of driving females.'

'Not if they's gonna screech and frighten the 'osses,'
muttered Sam, giving a reluctant tug of his forelock in
Dominique's direction.

'Mind your tongue, man!'

'No, he is quite right,' replied Dominique, cutting

across her husband's sharp reply and smiling at the groom. 'I hope I know how to behave myself in an open carriage and *think* I can promise not to screech, unless of course we are about to be overturned.'

'He ain't likely to do that,' opined Sam. 'Top o' the trees is Mr Albury when it comes to driving.'

'Ah, then I understand why you are happy to stay in his employ,' she said as Gideon helped her into her seat. 'And since *you* have such confidence in Mr Albury's driving, I am more than happy to drive out with him.'

'I think you have made a conquest,' murmured Gideon as the groom jumped clear of the horses and waited to scramble up into the rumble seat. 'Sam was not at all happy when he discovered I had fallen into the parson's mousetrap.'

Dominique said nothing, but she was pleased to have come safely over another small hurdle.

The spring sunshine had brought everyone out of doors and the journey to the park gates was slow. Gideon kept his attention on negotiating the busy roads and Dominique had plenty of time to admire his skill as he inched the curricle through the traffic. If she expected to enjoy a quiet drive, she was disappointed. As soon as they entered the park gates she saw the crowds. Ladies with parasols, gentlemen with their canes, all parading up and down beside a procession of carriages and riders. Their progress was very slow, for it seemed everyone wanted to stop and be introduced to the new Mrs Albury. Gideon was a little concerned at first about how Nicky would react to all the attention, but he discovered his worries unfounded. She was a little shy, but her manners were perfectly good and she turned aside the more impertinent comments and questions with a quiet dignity.

'How did they know I was in London?' wondered Dominique when they moved on from yet another introduction.

'There will have been something in the society pages.'

Gideon said no more. He had deliberately ordered Judd not to bring the newspapers into breakfast each morning after he had seen the first sly reference.

The Hon. Mr A—has brought his new bride to town, but there are rumours that this is not the Bride he had been expecting, his intended having been replaced at the very altar by Another. The ceremony took place at the seat of that well-known trickster, the Earl of M—

Gideon recognised Max's hand behind that entry and he did not doubt there would be more, which was why he had been so keen that his wife should make her first appearance in his company. He knew speculation would be rife, but he had not expected quite so much interest. Why, the carriages were queuing up to speak to them.

'A new bride always attracts attention,' he remarked after a pause.

'Undoubtedly, but I fear my cousin has been at work to advertise our situation,' she said shrewdly.

Gideon heard the uncertainty in her voice and briefly put one hand over hers.

'I have no doubt he has.' *Damn Max.* 'Do not worry. If we present a united front the gossip will soon fade, dismissed as idle rumour.'

'Of course, but...'

He glanced down and saw the crease in her brow, the way she caught her bottom lip between her teeth. He said gently, 'What is the matter, Nicky?'

'Max and his friends are still at Martlesham. Would he really send word all the way to London, to make mischief for us?'

'You should know your cousin doesn't like to be crossed.'

'True, and you did rather take the wind out of his sails by not calling for an annulment. I'm afraid he will make more trouble for you, if he can.'

For him? Did she have no worries for herself? He shrugged, wanting to reassure her.

'What can he do? When people see that we are perfectly happy together then the rumours will soon die away.'

'I fear that will inconvenience you greatly.'

'Me?'

'Why, yes, if you must be seen everywhere with me, instead of enjoying your own life as you have been used to do.

Gideon was startled at her matter-of-fact tone and rather alarmed, too. All her concern appeared to be for his well-being, while he had given very little thought to hers. He had been happy to leave his sister to look after Nicky, to provide her with the wardrobe she would need for her new life, but he knew most brides would consider him very neglectful. Not that Nicky wanted his attentions—she had been very reserved since their wedding night. True, she had seemed very willing then, but she had been an innocent and his passion must have frightened her as much as it had shocked him. It was not how he had expected to behave with his new wife.

It was one of the things his father had drummed

into him, that wives were fragile, delicate creatures and must be treated with great care and gentleness. Gideon had not visited her bed again and Nicky had shown no signs of wanting him to do so. He would need an heir, of course, but there was plenty of time for that when they were more comfortable together. Since they had arrived in London he had left her to settle in, seeing her only at breakfast and for dinner some evenings. He told himself it was for her sake, but there was something about his new wife that unsettled him, an unlooked-for attraction that stole up on him when he was too long in her company and he was determined not to take advantage of her again, but suddenly it all seemed incredibly selfish.

'I beg your pardon,' he said now, painfully aware of his shortcomings. 'I have been very busy, but you have every right to be angry with me for my lack of attention. Most new brides would be ringing a peal over their husbands for such behaviour.'

'But ours is a most irregular marriage. I do not expect you to—what is the term?—*live in my pocket*.' She shifted in her seat and looked up at him, her green eyes dark and earnest. 'I want to make you a good wife, Gideon.'

He did not know how to reply, but stared in silence at the serious little face framed by dark curls. No wonder the *ton* was so interested in his marriage. They had been in town for almost three weeks and this was the first time they had been seen out together. Well, he thought grimly, that would change. His friends would look for him in vain tonight. He would stay at home with his wife.

He did not realise he was still staring at her until he heard Sam's gruff voice, telling him to mind his horses. Nicky blushed and a shy twinkle appeared in her eyes.

'Yes, look to your driving, sir,' she admonished him, straightening in her seat. 'You are wandering all over the path.'

When Gideon informed Dominique at dinner that evening that he was not going out she could not conceal her surprise. It would be the first time he had spent the whole evening with her since the night they had arrived in Brook Street.

'Those who made your acquaintance in the park today will no doubt be sending you invitations very soon,' he told her, straightening the cutlery. 'This may be the last opportunity to enjoy a quiet evening together.'

When the meal was over Dominique left him to his port and went off to the drawing room. At first she nervously paced the floor, plumping cushions and straightening the ornaments, until she took herself to task for being so nervous. This was her home, too, and she should enjoy it. What would she really *like* to do? The beautiful pianoforte in the corner of the room gleamed enticingly, so she sat down and began to play. She was so lost in the music that she did not notice the time passing until she looked up and found Gideon standing by the door, watching her.

'Do go on,' he said, moving into the room and taking a seat by the fire.

Dominique continued until she had finished the Haydn sonata and, as the last notes died away, Gideon began to applaud.

'That was very good, Nicky. And to play without music, you are very accomplished.'

'Thank you, I have been practising here every day,

since I discovered this lovely instrument. I play the harp, too. My mother is very fond of music and insisted I should learn. When we came to England she badgered the earl into providing a tutor. The lessons continued until my uncle died three years ago.'

'And do you sing, too?'

'Yes, a little.'

'Then will you sing for me?'

A flush of pleasure tinged her cheeks.

'Of course. What would you like? An English folk song, perhaps?'

Receiving a nod of assent, she played an introduction, then added her voice, a little hesitant at first, but as the music took over she closed her eyes and sang with more confidence. It was a favourite of her mother's, a haunting love song about a young woman waiting for her lover to return. The thought of Mama, writing her endless letters, refusing to give up hope, gave an added piquancy to the song and when at last she had finished and opened her eyes again, for a moment she could not recall quite where she was.

'That was quite beautiful.' Gideon had moved closer. 'There is so much I do not know about you.'

His eyes were fixed upon her, dark and intense in the glow of the candles. A shiver ran down her spine and she felt desire curling deep inside her.

'We know so little about each other,' she said, trying not to think of the night they had spent together. He had seen her naked, explored her body in the most intimate way. Yet they were still strangers.

'Nicky—'

'I have asked Mrs Wilkins to bring in the tea tray,' she interrupted him hastily. 'And perhaps I should ring for Judd to build up the fire.'

He caught her hand as she walked by him and her fingers trembled in his grasp.

'You are afraid of me.'

She dared not look at him.

'Not afraid, no.'

'Then what is it?'

'You said it yourself. We do not know each other.'

'Then we must put that right.' His breath was warm upon her cheek. He must be bending, perhaps about to kiss the bare skin of her shoulder. If he did that she knew the slender rein she had over herself would snap, she would turn and throw herself at him again, and he would know what a wanton soul she had. She remembered the accusations against the late Queen of France: that she had been unable to control her lust. She had seen many such women at Martlesham since Max had become earl, not only actresses and whores, but also the wives of his so-called friends, all of them willing to share their favours. Her mother had kept her well away from those riotous gatherings, but she had heard Max's disparaging comments and knew the servants viewed them with contempt. Men despised such women and she was desperate that Gideon should not despise her any more than he did already.

She said with forced lightness, 'We can relate our histories over a dish of Bohea.'

'Yes, of course. And here is Judd now with the tea tray. Shall I light the spirit kettle?'

She uttered up a prayer of thanks at his friendly tone. This she could cope with, the ritual of making tea, sitting in separate chairs, their only contact the accidental touch of fingers when she handed him his cup. They conversed easily, but with a wary restraint, on guard lest any remark should cause offence or embarrassment.

'Your sister has invited me to her musical soirée on Thursday,' she said when he brought his cup to her for more tea. 'I would like to go, if you have no objection?'

'Of course not. May I come with you?' His brows snapped together. 'Now why should you look so surprised—would you rather I didn't?'

'G-Gwendoline thought you would not—she said I should not expect you to accompany me everywhere.'

'I think it might be expected that I would attend my own sister's soirée. That is, if you would like me to come with you.'

Dominique would like nothing better and wanted to say as much, but his next words stopped her.

'We are already agreed, are we not, that we must show the *ton* we are on the best of terms? You may be sure that someone will pass the word on to Martlesham.'

So that was it. They were to show Max that his little trick had failed. She forced herself to keep smiling.

'Quite.'

She made her excuses to retire as soon as she could after that, barely waiting for Gideon to kiss her fingers before pulling her hand away and hurrying off to her room. She heard Gideon's footsteps in the corridor some time later, but he did not even pause as he passed her door.

'Dominique, my dear, welcome to my little musical gathering. Ribblestone is at the House, but he will be back later to meet you.' Gwendoline bent to envelope her in a scented hug, the ostrich feathers in her turban quivering above her as she added in an excited whisper, 'I have never had such a crowd here before. Not one refusal to my invitations. This must be down to you, my love.'

'Don't put my wife to the blush before she is even through the door, Gwen.'

'Oh, tush, Dominique knows she is amongst friends here.' Gwendoline pulled Gideon to her and kissed his cheek. 'How are you, Brother? You are looking very fine this evening.'

Dominique thought so, too. Stealing another glance at her husband in his black coat and dazzlingly white linen, she thought he was easily the most handsome man in the room. His hair glinted with fiery red sparks in the candlelight, which also accentuated the strong angles of his lean face. He wore no jewellery save his heavy signet ring and a quizzing glass on a black-velvet ribbon around his neck, but the exquisite cut of his coat and artfully knotted cravat were the envy of many.

'My love, may I present to you…'

She found herself surrounded by gentlemen. Her instinct was to cling to her husband, but that would never do. She allowed him to make the introductions, accepted their compliments with a shy smile, but was relieved when, after a few moments' conversation, Gideon took her arm and guided her away.

'I can't have you falling into the clutches of those Lotharios tonight,' he murmured as he led her across the room.

'Are they all so bad, then?' She glanced back. 'They seemed perfectly respectable, save perhaps for Sir Desmond, who was whispering the most outrageous things to Gwen. The rest I thought were perfect gentlemen.'

'And so they are, as long as I am beside you, but leave them alone with a pretty woman—'

She felt her cheeks burn.

'Oh, do you mean that, Gideon, do you really think I am pretty?'

'As a picture,' he replied, lifting her gloved hand to his lips.

She knew it meant nothing, he performed the gesture with practised ease, as he had doubtless done hundreds of times before with other women, but she could not prevent her heart from beating just that little bit faster. Her body responded to his every look, every touch, but she had learned to hide it, so that she alone knew how much her skin tingled when he was close to her and how much she ached to feel his arms about her.

The gentlemen melted away, but the ladies were not so easy to escape. They clustered about the couple, trying to separate Dominique from her husband, ostensibly to sit with them for the forthcoming recital, but she guessed they really wanted to learn the circumstances of her marriage. She held tight to Gideon's arm and he turned aside every invitation, declaring with a laugh that he wanted to keep his wife to himself for this one evening.

When at length they sat down together she murmured her thanks to him and could not resist asking if he was merely staying by her for the sake of the gossip-mongers.

'Good God, no. I came here to be with you this evening. And besides, I want to know what you think. Many of my sister's guests have no musicality at all, and praise everyone to the skies, however dire the performance.'

He values my opinion!

Dominique sat up a little straighter. She had been apprehensive about the evening, but with Gideon beside her she began to relax and enjoy herself. They sat through some poor piano playing, and even worse poetry, but when they went in to supper Dominique could not agree with Gideon's remark that it was a wasted evening.

'I have made a number of new acquaintances and that will stand me in good stead in future. And,' she added, giving him a twinkling look, 'now I have heard the standard of music that is acceptable in town I shall not be afraid to play in public.'

'I am glad to hear that.' He grinned back at her. 'It has been particularly bad this evening. I shall have to have words with my sister.'

Later, however, when she brought her husband to their table, Gwendoline was unrepentant.

'They are friends, dear Brother, and desperate to perform. I get them over with first, so that we can all relax and enjoy the remainder of the evening.'

'Aye, that is why I am never here early,' agreed Lord Ribblestone in a grave tone that was decidedly at odds with the mischievous gleam in his eye. 'Gwen has too soft a heart when it comes to lame ducks and always likes to give them a chance to show their paces. You will learn, Mrs Albury, never to get to my wife's parties before suppertime.'

'*You* certainly do not,' retorted Gwen.

He smiled. 'Acquit me, my love. Tonight at least I would have come earlier, if matters had allowed.'

Gideon raised an eyebrow.

'Discussing the treaty, Anthony?'

Ribblestone's mouth twisted.

'This peace with France won't last the year.'

'Oh, I hope you are wrong there, my lord.' Dominique blushed at her impetuous words.

'My wife's father is French,' explained Gideon.

Lord Ribblestone's brows shot up.

'Is he, by Gad? But I thought—'

'Goodness, Anthony, if you took more notice of me and less of your dusty political papers, you would remember!' Gwendoline broke in hastily. 'I explained everything, so there is no need to go over it all again. Now, my lord, we still have any number of guests wishing to play for us tonight so you must help me get everyone back to the salon.' Gwendoline bore him away, giving Dominique a warm smile as she passed. 'I promise you the best players have yet to perform. I do not think you will be disappointed, my dear.'

Dominique tried to respond, but all she could think of was Lord Ribblestone's astonishment that Gideon should marry a Frenchwoman.

'My brother-in-law has many attributes, but tact is not one of them,' remarked Gideon. 'No wonder the government is in such disarray, if he is an example of their abilities.' He said gently, 'Your French connections are no secret in town, my dear, but I doubt anyone else will remark upon it.' He rose and held out his hand to her. 'Now, shall we gird our loins for more execrable music?'

She accompanied him back to the salon, but her new brother-in-law's shock had undermined her confidence. Everyone was watching her, wondering what could have persuaded Gideon to marry a penniless Frenchwoman without even beauty to recommend her. However, his continued presence at her side was reassuring, and since the musical offerings were indeed much improved she tried very hard to put her anxieties aside and enjoy herself. A particularly good duet between piano and harp had her clapping enthusiastically, as did a very funny ditty by Sir Desmond Arndale.

'Bravo,' cried Gwendoline, moving forwards to congratulate him. 'A splendid ending to our evening, sir. Now that everyone has performed—'

'Not quite everyone.' Sir Desmond interrupted her. 'Mrs Albury has yet to play.'

Dominique had been too busy applauding to take in his words until she found everyone looking at her.

'What? Oh, no—that is—'

'Come along, ma'am, I am sure everyone wants to hear you.' Sir Desmond was beaming and beckoning her forwards.

Gideon turned to her.

'I would like to hear you, very much, but if you wish I will tell them you would rather not.'

The kindly understanding in his eyes boosted her spirits. She squared her shoulders.

'No,' she said, smiling a little, 'I have been happy enough to listen to the others, it is only fair I take my turn.'

A smattering of applause went round the room as she rose and made her way to the pianoforte. Sir Desmond hovered around her, adjusting the candles and asking if he should search out any music for her from the pile of sheets on the table.

'Perhaps Mrs Albury will play us a *French* air,' sniggered someone from the audience.

Dominique affected not to hear, but she was heartened when Gideon responded with a laugh, 'Perhaps she will—whatever her choice I know it will be delightful. What is it to be, my dear?'

'A piece by Mr Mozart, I think,' she declared.

The 'Fantasia' was not long and not even particularly difficult. She had performed it many times for her mother and knew she could play it well, but her confidence wavered when she looked around the room and realised how many people were watching her. Then her gaze fell upon Gideon. He was smiling at her. Everyone else was forgotten. She would play for him and him alone.

As she struck the last confident chords she smiled, knowing she had done well. The applause was instant and the first 'brava' she heard was from Gideon. There were calls for an encore, but she shook her head, blushing, and would have joined Gideon, but Gwendoline carried her off to enjoy the praise and compliments of her guests.

'Gideon shall have you back in a while,' she told Dominique, sweeping her away. 'You must not allow him to monopolise you, my dear.'

'By Gad no,' declared Sir Desmond, accompanying them across the room. 'It's about time you gave the rest of us a share of your company, madam.'

When she glanced over her shoulder she saw Gideon smile and nod to her, before joining a group of gentlemen gathered about Lord Ribblestone, so she allowed Gwen to lead her to a lively little group who were enjoying a final glass of wine together before the carriages were called.

'I thought we should never get a word with you,' exclaimed Mrs Innis, a buxom matron swathed in mulberry silk. 'Albury has been guarding you all evening.'

'Not guarding,' Dominique protested with a smile. 'I enjoy his company.'

'La, madam, pray do not say such a thing!' cried Sir Desmond, throwing up his hands.

'At least not in front of Gideon,' added Gwen. 'It would make him horribly conceited, you know.'

'Yes,' declared Mrs Innis. 'A husband needs to be kept on his toes. 'You must not let him take you for granted.'

'You should set up a flirt,' whispered Gwendoline. 'As I have done.' She turned to Sir Desmond, who was hovering about her. 'My dear, will you be an angel and fetch me another glass of wine? I am quite parched this evening.'

As he lounged away Mrs Innis gave a fat chuckle.

'If only we were all fortunate enough to have such a devoted lap dog.'

'Desmond is very sweet,' agreed Gwen, smiling after his retreating form.

'But, does Lord Ribblestone not object?' enquired Dominique.

Gwen's smile slipped a little.

'I doubt he even notices.'

Mrs Innis tapped Dominique's arm with her closed fan.

'Lord bless you, Mrs Albury. A man don't want his wife to be forever clinging to his coat-tails, ain't that so, Lady Ribblestone?'

'No, indeed.' Gwen shook off her reverie and gave a bright smile. 'Pray do not look so shocked, dear sister. It is all the rage to have a cicisbeo, I assure you.'

'But I don't want a—a—'

'Not a case of what you *want*,' put in another lady, her eyes fixed rather wistfully upon a thin, bewhiskered gentleman on the far side of the room. 'Grayson only shows an interest in me if he thinks he has a rival.'

'Perhaps it is a little early for Mrs Albury to be setting up a flirt,' said Mrs Innis, considering. 'She is not yet married a month.'

'It is much too early,' Dominique replied emphatically. 'I mean to be an exemplary wife.'

'Very admirable, my dear, but you need to take care,' said the wistful woman. 'Nothing revolts a man more than an excessive display of affection from his spouse. Men are such contrary creatures, they are most attracted to the very thing they cannot have.'

And that would be the beautiful actress, thought Dominique, maintaining her smile with an effort.

'Very true, Lady Grayson,' averred Mrs Innis, the dyed ostrich feathers in her turban nodding vigorously. 'You must never appear too eager for his attentions— that way leads only to disaster.'

Dominique turned to Gwendoline, expecting her to say that was nonsense, but instead her sister-in-law nodded, saying slowly, 'You know, my dear, I think Gideon is very much like a dog with a bone. He may not want you at all, until someone else shows an interest.'

Dominique grimaced.

'I am not a piece of *meat*, Gwen.'

'No-o, but as his wife he may think he does not need to work for your affection.'

'Perhaps I should talk to him—'

'Fatal, my dear,' declared Gwen. 'You must keep Gideon at arm's length if you want to maintain his interest.'

'But surely—'

'Only a trollop would throw herself at a man,' stated Mrs Innis baldly, ignoring Dominique's attempt to speak. 'Give him your smiles, my dear, but never your sighs. Let him kiss you and make love to you, but never, *never* allow him to believe you care or it will be all over with you. He will be setting up his mistress and treating you like a bond slave. He will dominate and bully you until you are the unhappiest being in the world and he won't even *care*.'

'Who won't care?' demanded Sir Desmond, returning at that moment. 'If you are talking of Lady R, then I care very much.'

'Which just proves what we have been saying,' responded Gwendoline lightly. 'Men always want the one thing they cannot have.'

'What nonsense are you telling my wife?' demanded Gideon, coming up while they were all laughing.

'Merely a few home truths, Brother, regarding how best to remain happy.'

'My wife's happiness is, of course, my chief concern.' He made her a little bow and held out his arm. 'Our carriage awaits, ma'am. I think it is time we said goodnight.'

'I think that passed off very well,' he remarked as they drove home through the dark streets. 'And my sister introduced you to her friends?'

'Yes. Including Sir Desmond Arndale.' She drew a breath. 'Is…um…is he her lover?'

'I doubt it, but much of Anthony's time is taken up with government matters and Arndale is useful when Gwen needs an escort. A harmless fribble.'

'And is Lord Ribblestone jealous of him?'

'Lord, no.' He turned towards her. 'Why this sudden interest in Arndale?'

'I am curious to know how married women go on in London.'

'Many of them behave scandalously.' He leaned closer and reached out to cup her chin and turn her towards him. 'But I don't intend to allow *you* to behave like that, at least only with me.'

Her heart began to hammer as he kissed her and she raised her hand to touch his cheek, then pulled it back.

Men always want what they cannot have.

She must not show him how much she wanted him, yet surely he could hear her heart? She could hardly breathe it was thudding so heavily against her ribs. The carriage began to slow and he raised his head.

'We are home,' he murmured. 'Be ready for me to-night. I shall come to your room.'

If Dominique had thought waiting in the drawing room for Gideon to finish his port was nerve-racking, waiting for him to come to her bedchamber was almost unbearable. She allowed Kitty to dress her in one of the soft linen nightdresses she had chosen with Gwendoline, then dismissed her and sat on the edge of the bed with only the glow of the fire and a single candle to relieve the darkness. The trunk she had brought with her from Martlesham was just visible in the gloom and when a sudden flare of the candle flame glinted on its studded lid she went over and opened it, rifling through the contents to pull out a gossamer-thin creation. This is what the unseen and unknown Agnes Bennet would have worn, she thought. But Agnes knew exactly how to tease a man into submission—witness the way she had bewitched Gideon into offering her marriage.

Put it on, whispered the seductive voice in her head. *It will reveal your body and drive him to distraction.*

But Dominique knew her slender form could not compare with the voluptuous curves of Agnes Bennet. Gideon might be disgusted with her—worse, he might even laugh. Quickly she put the wispy confection away again. The trunk must be removed, it was a constant reminder of the woman Gideon had wanted for his bride.

She heard a soft noise somewhere in the quiet house and ran back to the bed. Straining her ears, she picked up the sound of footsteps getting closer and she clasped her hands together nervously.

Gideon had not entered this bedchamber since he was a child. It had been his mother's room and, apart from ordering that it was to be redecorated for his bride, he had not given it another thought—he realised a little ruefully that when he had issued those orders he had thought that his wife would spend most of her nights in his bed. But the woman he had envisaged sharing his life with was nothing like the woman he had married.

Something stirred within him when he saw the pale creature standing before the bed, her hair a dusky cloud around her shoulders. It was not the hot lust of their wedding night, more an urge to protect her, to make her happy.

'I...um...I hope this room is to your liking?'

'Yes, it is very comfortable, thank you.'

Silently he cursed his awkwardness. This was not a conversation for the bedroom. Why had he come here tonight? He recalled how beautifully she had played at Gwen's soirée, his pride in her performance, the possessiveness he had felt when the men had clustered round her. A spike of desire coursed through him and he tried again.

'You played like an angel tonight.' She smiled at that. Encouraged, he moved closer, holding out his hands. 'I did not know I had such an accomplished wife.'

Cautiously she reached out for him.

'I am glad that I pleased you, Gideon.'

'You do please me.' As he pulled her into his arms

he realised that he really meant it. 'You please me a great deal.'

She looked up at him, shyly accepting his kiss.

Gideon made love to her that night. Dominique returned his caresses but she kept her emotions in check and tried to respond as she thought a wife should, compliant and quietly accepting of his attentions. His lovemaking was gentle and restrained, as if he was afraid she might break beneath him, and although there was none of the hot heady passion of their first coupling, when it was over, Dominique found it immensely satisfying to have him lying with her, to hold him in her arms until he slipped from her bed to make the way back to his own room in the chill dark hours before dawn.

Chapter Seven

The following weeks were the happiest Dominique had ever known. Gideon bought her diamonds for her wedding gift and she wore them on almost every occasion. He took her driving in the park and escorted her everywhere, to balls, parties and breakfasts, introducing her to his friends and acquaintances. Whatever the news-sheets might say, he showed no signs of dissatisfaction with his bride, either in public or in private, when he came to her room at night. Dominique loved the special closeness of those nights and although he always returned to his own room before morning, when they met at breakfast, she thought his eyes had an added warmth when he greeted her.

As her confidence grew, Dominique began to make more changes to the Brook Street house. She ordered fresh flowers and arranged them in the hall and in the morning room, which had become her personal domain and where she was in the habit of entertaining her growing number of friends. The silent, tomblike atmosphere lifted, the servants looked happier and even Gideon remarked that the house felt much more like home. They were returning from a drive in the park when he said this and Dominique could not suppress a smile.

'Do you really think so? I am so pleased, because I was afraid you might not want me to change anything in your father's house.'

'You are mistress there,' he said, picking up her hand and kissing it. 'You may change whatever you wish.'

She felt the little bubble of happiness growing inside her. Gideon was more and more in the habit of such gestures and not only when they were in public. She was beginning to believe he genuinely cared for her. She wished she might respond in kind, but she could not forget Gwen's words of advice, that Gideon would find any such show of affection repellent. And Gwen was his sister, so she must know best.

When they reached Brook Street, Gideon helped her down and she felt his hand resting lightly on her back as he escorted her into the house. The butler opened the door to them, smiling broadly as he announced to Gideon that the delivery he had been waiting for had arrived.

'It has been set up, sir, just as you ordered.'

'Thank you, Judd.' Gideon relinquished his hat and gloves to the waiting footman, then put his hand under her elbow. 'Come, you should see this, too.'

He led her to the drawing room.

He said, as the butler closed the door quietly behind them, 'Well, what do you think?'

Dominique stared, blinked and stared again. Standing next to the piano was a golden harp and beside it a small stool covered with gold satin.

'Oh, Gideon,' she breathed, 'is it for me?'

'Of course. We have been in town for three months

now and it is something of an…er…anniversary present.'

She ran forwards and began to inspect it, running her fingers reverently over the strings.

'It is beautiful.'

'You said you used to play and I would like to hear you.'

'Yes, yes, once I have had time to practise a little.' She went back to him, unable to prevent herself from smiling. 'You are too generous to me, Gideon, thank you so much.'

Without thinking she threw her arms around his neck and kissed him full on the mouth.

'Oh! I beg your pardon.' She blushed and would have drawn back, but his arms slipped around her.

'Not at all. I must give you more presents, if that is the way you thank me.'

He was grinning down at her and suddenly all the careful restraint, the polite friendliness she had worked so hard to cultivate was forgotten. She could not speak for the heavy tattoo her heart was beating against her ribs and the sudden breathlessness that had overtaken her. She still had her arms about his neck and she could feel the silky softness of his hair against her fingers. The grin softened into a smile and the glint in his eyes heated her blood. She felt the tug of desire deep in her core and instinctively her body pressed against him.

Gideon's arms tightened as his body responded to the feel of her. It was the first time since their wedding night that she had taken the initiative and kissed him and he was surprised that her display of affection should please him so much. She felt so right in his arms and his sudden arousal was completed when he breathed in the scent of her, a mixture of summer flowers and an indefinable fragrance that he had come to recognise during those dark intimate nights as hers alone. The memory of her naked body heated his blood. He lowered his head to nibble at the tender lobe of her ear. She shuddered, but pressed even closer. A bolt of white-hot desire shot through him as he thought of the heights they might attain together.

'There is still an hour before we need change for dinner.' Dominique's very bones liquefied as his deep voice caressed her heightened senses. 'Would you like to—?'

A knock on the door interrupted them. As it opened Dominique quickly stepped out of his arms, but Gideon hung on to one hand, linking his fingers through hers. 'Yes, Judd, what is it?'

'The Earl of Martlesham, sir, wishing to know if you are at home.'

Gideon sighed. 'I suppose we must see him. Send him in.'

He cast a rueful look towards Dominique, who tried to hide her disappointment. Every fibre of her being screamed out that he should send her cousin to the devil, but the damage had been done, the magic of the moment was gone—perhaps Gideon had never felt it at all. The butler withdrew, to return a moment later and announce the earl in sonorous tones. Max came in, his fair features a little flushed from the heat of the day and his eyes going immediately to their linked hands.

Unhurriedly Gideon stepped forwards, saying calmly, 'Martlesham, good day to you. Have you come to see how we go on?'

Max returned Gideon's bow with a brief nod.

'Good day to you, Albury, Cousin. I thought I should call to let you know I was back in town.'

'How very good of you.'

Gideon's voice was heavy with sarcasm, which brought a dull angry flush to Max's face. Remembering her place as mistress of the house, Dominique invited him to sit down.

'Have you seen my mother?' she asked, when they had made themselves comfortable. 'Is she well?'

'Aye, as well as she ever will be. She came to see me just before I left Martlesham Abbey. Wanted me to use my influence to get her an audience with the Foreign Secretary. As if I had any! Told her she must look to you, Albury, for that sort of thing. As her son-in-law I have no doubt you would like nothing better than to seek out your new French relatives.'

The sneer in his voice was unmistakable. Dominique stiffened and opened her mouth to respond, but Gideon caught her eye and gave the slightest shake of his head.

'I shall of course do my best to assist Mrs Rainault,' he said evenly. 'Now we have signed the Treaty of Amiens I am sure there is a much greater chance of success.'

'Fustian,' Max retorted. 'Jerome Rainault's been dead these ten years. You of all people should know what savages the French are.'

Dominique flinched, but Gideon's smile did not falter. If anything, it grew as his eyes flickered in her direction.

'Not all of them.'

Max frowned, but after a moment he sat back in his chair, his brow clearing, and he addressed Dominique with at least a semblance of friendliness, 'So, how do you go on, Cousin? How do you like London?'

'Very much.' Dominique took her lead from Gideon and kept her tone light. 'I have made so many friends here. Everyone is very kind.'

'Well, perhaps they don't know—'

'Oh, everyone knows the circumstances of our marriage,' Gideon interrupted him, his voice dangerously quiet. 'The society columns of the news-sheets carried little else for weeks after we arrived. They were very well informed.'

A cruel smile curled Max's mouth.

'Were they, indeed? I wonder how that occurred.'

'Some malicious troublemaker,' replied Gideon. 'But their efforts were wasted. We have shown everyone that we are the epitome of domestic bliss. And you will be pleased to know my wife is becoming a firm favourite with all the hostesses. Ask anyone in town.' He smiled. 'But what are we thinking of? Perhaps you would like to take a glass of wine with us, to toast our felicity—'

'Thank you, no.' Max rose abruptly. 'I have an engagement to dine with friends.'

'Then Judd will show you out,' murmured Dominique, moving over to the bell pull. Max followed and took her hand.

'Accept my felicitations, Cousin. I am…pleased…to see you so comfortable.'

'Thank you.'

'And I have to thank you, too, Max,' said Gideon pleasantly. 'You have provided me with a perfect wife. Who could ever have thought things would work out so well?'

Without a word the earl gave another clipped bow and left the room.

Gideon smiled.

'I think we have done well, there, my sweet. Your dear cousin is not at all happy that his plans have misfired so spectacularly.'

She said slowly, 'We have made a fool of him, Gideon. He will not like that.'

'No, but he cannot alter it, so if he has any sense he will shrug and accept the situation.' Gideon glanced at the clock. 'I suppose we must change for dinner. We are engaged to join some card party tonight, are we not?'

'Yes, Lady Torrington's,' she said absently. 'Gideon— what you said, about helping *Maman*…would you mind if *I* tried to discover something about Papa? I was afraid to mention it before…'

He put his fingers under her chin.

'My dear, you should not be afraid to ask anything of me.'

His tone was light, but the warmth she had seen in his eyes earlier had disappeared.

'Are you angry with me, Gideon, because I want to find my father?' she challenged him. 'I cannot stop loving him, just because you have cause to hate all Girondins.'

His hand dropped.

'Who told you that?'

'Gwendoline. She—she told me about your aunt and uncle. And your brother.'

'Then you know my hatred is well founded.'

'But if you knew Papa—'

'I have no *wish* to know him,' he snapped. 'He was part of the regime which caused the death of three people very dear to me. That I can never forgive.'

'As you can never forgive me for being his daughter.'

There, she had said it. Dominique trembled at her own temerity. The colour drained from his face and his mouth became a thin line as he held back his anger. He turned away and walked to the fireplace where he stood with his back to her, staring down into the flames.

'I have tried to forget it, these past few weeks,' he said at last. 'But it is always there, a ghost between us.'

She walked up to him and put her hand on his shoulder.

'We have not fared so very badly, have we? We have to keep trying, Gideon. We have to make this work.'

'To prove Max was wrong? I am beginning to think that game is not worth the prize.'

'No, this is nothing to do with Max.' She ran her tongue over her dry lips and swallowed. She said, forcing the words out, 'I am carrying your child.'

He said nothing, but she felt a shudder run through him. She removed her hand and stepped back. The silence continued, unbroken, and at last, with a sigh, she turned and left the room.

Dominique fled to her bedchamber. Kitty was already there, waiting to help her change for dinner. She thought about dismissing her maid and indulging in a hearty bout of tears, but instead she fought down her unhappiness and allowed herself to be helped into the blue satin she had chosen to wear to Lady Torrington's card party.

Long after the door had closed Gideon remained staring down into the fire. So this was it, the last link in the chain that would bind him to his wife forever. A child. How ironic, that the heir to Rotham should have French blood in his veins, after all his family had suffered at the hands of that nation. It might be a girl, of course, but what did it matter? He would not cast off the mother of his child.

He raised his eyes to the mirror. It was as if the ghosts of his brother and his aunt were at his shoulders.

He waited, expecting to feel their disapprobation, but he felt...nothing. This baby was innocent of its history—as was his wife. He realised that he was in an impossible position: he could not turn his back on his marriage, any more than he could give up his inheritance. Nicky might not be the wife he had dreamed of, and he had never wanted to be his father's heir, but it was so. It was too late for regrets, he must move on and make what he could of his life.

There was a tangible lightening of the air around him, as if the shades of his brother and his aunt had disappeared.

Dominique was sitting at her dressing table while Kitty put the finishing touches to her hair when Gideon came in. Quietly she dismissed her maid, but remained in her seat, looking into the mirror as Gideon came to stand behind her.

'What you said. A baby. Are you—quite sure?'

She nodded. 'As sure as I can be.' She saw the dawning wonder and confusion on his countenance and turned to face him. He dropped on to one knee and took her hands.

'Then...perhaps you should be resting—do you want me to send our apologies to Lady Torrington?'

'No, no, there is no need for that.'

'Then, what shall we do? What do you *want* to do?'

His bewilderment dragged a shaky laugh from her.

'I want us to have dinner, Gideon, and to go to Torrington House. It is early days yet, no one need know that I am increasing.' She met his eyes. 'I want us to go on exactly as we are, Gideon.'

'Are you sure?'

'Yes, I am very sure.'

She did not have the courage to ask him not to avoid her bed and could only hope he understood her.

'Then I will go and change.'

'Please do.' She smiled. 'You will incur Cook's wrath if his dinner is spoiled because he has to wait for you.'

She turned back to her mirror, to pin up the last few curls.

'One more thing.' He stopped at the door. 'Of course you must do everything you can to find your father. You do not need to involve me—I will direct Rogers, the family lawyer, to come and see you.'

Even as she struggled to find the words to thank him, he was gone.

Gideon was more attentive than usual at dinner and towards the end of their evening at Torrington House, instead of going off to join his friends at White's and leaving his wife to make her own way home, he elected to accompany her back to Brook Street. When she remonstrated with him, declaring that she did not wish to curtail his pleasure, he replied with perfect sincerity that escorting her home *was* his pleasure.

They were in the hall, waiting for their carriage, and as he took his wife's cloak from the footman and gently placed it about her shoulders, Gideon reflected on the change that had come over him in the past few months. By heaven, he was becoming quite domesticated! His wife's soft voice brought him back to the present.

'I heard Mr Williams say you had been invited to Martlesham House.' There was a note of uncertainty in her voice.

Gideon gave her shoulders a little squeeze.

'I have no interest in associating with Max or his friends.' He escorted her to their waiting carriage and settled himself comfortably beside her before adding, 'I think I have outgrown such company.'

'I am glad. I fear Max has little regard for the feelings of others.'

'None at all, but it was not until he hoaxed me that I saw just how thoughtless he is.' He turned towards her, saying earnestly, 'I was careless, too. It was wrong of me to punish you for his trickery. I was a fool, Nicky, but I hope I have learned my lesson now.'

'Oh, Gideon—'

'I know this marriage is not what either of us wanted,' he rushed on, needing to explain, to make amends. 'But it will not be so bad, I promise you. I have no doubt we will rub along very well. And once the little matter of an heir is out of the way I shall not importune you with unreasonable demands.'

She had twisted in her seat and raised her hand, as if to touch his cheek, but now it fell again.

'Un-unreasonable?'

'Yes. I shall not expect you to submit to my... attentions.' He frowned. 'What is it, Nicky? Have I upset you?'

'No, no.' She shook her head quickly. 'I am merely tired, that is all.'

She drew back into the shadows of the carriage and they lapsed into silence. Gideon hoped she understood what he had been trying to say. He feared he had phrased it very badly, yet he could not bring himself to state it quite as baldly as his father had done. Gideon could still remember his father's words as they had lowered the wasted body of the viscountess into the family vault. 'So many years of pain, the stillborn babes, the illness—if I had taken a mistress for my lusts I would have spared your poor mother a great deal of suffering.'

His father had been at pains to impress upon him a husband's responsibilities: his wife would expect to give him a son, perhaps two, but childbearing was a perilous occupation and a gentleman would not overtax his wife's delicate body with his demands. That was twelve years ago. Gideon had been a mere boy of sixteen and devastated by the death of his kind, gentle mother. He had dreamed of joining the army, but his widowed father had insisted upon keeping him close, and when James had died two years later, Gideon's fate had been sealed. Not for him the glories of the battlefield. The title and the heavy responsibility of the estate and its people was his fate. Was it any wonder, then, that when the inheritance from his godmother had given him his independence he had rushed to town and proceeded to kick up every kind of spree and lark? That was when he had fallen in with Max's set and proceeded to prove to his new friends that he could drink, gamble and wench with the best of them. Or perhaps that should be the worst. His father clearly thought so.

When they reached Brook Street, Gideon suggested they should take wine together in the drawing room, but Nicky declined and with a brief goodnight she disappeared up the stairs. He watched her go and a shard of disappointment pierced him. She did not want his company, and, now she was carrying his child, she would not want him in her bed.

Invitations were flooding into Brook Street for balls, routs, riding parties and soirées and Dominique acknowledged that her sister-in-law was in no small measure responsible for her popularity.

'If you had not taken me in hand, I should not go on

half so well,' she said to Gwendoline when they sat together in the supper room during Lady Grayson's summer ball. 'You have shown me just how to go on here.'

'Nonsense, you would have come about,' replied Gwen, justifiably proud of her protégée.

The shy little sparrow, blown into town on the icy spring air, had been transformed into an exotic creature, dressing in hot, vibrant colours that made the most of her dusky curls and emerald-green eyes. Her liveliness and appealing manners charmed the hostesses, who considered her an asset to any gathering. She had also attracted the attention of a considerable number of gentlemen, but watching Dominique now, as Gideon led her on to the dance floor, Gwendoline concluded that her vivacious sister-in-law had eyes only for her husband.

Not that Dominique doted upon Gideon: on the contrary, she never clung to his arm and smiled complacently when he went off to the card room, or partnered another lady in the dance, but Gwendoline noticed those occasional, unguarded moments when Dominique's eyes would rest just a fraction too long upon her husband. She had seen that same look upon the faces of other young brides and it rarely survived the first year. After that they found other men to amuse and divert them. She sighed. As she had done in a vain attempt to pique Ribblestone's interest.

Dominique went down the dance with her husband, wishing the moment could go on forever. She knew no greater felicity than to stand up with Gideon. He was always most attentive when they were in public and she could pretend at such times that they were really the doting couple society thought them. It was a game

they played, but this evening her confidence had been
badly shaken, following an encounter with her cousin.

It was inevitable that they should meet Max occasionally, but they generally contented themselves with
a brief nod in passing. However, this evening Max had
sought her out. She thought he must have been waiting for his opportunity, because it was one of the rare
occasions during the evening when she was standing
alone. He asked her to dance with him and when she
hesitated he gave a rueful smile.

'I suppose you think me too bad a person to partner
you, but can we not put aside our animosity, just for
half an hour? We are family, after all.'

'Very well, Cousin.' She took his hand and let him
lead her on to the dance floor, well aware of the curious glances of those around them. The rumours might
have died down, but the circumstances of her irregular
marriage to Gideon were not yet forgotten. She held her
head up and smiled at her partner. 'Perhaps this will
show we are not at daggers drawn, my lord.'

It was a lively country dance and, by the end of it,
the earl's countenance was more ruddy than ever and
he was wheezing a little.

She went to move away, but he caught her hand.

'Not yet. I want to talk to you.'

'I do not think there is anything to talk about.'

He drew her towards the long windows which had
been opened to allow in the balmy night air.

'Are you not interested to know what is going on at
Martlesham?'

'My mother is a frequent correspondent. She tells
me all I want to know.'

'Let us step out on to the terrace a moment—'

'No.' She stood her ground. 'I do not trust you, Max. You are wont to make trouble.'

He looked pained. 'I merely want to get a little air. Dancing is so exhausting.'

'You should dance more, Cousin, not less.' Her eyes fell on the bulging front of his waistcoat. 'The exercise would be beneficial.'

He scowled at that.

'Aye, you may mock me, madam, but I know this marriage of yours is not as it seems.'

'You know nothing. We are very happy together.' She added, a touch of relief in her voice, 'My husband is over there and he is looking for me. Do not detain me, Cousin, if you do not wish to anger him.'

He reached out and caught her arm as she went to walk away.

'Happy, are you?' he muttered, his lip curling. 'Well, enjoy it while you can, Cousin. As soon as he has got you with child, Albury will pack you off to Rotham so he can take up his old life again.'

With a great effort of will Dominique kept her hands from sliding protectively across her belly. It was two weeks since she had told Gideon about the baby and so far they had kept it a secret from everyone else. With a scorching look she pulled herself free and hurried away to join Gideon.

'I saw you with Martlesham,' he said as she came up. 'I hope he did not upset you?'

'No, he wanted to dance and I thought we should, to show the world there is no bad feeling between us.'

'And after?' He was watching her carefully. 'He tried to take you outside.'

She shrugged.

'He would make mischief if he could, but I am wise to him.'

'Perhaps I should warn him off—'

She put her hand on his arm.

'Please, Gideon, let it be. He is my cousin and I would rather we ignored him than quarrelled.'

'Perhaps you are right,' he said. 'After all, he has done his worst. He cannot hurt us now.'

Dominique allowed him to lead her away, but despite her smile and Gideon's assertion, the earl's warning remained with her.

Chapter Eight

Max's words were still in her head the next morning, when she stood naked before the mirror and placed her hands on her thickening body. Gideon had insisted she should see his doctor and she had just endured a lengthy examination, after which Dr Harris, a blunt, jovial man, confirmed what she already knew.

'Carry on with your life as before,' he said. 'I don't believe in ladies mollycoddling themselves just because they are increasing. You are a healthy young woman, exercise and fresh air will do you more good than lying on a daybed. Your body will tell you what you can and cannot do, but you should not need to make any changes just yet.'

She had no intention of making changes, but Gideon had already done so. He had not shared her bed since the day she had told him about the baby. She could only assume that he considered his duty done now, until she had given birth. Her hands moved over her belly: in a few months it would be swollen with their growing child.

A knock at the door interrupted her thoughts and she reached quickly for her dressing gown.

'Come in.'

Gideon entered. He was smiling.

'I have been talking to Harris. He agrees with your assessment that the child is due in December.'

'Are you pleased, Gideon?' she asked him shyly.

'Do you doubt it?' He came forwards and put his hands on her shoulders. 'I am delighted.'

'Then so, too, am I,' she said, smiling up at him.

He hesitated before lowering his head to kiss her. Tentatively she put her arms about him and felt his hands tighten on her shoulders. Her body tingled with anticipation as she felt his fingers close upon the wrap, as if he was about to push the thin silk from her shoulders and expose her nakedness. Her disappointment was searing when instead he gently put her away from him.

'Delighted,' he said again, smiling awkwardly down at her. 'I must go. I have work to do. How do you amuse yourself today?'

She turned away so that he should not see how his rejection had hurt her.

'I am going to Grosvenor Square to take tea with Gwendoline before we drive in the park.'

'Then we shall meet again at dinner.' He walked to the door.

'You haven't forgotten that we go to Knightson House tonight?'

He turned to look at her. 'You won't be too fatigued?'

'Of course not.' *But I would much rather stay here with you.*

She drew a breath, trying to frame her thoughts into words. 'But I would happily remain here, if you would rather not go?'

'No, no, you wish to go and I shall be delighted to escort you.' He smiled, gave a little bow and left her.

* * *

Dominique sank down on to the stool and stared into the mirror. Gideon was so polite, so distant. Not only did he avoid her room at night, but he rarely touched her now—the kiss he had just given her was a mere brushing of the lips. Her own had parted, but he had immediately drawn back, as if repulsed by the contact. Was Max right—did he want to go back to his bachelor existence? She wondered if she should tell him how much she missed his attentions, but she was afraid the admission would push him still further away. If the married ladies of her acquaintance were to be believed then a wife should keep her husband at a distance, never for one moment let him think *she* desired *him*. She must remain aloof, unattainable. Could that be true, when all her instincts told her the opposite?

Whenever she was with Gideon she wanted to put her arms about him, to touch him and kiss him. Such public displays were frowned upon. It might have been thirty years ago, but the Duchess of Devonshire's scandalous behaviour was still talked of—when, as a young bride, she had danced across the room to sit upon her husband's knee. If a duchess could not indulge in such forward behaviour, how much worse would it be for an ordinary lady, and one who was only half English? Gideon already had a deep hatred for the French, she must not give him even more cause to despise her. Sighing, she pushed herself up off the stool and went into the dressing room. She would talk to Gwendoline. When they were alone she would ask her again just what was and wasn't acceptable behaviour in a wife.

Dominique had lost no time in unburdening herself to her sister-in-law and had finished explaining her di-

lemma even before her teacup was empty. Lady Ribblestone was sympathetic.

'You are in love with Gideon.'

Dominique nodded miserably.

'Yes, I believe I am.'

'Oh, my poor girl.'

'I know,' murmured Dominique, trying not to cry.
'If Gideon knew of it, he would feel sorry for me and I
do not think I could bear that.'

'Of course not.' Gwendoline sat for a moment, staring into space. 'Now, let us consider your problem.
What is it you want from Gideon?'

'I suppose it is too much to hope that he might fall in
love with me.' Seeing Gwen's doubtful look, she sighed.
'I know I cannot expect him to spend all his time with
me, but I should like us to be...to remain friends.'

'Then you must make a life for yourself, show him
you go very well without him. A man does not like
a miserable companion, but if he sees you are cheerful and content then he will be happy to spend time in
your company.'

'Is that possible?'

'Oh, Lord, yes. It is the best one can hope for.' Gwendoline went quiet, as if contemplating what she had just
said, but after a few moments she shook off her reverie.
'You could take a lover.'

'I do not want a lover,' retorted Dominique, her
cheeks burning.

'No, perhaps that is for the best,' Gwen agreed with
her. 'Gideon would be very likely to blame it on your
French blood. However, it will do no harm if the gentlemen show a preference for *you*, my love, and they are
already doing so. My efforts to turn you into a success
seem to be working. Why, Lady Grayson told me how

many gentlemen wanted to dance with you last night. But it is not just the gentlemen, every hostess in town is eager for your presence.'

'They are curious to see the bride Max foisted upon Gideon,' said Dominique bitterly.

'Those rumours are well and truly forgotten now, I assure you. They see you as the rich and fashionable Mrs Albury and, of course, as a future viscountess. Everyone is charmed by you and there is no better way to punish your mischievous cousin than to become society's darling.'

'I do not think I shall be going about in society for very much longer,' admitted Dominique. 'You see, I am…I am in an interesting state.'

'*Already*? Are you sure?'

Gwendoline's shocked response brought the colour flooding to Dominique's face again.

'Yes, but I would be grateful if you kept it to yourself, at least for a while.'

'Of course, my dear—but that is wonderful news. Does Gideon know?'

'Yes, I told him immediately.'

'And is he pleased?'

'I think so.'

'Well, that is a relief. I have no doubt he will want to take you to Rotham soon, to make you known to Papa. And you had best get used to standing up for yourself, for I doubt if Gideon will stay long with you there.'

Dominique felt her spirits sinking.

'That is what Max said. He s-said Gideon would be glad to be rid of me, so he could go back to his old life.'

'The Earl of Martlesham is an odious mischief-maker,' said Gwendoline frankly. 'Gideon's behaviour since he brought you to town cannot be faulted. He has been a model husband in public.'

'But only because he wants to show everyone that we are happily married. What if…what if he comes back to town and sets up a mistress?' stammered Dominique, voicing her deepest fear.

'That is a risk we all have to take,' said Gwendoline. She sighed. 'Not that Ribblestone has one, he is far too wedded to his politics. No, be advised by me—you must not show any tendency to cling to Gideon. And enjoy your remaining time in town as much as you can. Once you are immured in Buckinghamshire there is no telling when you will get away again. Heavens, is that the time? My coachman will be at the door any moment to take us to the park. And after that I shall drop you at Brook Street. You and Gideon are promised to attend the Knightsons' ball this evening, are you not? You must have plenty of time to change into another of those delectable gowns of yours. Everyone will be watching to see what new creation you will be wearing.'

Dominique laughed.

'There will be dozens of ladies there equally well dressed.'

'One or two, perhaps, but few can carry off the vibrant colours we have chosen for you. It makes you stand out in the crowd.'

'I am not sure I want to stand out, Gwen.'

'Of course you do. Gideon has already told me how proud he is of his fashionable wife.'

'Has he? Has he really?'

Gwen laughed and patted her hands.

'Yes, *really*, so let us not disappoint him!'

The Knightsons' midsummer ball was a crowded affair, but Dominique had so many acquaintances in town now that she was not overawed by the throng of people jostling to get into the ballroom. Her confidence was boosted by Gideon's compliments when they had arrived at Knightson House and she removed her cloak. She was wearing a new gown of green silk, a perfect match for the emeralds Gideon had given her on their first night in town, and she had piled her dark hair upon her head with just one glossy curl falling upon her bare shoulder.

'You continue to delight me, my dear,' he said, raising her hand to his lips.

She blushed at the compliment. He might well have spoken for the benefit of the other guests milling around them, but there was no mistaking the warmth in his eyes when he looked at her and she entered the ballroom with a smile on her lips and a song in her heart.

Her happiness continued when Gideon led her out for the first two dances and after that she was content for him to dance with his sister and other ladies of their acquaintance. Dominique herself was not short of partners, but by supper time she was eager to find her husband again. Her diminutive height proved a disadvantage as she pushed her way through the crowd, standing on tiptoe to try to see Gideon's tall figure. A slight jostling occurred and as she stepped back to avoid a cheerfully inebriated couple her heel came down upon someone's toe.

'Oh, I beg your pardon!' She swung around, an apologetic smile on her lips. The gentleman standing behind her was a stranger, but he was laughing.

'*C'est rien.* Madame…Albury, is it not?' He made her a bow. 'We have not been introduced, but in such circumstances…Raymond Lamotte, *madame*, *à votre service*. This is most fortunate. I have been wanting to talk to you.'

'To me?' She studied the young man before her. He was of average height and darkly handsome with his raven hair, cropped à la Brutus.

'*Mais oui, madame.* One could not help hearing the rumours…' He looked a little self-conscious. 'You are the daughter of a Frenchman, are you not?' Dominique was no longer concerned for the man's appearance. Seeing her intense look, he spread his hands. 'I fled from my beloved France several years ago. It broke my heart to do so, but…' he gave a shrug '…it is not the great country it once was.'

'N-no, indeed,' she murmured.

He glanced around.

'It is difficult to speak here, it is so crowded. Perhaps, could I beg the honour of escorting you to supper?'

It took Dominique only a moment to decide. Gideon was nowhere to be seen and this young man was watching her so hopefully.

'Of course, *monsieur.*'

The supper room was very busy, but her companion led her to a small table in one of the alcoves. An elegant supper was laid before her, but Dominique hardly noticed, for she was soon lost in reminiscences about France. Raymond Lamotte was eager to talk and she guessed that he was homesick, as she had been when she first came to England.

'Of course it was easier for me,' she told him. 'I was a child, just ten years old, and my English mother had tried to ensure that I was familiar with the ways of this country. For you, *monsieur*, it must have been so much more painful.'

'It was. I did not wish to quit France but what could I do? My friends were imprisoned, or worse. At first I was in favour of the revolution. The country needed to change, *mais oui*, but then came the Terror and the execution of the poor King and Queen—it was too much. The change was going too far.'

'That is exactly what Papa thought,' exclaimed Dominique. 'But his views were too moderate and no one wanted to listen.'

'So he brought you to England?' He raised his hand and signalled to the waiter to refill their glasses.

'No.' Dominique waited until they were alone again, pleased for the delay so that she could muster her thoughts. 'He arranged for Mama and me to come here while he remained in France.' She added quietly, 'We have not heard from him for ten years.'

'Ah, I see. *Je regrette*—'

She raised her hand, fending off his sympathy. Glancing up, she noticed with surprise that the supper room was almost empty.

'Oh, dear, how the time has flown,' she said. 'The dancing will begin again soon. Thank you, Monsieur Lamotte, I have enjoyed our conversation, but I must get back.'

'Of course, I shall escort you.' He rose and held out his arm to her. 'If you will permit, I should like to talk more with you. It is so refreshing to be able to speak freely about my country with someone who loves it as I do.'

She nodded, saying shyly, 'I should like that too, sir.'

'May I call upon you tomorrow morning?'

'No!' She stopped in alarm, imagining Gideon's anger if a Frenchman should arrive at his door. 'No, that is not possible.' She swallowed, aware of his disappointment. 'But perhaps…perhaps you will be walking in Green Park tomorrow, sir, at ten o'clock? It is a popular promenade.'

'And…will you be there, Madame Albury, at ten o'clock?'

'I will,' she declared, stifling her conscience. After all, there could be no harm in them meeting in public. 'I will be there.'

'Then so, too, shall I,' declared Monsieur Lamotte. They were entering the ballroom, where the musicians were already tuning up for the next set. He said, a laugh in his voice, 'I would ask you to dance with me, but I fear I have taken far too much of your time already and see several gentlemen giving me the angry look.'

She blushed and disclaimed, but did not seek to detain him. Even as she watched him walking away two young gentlemen came up, cheerfully vying with each other for the privilege of leading her out. Smiling, Dominique turned her thoughts away from Raymond Lamotte and gave herself up to the enjoyable task of choosing a dance partner.

'I am sorry I was not able to take you in to supper,' said Gideon as they rode home later that night. 'Anthony and I were caught up in a political discussion and I did not like to abandon him. I hope you found someone to look after you?'

'Yes, I did, thank you.'

Dominique struggled briefly with her conscience, wondering how she could explain to Gideon about Monsieur Lamotte, but even as she tried to frame her reply he took her hand, saying, 'That's good. I am glad you are finding your feet in town, Nicky.'

'Oh, yes,' she replied. 'I go on much more comfortably, now I know so many people.'

'Aye, I noticed you were never without a partner tonight.' He laughed. 'It will soon be that you will not have need of me to accompany you at all.'

She turned, looking at his dark shape beside her as she said earnestly, 'Oh, never say that, Gideon. I would not be half so comfortable if you were not with me.'

He laughed and raised her hand to his lips.

'Flatterer!'

Did he really think that, or was he perhaps looking forward to the day when he could leave her to fend for herself and return to his old bachelor ways? Dominique longed to ask him, but she kept silent, fearful of his answer.

Chapter Nine

Dominique met Raymond in Green Park the following morning. They spoke only briefly, but arranged to meet again the next day, and the next. Raymond was a charming companion. Not only were his recollections of France quite riveting, but he was also interested in her own childhood memories, and since she dared not mention her French connections to Gideon it was a relief to be able to talk about her family with someone who understood what she had been through. Soon she felt that they were firm friends.

However, they had very few acquaintances in common, so it was some weeks before they met again socially, at an evening party given by Lord and Lady Dortwood. Dominique spotted Raymond in the crowd, but although he acknowledged her with a faint nod the evening was well advanced before he came over to greet her.

'I thought you would never ask me to dance,' she said, when he led her out to join a new set.

'I was not sure you would wish to acknowledge me,' he murmured. 'I see you are with your husband.'

'Of course I will acknowledge you,' she said, feeling the heat burning her cheeks. 'I am not ashamed of knowing you!'

She danced on, unsettled by the realisation that she had not mentioned her friendship with Raymond to anyone. Their morning walks in Green Park had so far excited no comment since they had never met anyone with whom Dominique was acquainted. Now it occurred to her that others might consider such meetings to be clandestine. That would not do, at all.

When the dance ended she took Raymond's arm and firmly led him across the room to where Gideon was waiting. She performed the introduction and after a short exchange Raymond moved away. Gideon lifted his quizzing glass to watch him go.

'Where did you say you met him?'

'At the Knightsons' ball.' She frowned up at him. 'Really, Gideon, was it necessary to be so cold towards Monsieur Lamotte? You barely spoke half-a-dozen words to him.'

'I beg your pardon, my dear, but we have so little in common.'

'It was more than that. You were positively arctic!'

'I am certainly surprised by your friendship with the fellow.'

'You are offended, because he is French,' she declared hotly. 'Your hatred of the whole race is quite unreasonable.'

He did not reply and with a toss of her head she turned away.

'Nicky!' She stopped and he said quietly, 'I would rather you did not pursue your acquaintance with Monsieur Lamotte.'

She turned, her brows raised in haughty surprise.

'That is outrageous! You cannot dictate with whom I shall associate.'

'I was not aware I was dictating to you, my dear, merely making my wishes clear.'

'It is the same thing.'

'Not at all.'

'And if I refuse to comply?'

His eyes narrowed. He leaned closer so that his words were for her alone.

'Do not forget, madam, that you are my wife.'

Her head went up.

'But I am not your slave!'

With a swish of her skirts she flounced away from him.

How dare Gideon dictate to her! It was nothing but prejudice, because Raymond was French, and she was tired of it. She wished Gwendoline was here, but she was attending some tedious political dinner with Ribblestone. There was no one else present to whom she could pour out her anger and frustration, so she took herself off to the card room and proceeded to lose a large portion of her pin money.

However, by the time she left the card room her temper had cooled, so that when she saw her husband in the ballroom she went straight up to him, saying penitently, 'I beg your pardon, Gideon, I should not have ripped up at you so.' His brows went up, but the harshness left his face as he took her outstretched hand and she was emboldened to continue. 'I understand why you might not like Monsieur Lamotte, but he is a link with my childhood, the life I knew before we moved to England.' She clung to his fingers. 'Please do not ask me to give him up.'

He stared down at her, a look she could not interpret in his hazel eyes.

'Is he merely an acquaintance, Nicky, nothing more?'

'Of course. What else should he be?'

'And your morning meetings with him in Green Park?' When her eyes flew to his face he gave her a wry smile. 'You were seen, by Anthony. I told him it was nothing and the fact that you had your maid with you gives weight to my belief.'

'And it *is* nothing, Gideon, I give you my word.' She sighed. 'But I quite see how it must look, so I shall not meet him there again.'

'Thank you.' He squeezed her hand. 'I will not have the fellow call at Brook Street, but if you meet him at such parties as this and wish to dance with him, I will not object.'

A compromise. She was aware of how much ground he was giving.

'Very well, Gideon. Thank you.' She suddenly felt very tired. 'Do you think our hostess would object if I went home now?'

'No, of course not. I shall escort you. Go downstairs and collect your wrap while I give our excuses to Lady Dortwood.'

Dominique made her way to the hall, where a lackey was sent scurrying off to fetch her cloak.

'I fear your husband does not like me.'

Dominique whirled about to find Raymond Lamotte standing behind her.

She gave a sad little smile. 'It will be best if we discontinue our walks together, *monsieur*.'

He shook his head. 'Ah, that is a sadness, because I have something to discuss with you.'

'We will have to do so the next time we meet—'

'It concerns your father.' His words brought her eyes flying to his face. He continued, 'You told me you were trying to find him, so I have made the enquiries. I have friends in France who still have influence with the *Directoire*. They will know how to find the missing person. Some have been imprisoned for many years and it is not easy to gain information, but there is a man who knows how to do these things. He moves regularly between France and England, but secretly, so the less people who know of this the better. I have spoken to him about your father and he thinks we may be able to find him.'

She shook her head, hardly daring to hope. 'Then you must come to the house. Gideon could not object to that—'

'Oh, but I fear he would, *madame*. You have told me yourself he is not a friend to my country. He would think it a—how do you say it?—a ploy. *Non*, I would rather discuss this with you alone. I need information from you.'

'Anything,' she said eagerly.

'*Eh bien*, you must write down everything you remember of your father—where he lived, what he looked like, who his friends were. No little detail is too small. When you have done that, you must bring it to me at my lodgings and I will pass it on to my friend.'

'Yes, yes, I will, of course.'

'Good. I need the information by tomorrow evening. My contact is returning to France the following morning and he has promised to seek out news of your father.'

'Oh, oh, thank you.' She felt the hope bubbling up within her again. *Maman* would be so pleased when she told her! 'I shall begin writing it all up tonight and send it round—'

'No, you must bring it yourself. Can you be there at five o'clock? Then I can read it and if there are any things that are not clear, any questions, you will be there to answer them.'

'Yes, of course, I understand.'

'Good.' He gave her his direction, looking over his shoulder as the servant hurried up to them carrying her rose silk wrap over his arm. 'I must go now. Remember, my contact relies upon secrecy—if he is discovered, then all is lost.'

She nodded. 'You may trust me to tell no one.'

'Thank you, *madame*.' He smiled and pressed a final kiss upon her fingers. 'Until tomorrow, then. Five o'clock. Do not be late!'

He hurried away and Dominique absently fastened her cloak about her shoulders. *Maman* had been trying for years to find news of Papa without success. To have someone else searching, someone who knew the workings of the French government, surely they would have far more chance of finding out the truth? She had never quite given up hope, but it had lain dormant and now, suddenly, it was blossoming again. She could not wait to get back to Brook Street and write out everything she could remember about her father.

Gideon found his wife very distracted on the homeward journey. He wondered if she was regretting her promise to give up her walks with Raymond Lamotte. When Ribblestone had mentioned that he had seen Nicky walking with a French émigré in Green Park Gideon had shrugged it off. He guessed it was a chance meeting, and he quite understood why she had not mentioned the matter to him, but a casual remark to Kitty when he met her on the stairs two days later elicited the information that her mistress was in the habit of walking in the park every morning. And, yes, the French gentleman was always there.

Intrigued, but not yet alarmed, Gideon had asked Anthony to make discreet enquiries and found that the émigré was an impecunious young man from an obscure but perfectly respectable French family who had fled the Terror and was now living in bachelor lodgings in Cleveland Row. The worst that was known of the young man was that he frequented a gambling hell in King Street that Ribblestone himself favoured. However, Gideon knew that if his wife continued to meet with Lamotte it would only be a matter of time before the gossipmongers heard of it and began to speculate upon the nature of their acquaintance. Their liaison might be quite innocent, but it would not do and Gideon had known he would have to speak to Nicky about the matter.

However, he had been reluctant to do so—until he had seen Lamotte dancing with his wife. Then Gideon had been aware of a sharp stab of disapproval. He had watched Nicky dance with dozens of fellows since they had come to town and thought nothing of it—after all, he was a reasonable man—but Raymond Lamotte was a Frenchman and to see the handsome young dog paying such attentions to his wife had roused Gideon's temper. In fact, in any other circumstances he would have thought the emotion he felt when he saw them together was jealousy, but how could one feel that for a wife one did not love?

No, he did not love his wife, he thought as the carriage pulled up in Brook Street and he escorted her into the house. How could he? She was a constant reminder of the loss his family had suffered. He felt a tiny kick of guilt. Perhaps his disapproval this evening of her friendship with Lamotte had been a little severe. In an effort to make amends he invited her to join him in the drawing room. She gave a little start.

'Oh—no! That is, how kind of you, Gideon, but I—I am very tired. I think I will retire....'

He covered his disappointment with a smile.

'Of course, my dear, if that is what you wish.'

He raised her hand to his lips and her fingers trembled in his grasp. As he looked up he was surprised to find something in her green eyes that made his brows snap together. A wistfulness, a longing that touched a chord inside him and roused the desire for her that was never very far away. How long had it been since he had been in her bed?

'Perhaps you would like me to come up with you?'

Her recoil told him immediately how wrong he had been.

'Oh, I— If only... Not tonight, if you please, Gideon. I am nigh on dropping with fatigue.'

With a shy, apologetic smile she wished him goodnight and hurried away.

Gideon waited until she was out of sight before walking into the drawing room. It was perfectly reasonable for her to be tired. After all, she was increasing, although no one watching her lithe figure skipping around the dance floor this evening would have guessed it. She had looked quite animated, too, never more so than when she had been dancing with Lamotte. Quickly Gideon dismissed the thought. He glanced around him. It was the custom to keep this room in readiness every evening with a good fire and candles burning in their wall-brackets, but despite the room's cheerful aspect

Gideon found that he had no desire to drink alone, so he went up to bed. When he reached Nicky's room he stopped. A strip of light shone beneath the door, showing that she was still awake, but there was no sound from the room, and after a few seconds he went on to his own bedchamber, disturbed by a vague, niggling dissatisfaction.

At breakfast the next morning Nicky greeted him with her usual good humour and Gideon's day brightened immediately.

'You are not fatigued by last night's exertions?' he asked her as she poured coffee for him.

She gave him a sunny smile.

'Not in the least. You know Dr Harris said I could carry on very much as before.'

It was on the tip of his tongue to ask her if she thought that included her wifely duties in the bedchamber, but he was afraid to bring that haunted, frightened look back into her face, so instead he asked casually what she planned to do today.

'I have some letters to write, and after that I am taking Kitty to Grosvenor Square with me. Gwen's dresser is an excellent coiffeuse—'

'You are not going to cut it short?' He frowned, recalling the way her dusky curls cascaded over her shoulders, a perfect foil for the creamy whiteness of her skin.

He remembered her standing naked before him while he pulled the pins from her hair so that it fell in a dark curtain to the small of her back, almost resting on her gently rounded buttocks. He remembered pulling her towards him and tangling his hands in the thick skeins of silky hair, holding her fast while his tongue plundered her mouth.

His body responded immediately to the memory and he struggled to give his attention to her reply.

'Heavens, no. Kitty is merely going to learn a new way to put up my hair.'

'Ah, I see. And what do you do after that? I am busy this morning, but perhaps later you would like to drive out with me.' He grinned at her. 'We might go to the Park at the fashionable hour and show off your new hairstyle.'

A shadow crossed her face.

'Oh, I would enjoy that, only I… um… We are going to visit a new tea garden in Hampstead and I shall not be back until dinnertime.'

'Of course. Then we shall meet again at dinner.'

Gideon pushed his plate away and rose from the table. Why he should feel disappointed he did not know. The notion of driving out with his wife had only just occurred to him and was easily dismissed. However, after spending the morning poring over his accounts, he found the sun shining in through the study window was too tempting to ignore. It was not yet the fashionable hour for the promenade and Gideon decided he would exercise his greys in the Park before it became too crowded. He sent a message to the stable and ran upstairs to change into his riding coat and buckskins and to thrust his feet into his glossy top-boots.

By the time he came down again Sam was waiting at the door with the curricle. The greys were fresh and leaped into their collars as they set off, but as they swept through Grosvenor Square Gideon spotted his sister approaching in her open carriage. He waved to her coachman to stop, bringing his own team to a plunging halt when the carriages were alongside each other.

'Really, Gideon, we cannot hold up the traffic in this way, I shall be hounded out of the square!'

'I thought Nicky was with you,' he said, ignoring her laughing protest.

'She was, until half an hour ago.'

'Oh. Are you not going to Hampstead with her?' Gwen's brows rose.

'Hampstead? No, indeed. Why should she go to Hampstead?'

'There is a new tea garden, I believe.' Gwen's blank look made him frown and the horses jibbed as his hands tightened involuntarily on the reins. He said, 'She has her maid with her, I take it?'

'No, we sent Kitty home as soon as Dominique's hair was finished. Gideon, what—?'

He cut her short, not wishing to explain anything. With a hasty farewell he drove on. Plans for Hyde Park were abandoned. He considered driving to Hampstead, but something told him he would not find Nicky there. Instead he drove back to Brook Street, and with a curt order to Sam to walk the horses he went indoors to look for the maid.

He found her in Nicky's bedroom, mending a flounce, and asked her without preamble if she knew where her mistress would be.

Kitty jumped to her feet.

'I—I don't know, sir,' she stammered, dropping a wobbly curtsy. 'She sent me off from Lady Ribble-stone's and said she'd be making her own way home later.'

'And she didn't say where she was going?'

'N-no, sir.'

'Are you sure?' Gideon bent his frowning gaze upon her. 'Think, girl!'

Kitty stared at him, wide-eyed as she screwed her apron nervously between her hands. Gideon drew a breath and forced himself to speak quietly, 'Did she give you no idea of where she might be going?'

The maid chewed her lip, frowning in concentration. At last she said, 'She—she did ask me where Cleveland Row might be.'

A cold hand clutched at Gideon's heart. Without a word he strode out of the room, thundered back down the stairs and out to his curricle. It did not take him long to find the lodging house, but the servant who opened the door told him that Lamotte was not at home.

'Has a lady called here for him?' demanded Gideon.

The servant looked blank and shook his head. Even a generous bribe could not elicit anything more than the information that *'monsewer'* had been out all day, but that he was expected back later, since he had sent out for a special dinner to be prepared and brought to his rooms that evening.

Gideon drove back to Brook Street, a mixture of fear and anxiety fermenting in his head. He tried to think logically. Perhaps he had misunderstood Nicky. She had many friends—it might well be that she was on a perfectly innocent outing. After all, she had said she would be home in time to join him for dinner. Gideon faced up to the fact that there was little he could do, save go home and wait for Nicky to turn up.

However, after he had dismissed his curricle and paced once through the empty house Gideon realised he could not be idle. He changed into his evening clothes, picked up his hat, gloves and cane and strode off to St James's Street. If he could find Lamotte, then his main worry about Nicky would be assuaged.

* * *

No one in any of the hells he visited had seen the young Frenchman that day. In growing desperation he made for the last one on his list, the narrow house in King Street that Anthony patronised.

Despite the early hour the rooms were quite full, the heavy curtains pulled across the windows and the room bathed in candlelight. Gideon recognised several of the players and was hailed merrily and invited to join them. He declined politely and continued to ask after Lamotte, but his enquiries drew nothing but blank looks. No one had seen him.

The Earl of Martlesham was presiding over the faro table in the final room and he looked up as Gideon came in.

'Albury, this is a new departure for you. Will you join us?'

'No, thank you,' he replied shortly. 'I am looking for Raymond Lamotte, do you know him?'

'Lamotte, Lamotte…' Max considered for a moment. 'No, I don't think I do.'

Two of the players glanced up and exchanged looks, their brows raised. Gideon said nothing and after a moment Max continued. 'What do you want with the fellow?'

'Ribblestone gave me a message for him,' he said casually. 'It doesn't matter.'

'As you will.' Max waved a hand. 'We are about to go in search of our dinner. Why not come along with us?'

'Thank you, no. I dine at home tonight.'

'With your lovely wife? Gad, sir, but the two of you are inseparable.'

Gideon misliked the smile that spread over the earl's face and his hand tightened on his cane. Did Max know something? How he would like to choke the truth out of him! Gideon left them to their play and went back out into the sunshine. He glanced at his watch. It was past six o'clock. Perhaps Nicky was home now and waiting for him.

And perhaps not.

He glanced up and down St James's Street, doubt and indecision crowding his mind. Now she was with child his wife might consider it safe to take a lover. His hand tightened on the head of his cane. By God, if that was the case she would soon learn her mistake! Eyes narrowed, his jaw tight with anger, Gideon strode off.

Dominique had never spent such a long afternoon. When she had left her sister-in-law there were still two hours until she was due at Cleveland Row. She wished she had asked Kitty to wait for her, but Monsieur Lamotte had told her to come alone and she was afraid that Kitty might not understand the need for total secrecy. She whiled away her time wandering in and out of the various shops in Bond Street. She was ill at ease on her own and found herself purchasing various items— gloves, ribbons and parasols, as well as a quite hideous bonnet in puce satin—all of which she ordered to be sent to Brook Street. At last she judged it time to make her way to Cleveland Row for her rendezvous.

She was admitted by a respectable-looking servant, who then directed her to Monsieur Lamotte's rooms on the first floor. Dominique knocked on the door and was a little relieved when the gentleman answered in person. She drew a folded paper from her reticule.

'This is all the information I have on my father.'

He held the door wide.

'Please, come in, madame.' Observing her hesitation,

he said gently, 'I will need to read this through and we can hardly discuss the contents here on the landing.'

'No, of course.'

She stepped across the threshold into the small, sparsely furnished room. An old-fashioned armchair and a sofa crowded the empty fireplace, a sideboard stood against one wall and a small table was placed beneath the window. A haphazard pile of newspapers and gentleman's magazines on one of the dining chairs suggested that the table had been hastily cleared.

Raymond closed the door.

'Pray, madame, let me take your coat. *Eh bien*, sit down, if you please, and be comfortable.'

Swallowing, she allowed him to remove her pelisse and guide her to the sofa, where she perched on the edge, her hands clasped nervously in her lap. Raymond dropped the paper on to the table and went to the sideboard, where he proceeded to pour wine into two glasses.

'No—not for me,' she said hastily. 'I cannot stay.'

'Just a glass, madame, that we may raise a toast to France.'

She took the glass from him and solemnly repeated the toast, but she was relieved that her companion then sat down at the table to read her document. She waited impatiently as he scrutinised every line, asking the occasional question, and making notes on the edge of the paper with a pencil. She glanced at the clock on the mantelpiece. It was nearly six. She must get back soon. A soft knock upon the door made her jump. Raymond answered it and after a muted conversation he stood back and a number of waiters came in, bearing trays.

'My dinner,' explained Raymond, smiling. 'I ordered

it earlier. I hope you do not mind if they set it up now, while I finish reading this?'

He threw himself into the armchair and continued to read. Dominique clasped her wine glass before her, wishing she had thought to wear a veil. She felt very out of place sitting there, while the servants marched in and out.

As soon as they were alone again she put down her glass and rose.

'Monsieur Lamotte, you have read every word now. I must go—'

'No, no, madame, not quite yet, if you please.' He was on his feet and standing between her and the door. 'I was hoping that you would do me the honour of dining with me.'

He reached out for her hand, but she snatched it away.

'Out of the question,' she declared. 'It would be most improper to dine alone with you.'

'But you are already here and alone,' he pointed out, coming closer.

'That is very different.'

'Is it?' He gave her his charming smile, but she was more alarmed than attracted.

Dominique retreated a few steps. She had placed herself in a most precarious situation. To visit a gentleman's lodgings, without even her maid in attendance, was the height of impropriety. Gideon would never forgive her, if he found out. She took a breath.

'Monsieur Lamotte, I think you misunderstand. You promised you could help me with news of my father.'

'And so I can, Madame Albury, but I would like you to show a little gratitude. Would dinner be such a trial?'

'Sir, it is impossible. Please stand aside and let me leave.'

His smile became predatory.

'Well, if you cannot dine with me, perhaps a little kiss—'

He lunged at her. Dominique whisked herself away, but not before his fingers caught the muslin fichu tucked decorously into the neck of her summer gown. It slipped from her shoulders as she retreated behind the sofa, anger blazing through her.

'How dare you?' She glared at him. 'I came here in good faith, monsieur. I thought as a fellow countryman I could trust you!'

'And so you can, madame.' He held out his arms. 'All I ask is a little kiss from you and I shall let you go.'

'Do you think I am a fool?' She snatched up the poker from the hearth. 'Stand away from the door, monsieur.'

He looked a little startled, but made no attempt to move out of her way. Dominique was enraged, but she was well aware that the Frenchman had the advantage of strength and size. She was debating what to do next when swift footsteps were heard on the stairs and a familiar voice sounded from the landing.

'No need to come with me, my man. I know the way.'

The door opened and with a smothered exclamation Raymond jumped aside, his eyes narrowing as Gideon appeared, his frame almost filling the doorway.

Dominique stared. To her amazement her husband merely smiled at her.

'My apologies, my dear, have I kept you waiting? I was delayed, don't you know, in Piccadilly.'

Chapter Ten

Gideon uttered the words cheerfully as he came in and closed the door behind him. He had entered the room with every nerve-end tingling, prepared for a brawl, but when he had opened the door to see his wife brandishing a poker to keep her would-be seducer at bay his worst fears were alleviated. In fact, he had a strong inclination to laugh.

'I think, my dear, you can dispense with the weapon now.'

She lowered the poker.

'How did you know where to find me?'

'A simple deduction.' He glanced at Lamotte, who was silently watching him, a guilty scowl darkening his countenance. 'What inducement did you use to entice my wife here?'

Nicky said quickly, 'He told me he could help me find my father.'

Gideon raised a brow. 'And can you, monsieur? I thought not,' he added drily as Lamotte shrugged. He picked up the fichu from the floor and handed it to Dominique. 'Here, madam. Put this on and your coat, too. I shall escort you home.'

She took the muslin scarf from him, but made no move to put it on. Instead she stood twisting it between her hands, her dark anxious gaze fixed on his face.

'B-but I have been seen here. The landlord and the waiters who brought in the dinner—'

'The landlord now believes you came here looking for me and as for the waiters, I think our friend here will be able to silence them.' He turned to Lamotte, placing the tip of his cane against the Frenchman's silk waist-coat. 'Let me make myself very clear,' he said icily. 'If the slightest hint of scandal attaches to my wife's being here, monsieur, then I shall take great pleasure in calling you out and despatching you. Do you understand me?'

Lamotte shook his head.

'Believe me, I never meant any harm to madame.'

'No.' Gideon's eyes narrowed. 'You were put up to this by another, were you not?' The flash of fear that crossed the Frenchman's face gave Gideon his answer. His lip curling, he gave the cane a little push, sending Lamotte staggering back.

Dominique had put on her pelisse and was now watching them. Gideon opened the door, saying loudly,

'I am very grateful to you, monsieur, for looking after my wife until I could join you. But we will not keep you any longer from your dinner. Adieu, sir!'

He flourished a bow and held out his hand to Domi-nique. She picked up a sheet of paper from one of the armchairs and stuffed it into her reticule before cross-ing the room to join him.

'It is the information about my father,' she said in response to his enquiring gaze. 'It will not be needed now.'

She bent a look of burning reproach upon Lamotte, who had the grace to hang his head.

'I beg your pardon, madame.'

Gideon took her arm.

'Come, my dear.'

He escorted her down the stairs and out into the street. As they walked away from the lodging house Dominique gave a little sob.

'I am so very sorry, Gideon. It was foolish of me to go there alone. I should have told you…'

'And why did you not?'

'B-because he said that success in finding out about Papa depended upon the utmost secrecy.'

Gideon looked down at her bowed head.

'But that is not all, is it? You thought I should refuse to sanction this line of enquiry.'

'Yes.' Her reply was so quiet he almost missed it. He sighed.

'Am I such an ogre, Nicky?'

'Oh, no, no!' She stopped and turned towards him. 'You are not an ogre at all, but your abhorrence of all things French—' She bit her lip. 'But in this case you were right to be suspicious of Monsieur Lamotte and—and I beg your pardon.'

He squeezed her hand.

'It was not totally your fault, Nicky.'

She was silent for a while, but as they walked out into St James's Street, she said slowly, 'You said someone else was behind this. Do you think it was my cousin?'

'I not only think it, my dear, I am sure of it.'

She gave an angry little growl.

'Ooh, of all the odious—' She stopped. 'There he is now, across the street with his cronies! And he has seen us. Let us confront him. I would like to scratch his eyes out!'

'I have a much better idea,' he said, catching her chin

between his thumb and finger. 'We will show him that his plan to cause trouble between us has not worked at all.'

He lowered his head and kissed her.

Dominique's heart stopped and she forgot all about being angry with Max. She forgot about everything, save the soaring pleasure that filled her whole being. Gideon was still holding her chin so she could not pull away, even if she had wanted to do so, which she did not. His lips were gentle, it was the lightest of kisses and she found herself standing on tiptoe to prolong the moment. When at last he raised his head he was smiling down at her, such a glint in his eyes that she wanted to reach up and pull him down so she could kiss him again.

'Is he still watching us?' he murmured.

'Who?' She ran her tongue round her lips, trying to drag her mind away from the distracting cleft in his chin and the seductive curve of his lips.

He laughed, settled her arm firmly in his and began to walk on.

'Your cousin is standing on the far pavement and staring at us as if he cannot believe his eyes. Look across, my dear, and smile while I tip my hat to him— like so. There, is that not more satisfying than, er, scratching his eyes out?'

Dominique chuckled even as she smiled and nodded at Max, who was glowering across the road at them.

'It is amusing to see him so dumbfounded,' she agreed, 'but I am so angry with him! He will be fortunate when we meet again if I do not box his ears!'

'What a violent creature you are,' marvelled Gideon, a laugh in his voice. 'I find you brandishing a poker at Lamotte and now you want to assault your cousin.'

'When I am in a passion I hardly know what I am about,' she confessed ruefully.

'No, you don't, do you?'

She looked up at that, a laughing question in her eyes, and found him watching her with such an arrested expression that her laughter died. Had she angered him, perhaps?

'Can you really forgive me for my foolishness today?' she asked him anxiously. 'I promise you I shall not keep anything from you again.'

The serious look disappeared and he smiled, flicking her cheek with one careless finger.

'Of course I forgive you,' he said lightly. 'Now let us hurry back to Brook Street. All this excitement has given me an appetite!'

It was almost an hour later when Gideon sat down to dinner with his wife, but despite his earlier protestations he only picked at the array of sumptuous dishes spread before him. His thoughts went back constantly to the events earlier that evening. Max's attempts to discredit his wife had angered him, but that was not the only reason for his distraction. He was shocked by the jealousy that had consumed him when he had suspected Nicky had taken a lover.

That had been superseded by fear for her safety when he realised Max's involvement, but more than anything he was confused by the overwhelming desire that had come over him when he had kissed her. It had been every bit as strong as on their wedding night. *Then* he had put it down to an excess of wine. Kissing his wife in broad daylight and in such a public place as St James's Street should not have had anything like the same effect, but the touch of her lips had shaken him to the very core. He had covered it well, of course, but then, when they were walking home and she had mentioned her passionate nature, the memory of her response to his lovemaking on that first, momentous night had hit him so forcibly that for a few moments he had not been able to speak and had only been aware of a strong desire to rush home and repeat the performance.

Since their night together at Elmwood he had tried to treat her as a wife should be treated. He visited her bed for the sole purpose of producing an heir, keeping all other feelings well under control and it shocked him, as they entered the shadowy portals of his Brook Street house to find that he wanted to pick her up and carry her to his room, to rip off her clothes and make love to her as violently, as passionately as on that first, tempestuous occasion.

It could not be, of course. Now she was carrying his child he had no excuse to make love to her. His father had told him to take a mistress, but Gideon knew now that he did not *want* a mistress, he wanted his wife.

He struggled through dinner, trying to converse, attempting to entertain Nicky with amusing anecdotes while all he could think of was the softness of her skin, the warmth of her limbs when they were wrapped around him. When she went off to the drawing room he lingered over his port, wondering if the excitement of the day would make her too tired to wait up for him, but as he reached the drawing-room door he heard the soft lilting strains of the harp.

He watched her from the doorway, marvelling at the concentration on her face, and when his eyes moved to her hands caressing the strings he found himself re-membering how gently those same fingers touched his body. Gideon shifted uncomfortably. It would not do.

She was with child and as such would not welcome his advances. Indeed, he knew that such behaviour was downright dangerous. Father had made that quite clear. Looking across at the delicate little figure before him, Gideon knew he would not risk such a thing happening to Nicky.

Yet it took all his resolution to part from her that night and not to make his way through the dressing room to her bedchamber.

'I think we should go to Rotham,' Gideon announced at breakfast the next morning. 'It is time you met my father.'

Dominique continued pouring her coffee. It was not unexpected, but his next words caused her to heart to sink.

'You will remain there until the baby is born.'

'And will you stay, too?' she asked, trying to keep her voice casual.

'For a couple of weeks.'

So it had come. He had had enough of her—and how could she blame him, after her foolishness yesterday? There could be no arguing. Of course he would want the child to be born at Rotham, especially if it was a boy.

'When do we go?'

'In three weeks.'

'Gwen has invited us to join her in Brighton.'

'Impossible,' he said shortly.

She accepted this, but he must have observed her disappointment for he added in a kinder tone, 'Perhaps next year. Dr Harris is very good, but I should like you to have the services of my father's medical man, a very experienced doctor. He delivered both of my sister's children. Ribblestone's country seat, Fairlawns,

is but five miles from Rotham and Gwen will vouch
for him, I am sure. That is, have you told her that you
are increasing?'

'Yes, but I swore her to secrecy.'

He gave a wry smile. 'Then I doubt it will remain a
secret much longer.' He pushed back his chair. 'If you
are in agreement, then I shall write to my father today
and tell him we shall be at Rotham by the middle of
July.'

What could she say? It was good of him to pretend
she had a choice.

When Gwen heard that they were going to Rotham
she screwed her face up in distaste. Dominique blinked
away a rogue tear that threatened her eye.

'Gideon says I am to stay there until the baby is
born.'

'Six months! You poor thing.' Gwen added quickly,
'I am sure he is thinking of your well-being, my love.'

'He says the doctor there is very good.'

'Oh, yes, indeed, you will like Dr Bolton, I am sure.
Did Gideon tell you he delivered my babies? Perhaps
if he had been our doctor when Mama was carrying
that last child…'

'What happened?' asked Dominique.

Gwen sighed. 'When we were young Mama was
never well. She was always enceinte, or recuperating
after a miscarriage. She had six more children after
Gideon, but they all died within hours. Not that she
ever complained. I believe she loved my father passionately. But the last time she was brought to bed she
did not recover. Papa was heartbroken. I did not understand at the time why he should blame himself, but

now that I am married I understand that a man can be too…physical.' Gwen blushed.

'And when did she die?'

'Oh, it must be twelve years since. It was a bad time, we were all at Rotham, we all knew her suffering.'

'Poor lady,' murmured Dominique. 'Perhaps Gideon really is concerned for my health.'

'How can you think otherwise? You are still fretting over your cousin's words, is that it? You are worried Gideon wants to be a bachelor again. I do not think he has any such intention.'

'He did say he had outgrown Max and his circle,' said Dominique, hopefully.

'I am sure he has.' Gwen said slowly, 'Gideon's wildness in recent years was more a rebellion against Papa, I think. You see, after Mama died Father changed. I was engaged to Ribblestone at the time, so I never suffered too much from his melancholy, and James, too, was of age and spent most of his time in town, but poor Gideon—Papa tried to turn him into a pattern card. It became even worse when James was murdered in Paris, and then Tante Gwendoline and the *duc* were guillotined. Gideon remained at Rotham, Father said it was his duty, now he was the heir, but the constraint irked him a great deal. It was no wonder that when he inherited a small fortune he took the opportunity to escape to town. He spent recklessly and seemed intent on committing every folly imaginable…' She smiled. 'So you see, my love, marriage to you could well be the making of my brother!'

Dominique clung on to that small ray of hope as she prepared to leave London. It was not to be expected that her interesting condition would remain a secret, al-

though Gwen had assured her sister-in-law that she had
told only her closest friends. By July it was all over town
and Dominique had to accustom herself to beaming
smiles and knowing looks. She saw Raymond Lamotte
occasionally, but afforded him no more than a distant
bow. She was still very angry with Max, but thankfully the one time they met she had Gideon by her side.

They were attending a musical recital and she was
coming out of the supper room on Gideon's arm when
the earl appeared before them.

'Martlesham.'

As Gideon bowed she made her curtsy to the earl.

'Good evening, Albury. Cousin.' He held on to her
fingers after kissing them. 'I understand I am to congratulate you.'

'Thank you, Max.' She withdrew her hand as she
gave him a glittering smile. He responded with one
equally false.

'It explains why you can do no wrong in your husband's eyes at present.'

Gideon gave a soft laugh.

'You are thinking of our embrace in St James's
Street.' He pulled her hand on to his arm again and
patted it. 'An outrageous display of affection in public,
of course, but I could not help myself.'

'Could you not?' Max's lip curled. 'I thought it might
be for my benefit.'

'Good Gad, no,' exclaimed Gideon, recoiling artis-
tically. 'Whatever gave you that idea?'

'Oh, I don't know,' returned Max, considering. 'I
think it was something Lamotte said to me.'

Dominique froze. A furious retort rose to her lips,
but Gideon's hand was still covering hers and he gave
it the slightest squeeze. She remained silent.

'Ah, yes, Monsieur Lamotte.' Gideon's voice was quiet, silky, but no less menacing. 'Odd that you should deny him one day and the next he is a friend.'

'I should say he is more of an acquaintance.'

'A charming young man,' said Gideon lightly. 'But French, you know. He is unfamiliar with the way we do things here, especially when it comes to husbands. They can be the most unaccountable creatures, you see.'

'Can they?'

Max sounded wary and, casting a quick glance at Gideon, Dominique thought that despite his pleasant tone his eyes had never been so menacing.

'Oh, yes,' he said softly. 'I did not realise it until I became one myself, but it seems now that if anyone should try to harm my wife, or even to upset her, then I should be obliged to wreak the most terrible vengeance. I just couldn't help myself.'

Despite the noise and chatter of the room, a dangerous silence hung around the two men. Dominique could feel the tension and remained still, not daring to do anything that might precipitate violence. At last Max gave her a tight smile.

'You are to be congratulated, Cousin, you have found yourself an admirable protector. I wish you joy of your bulldog.'

With a curt nod he stalked past them.

'Do you think he understood you?' she asked as they continued back to the music room.

'Oh, yes,' murmured Gideon. 'I think he understood me all too well. He will not bother us again.'

Recalling the fury in Max's eyes, Dominique could not be easy.

'Gideon—'

'Hush.' He held up his hand. 'We have given your

cousin quite enough time this evening. Let us instead listen to the music. This next soprano, I have been told, is quite matchless.'

Their last weeks in town were very busy. Dominique felt quite low when Gwen departed for Brighton, but she left Dominique a long list of things she considered necessary for a protracted stay in Buckinghamshire.

'Buy your loose gowns before you go, for there is but one dressmaker in the village, and although you will want to put some work her way you will need more gowns than she can provide. And make sure you buy some warm petticoats. Flannel ones, my love, because the corridors at Rotham can be icy in winter! Then you will need books,' Gwen continued, counting off the items on her fingers. 'I left one or two novels at Rotham, but I doubt my father will have anything new, and it is *such* a fuss to send to London every time one wants a diversion. If you wish to paint, then you should find everything you need in the old nursery.' She pulled a face. 'Poor Papa, he insisted we have the very best— tutors, materials, paints, charcoal and sketchpads—but I was a sad disappointment and not at all proficient at drawing or painting. Oh, and buy at least two pairs of stout boots, the lanes become prodigiously muddy...'

She went on for some time and when she had finished Dominique gave an uncertain laugh.

'You make Rotham sound like something from a Gothic novel, all gloomy shadows and empty, echoing halls.'

'Well, it is,' replied Gwen with alarming candour. 'Since Gideon escaped, Papa has rattled around in that great house all alone, with only an elderly neighbour to visit him.' Gwen noticed her sister-in-law's dismay and quickly assured her that Rotham was in no way as bleak as it sounded. 'The local families will be glad to welcome you, I am sure, and Ribblestone and I will be returning to Fairlawns in December, so we shall only be a few miles away.'

To Dominique, December sounded a very long time ahead, but she put aside her worries and threw herself into preparing to travel to her husband's family home.

Travelling in easy stages, they took two full days to reach Rotham. A baggage coach was hired to follow them, the roof piled high with trunks and Dominique's precious harp packed inside. Dominique rode in the elegant chaise sent up from Rotham for her comfort. Her only disappointment was that Gideon preferred to ride, but since this meant that Kitty could join her in the carriage she was not lonely on the journey, and when they stopped overnight at a prosperous coaching inn there was no lack of conversation with Gideon.

They dined in a private parlour served by the well-trained staff of the inn, who were efficient and unobtrusive. Even so, Dominique kept the conversation to innocuous subjects until at last the covers were removed and they were alone.

'Tell me about your father,' she said, putting her elbows on the table and resting her chin on her hands. Gideon looked nonplussed and she added with a smile, 'Are you very like him?'

'In looks, perhaps, but in temperament—my father is very reserved.'

She thought of the long silences she had endured with Gideon, but did not comment upon it and said instead, 'Is his health poor? Is that why he lives so quietly? Gwen told me,' she explained, when he raised his brows at her. 'She warned me that Lord Rotham rarely entertains.'

Gideon gave a crack of laughter.

'Rarely? He *never* entertains. However, that must change if you are living there. You must invite whom you please.' He was silent for a moment. 'You must not be frightened of my father, Nicky. He might appear cold, but his heart is very generous.'

'It will need to be,' she murmured. 'I bring no dowry.'

'You must not let that worry you.'

'But it does, Gideon.'

'I think Father will be too relieved to know I have settled down to worry about your lack of dowry. You see, he was sorely disappointed when I went off to make my own life in London.' He was silent while he poured himself another glass of wine. 'I did not behave well, I admit it. And once in town I fell in with your cousin and his friends. I am not proud of that time.'

After the suffocating discipline of Rotham, Max's mischievous merrymaking had seemed very attractive. Gideon had willingly participated in the pranks and jokes they played on each other and even on total strangers—boxing the Watch, stealing an old gentleman's wig, holding mock duels, bribing the coachman to let them take the reins of the stage and race it against one of their own carriages... It had all seemed like harmless fun at the time, but looking back he saw how childish it had been. When he stole that little lightskirt from under Max's nose it was inevitable that the earl would retaliate, but bullying his innocent little cousin into marriage—!

Glancing up, Gideon saw Nicky's anxious face and

he added quickly, 'That is no reflection upon you, Nicky. I could not want for a better wife.'

'But perhaps you could want a more beloved one.'

Gideon frowned.

'We will not discuss that, if you please. The actress Max employed to impersonate you would not have been acceptable to my family.'

Dominique met his eyes across the table, the wine making her brave.

'And am I any more acceptable?'

To her surprise the coldness in his gaze was replaced by something warmer, including a hint of laughter.

'With your grace and dignity and your indomitable spirit—yes, you are, my dear.'

She was inordinately pleased with his answer even though it made her blush rosily. At the same time she felt that strong tug of attraction to the man sitting opposite. His look seemed to burn right through her decorous gown and she could feel her body responding, the breasts tightening, pushing against the restricting material as she imagined his hands caressing her body. It had been weeks since he had touched her like that and she was filled with an indescribable ache to feel his arms around her. She longed to say so, but the words would not come. The silence stretched between them, becoming ever more uncomfortable.

'It—it has been a beautiful day,' she said at last, glancing out of the window. 'It seems a shame that we spent it travelling.'

'I at least had the benefit of riding. You were shut up in the chaise all day. Perhaps you would like to take a little stroll with me now and catch the last of the sun?'

'I would like that very much,' she said, reaching for her shawl.

* * *

The inn was situated on a busy street, but Gideon had noticed a lane to one side and once they had walked a few yards the noise and bustle were left behind. They strolled side by side in companionable silence. The lane was bounded on each side by large fields of ripening corn, gleaming and golden in the setting sun.

'How long will you stay at Rotham?' she asked him.

'Until you are established. I shall drive down to Brighton to see Gwen, then I shall go to Chalcots and see what is needed to make it habitable. I have been thinking we might set up home there.'

'That is your godmama's house, near Hampstead? I should so much like to see it.'

'And so you shall, once your confinement is over. Too much travelling will fatigue you and I would not risk your health.' His voice was kind, but Dominique's spirits sank. He did not want her with him.

'I shall write to you,' he continued. 'You shall have your say about the furnishings and the decoration.'

But from a distance.

'Thank you.' She could not keep the note of disappointment from her voice and Gideon's next words told her he had noticed.

'Believe me, it is best that you remain at Rotham, where Dr Bolton will be on hand if you need him.'

'But your father will not want me.'

'You are the mother of his grandchild, of course he will want you at Rotham.'

She nodded. Her first consideration now must be for her unborn child. She shivered.

'The sun has gone down. Shall we return to the inn?'

Her shawl had slipped to her elbows and as they

turned to make their way back to the inn she struggled to rearrange it.

'Here, let me.'

He pulled up the shawl and her spine tingled with the familiar touch as his hands rested on her shoulders.

Hold me, she begged him silently. *Kiss me*.

Gideon's hands stilled. He could feel the delicate bones of her shoulders through the thin folds of the shawl and the summer gown beneath. Her hair was caught up in a knot, but a few wisps curled darkly against the creamy skin at the back of her neck. He knew an impulse to place his lips there and taste her sweetness, but he feared that would lead him on to a more passionate exchange, so he quelled the desire rising in him and instead lifted the shawl a little higher.

'There, is that warmer?'

'Yes, thank you, Gideon.' She put her hand up over his, where it rested at the side of her neck, and turned to smile up at him.

It was as if someone had knocked the breath out of his body. When had she become such a beauty? Those green eyes with their lush fringing of dark lashes, the straight little nose and soft, full mouth—desire leaped inside him and the blood pounded through his veins. It was all he could do not to drag her roughly against him and ravish her here and now, in this secluded lane.

No! He reeled back. What was he thinking of? This was summer madness, the proximity of a pretty girl combined with the effects of the wine, a good dinner and the balmy summer evening. She had been trapped into marriage with him through very little fault of her own and she deserved more respect than that. In an effort to quell his desire he reminded himself that she was not the woman he had set his heart on, although it was strange that now, when he thought of the bewitching actress called Agnes Bennet, he could hardly recall her face.

Dominique saw Gideon's eyes darken, felt the jolt of mutual attraction, as if some invisible wire hooked them both, but the hot desire in his glance was quickly replaced by shock and he recoiled from her. She did her best to ignore the chill that filled her soul. She might be his wife, but she was not his love.

Hiding her own disappointment, she suggested they should go back to the inn and immediately turned her steps that way, head held high. This was her life now and she must be content.

Chapter Eleven

Dominique's image of Rotham as a sinister Gothic pile faded with her first view of the house. It was bathed in the golden glow of a summer's evening, a many-gabled Jacobean mansion built of red-brick and creamy stone and the windows of the three-storeyed house flashed a fiery welcome, reflecting the glorious sunset.

'Why, it is quite enchanting!' she exclaimed involuntarily.

'Is it?' Gideon leaned forwards to gaze at his old home. 'Yes, I suppose you might think so.'

As the coach pulled up at the front steps he leaped down, ready to hand out his bride. An elderly butler came out to meet them, bowing slightly as he announced that Lord Rotham awaited them in the drawing room.

'Thank you, Colne. I shall take Mrs Albury to him.'

Silently Dominique accompanied Gideon through the small stone porch into an ancient-screens passage. After the sunlight, the passage with its unpolished wooden panelling was very dark and she stopped to let her eyes grow accustomed to the gloom before stepping into the hall. The wainscoting here was equally dull, but the sun streamed in through the windows, the bars of sunlight full of golden dust motes. Swords, shields and antlers adorned the walls. The whole room had the feel of another era, but it looked sadly neglected.

'Is this room never used?' she asked.

'Rarely. When we had house parties everyone would gather here before going out for a day's hunting or riding and we used to hold a harvest supper here for the tenants and their families, but that stopped when my mother died.'

'And where is the drawing room?' she asked as they followed the butler out of the great hall and into another, inner hall.

'Upstairs,' he told her. 'All the principal rooms are on the upper floor.'

'Including the dining room?'

'Of course.'

'And the kitchens?'

'In the basement.'

'A twenty-minute walk, no doubt,' she murmured.

Gideon laughed.

'Exactly!'

They ascended the grand staircase to a wide landing. The house was built around a central courtyard and a series of windows allowed plenty of light into the upper rooms, which led one from the other. The drawing room was the first of these chambers to be entered.

Even to one used to the grandeur of Martlesham Abbey, the drawing room was impressive. Ornately carved panelling covered every wall and the patterns were repeated in the plaster moulding on the ceiling. An elaborate stone chimneypiece dominated the room, the Albury coat of arms emblazoned at the centre of the overmantel. Dominique took in the faded grandeur of the room and the heavy, old-fashioned furniture as Gideon led her forwards to meet her host.

Viscount Rotham had risen from a wooden armchair set on one side of the fireplace and now stood waiting to greet her. She dropped into a deep curtsy, but as she rose she looked up to study her father-in-law. The likeness between the viscount and his son was marked. Both were tall and lean, with the same finely sculpted lips and high cheekbones. Each had hazel eyes set beneath dark brows, but where Gideon wore his auburn hair unpowdered and just touching his collar, the viscount preferred the old style of a curled and powdered wig. He was dressed all in black, save for the narrow ruffles at his wrists and the linen at his neck.

'Welcome, madam,' he said politely. 'Pray sit down. I trust the journey was not too onerous for you?'

'Not at all, my lord. We made one stop overnight.'

'Just one?' Those dark brows rose and he bent his gaze upon Gideon. 'Was that wise, my son? Another night would have given your wife more respite from the rigours of the road—'

'But it was not at all necessary.' She knew an urge to turn and run as two pairs of hazel eyes turned towards her in surprise, but she held her ground. 'Your carriage is so well sprung, my lord, that the miles flew by. I am not at all fatigued, I assure you.'

She was rewarded by a smile from Gideon as he guided her to a sofa, the only padded seat in the room.

'Indeed, Father, we saw Dr Harris before we left town. He assured me that there was no danger in the journey.'

'Nevertheless, I have ordered dinner to be put back, to give you both time to rest…'

The exchanges continued, polite enough, a little

stilted, but not unfriendly. Dominique mentioned this
to Gideon when he escorted her to their apartments on
the top floor and he concurred.

'I am glad you were not intimidated,' he continued.
'Father's style is a little formal, but he is perfectly kind,
I assure you.'

She had to remind herself of this fact when they went
down to dinner. It was served in the dining room, another grandiose chamber beyond the drawing room.
The long table in the centre was set with all the pomp
and formality one could desire. Only Dominique did
not desire it.

Conversation was almost non-existent, the food cold,
and by the time Dominique returned to the empty drawing room while the gentlemen enjoyed their brandy she
was beginning to long for the cosy comfort of Brook
Street. Not one to repine, she spent the time alone tuning her harp, which had been set up in one corner of the
room, where the big windows overlooked the gardens.
She had completed her task and was gently strumming
the strings when Gideon came in with his father.

'Since there is no pianoforte here we brought Nicky's
harp with us.' Gideon explained in response to his father's look of surprise.

'Indeed?' The viscount's response was cool.

'I hope you do not object, my lord?' asked Dominique quickly.

'On the contrary. Gideon's mother was musical, but
when Gwendoline married I had the pianoforte sent to
Fairlawns. However, it will be pleasant to have music
at Rotham once more.' He gave her a little bow. 'This
house has been too long without a mistress, madam.
I should be honoured if you would take on that role.'

'Th-thank you, my lord.'

Gideon touched her arm. 'Perhaps you will play for us now, Nicky.'

She complied, happy to avoid the long, awkward silences that had accompanied their dinner. No tea tray had been ordered. When the clock struck eleven she excused herself and retired. She and Gideon had been allocated adjoining rooms, with a connecting door, and she was not displeased when Gideon knocked and entered a short time later.

Dominique was sitting at her dressing table while Kitty unpinned her hair, but she dismissed her maid immediately. She was wearing only her nightgown and suddenly felt a little shy to be alone with her husband. To hide her embarrassment she kept her eyes on the mirror as she removed the last of the pins.

'I think that went off very well,' remarked Gideon, coming closer. 'Father was very complimentary about you.'

She was pleased, but could not resist asking him if all meals were taken in the dining room.

'When Father is alone he dines in his room and his man, Warner, takes him his breakfast, too. It is the custom here for all guests to break their fast in their room. Kitty will bring yours to you in the morning.'

The idea of sitting in bed with Gideon while he fed her tiny morsels of toast was very appealing—in fact, it sent a little shiver of excitement rippling through her—but that was something lovers might do and she and Gideon were not lovers. Instead, she knew she would be breaking her fast in a lonely state.

Dominique dragged the brush through her hair, sitting tense and upright. Gideon walked up behind her and held out his hand.

'May I?' Silently she handed him the hairbrush. He said quietly, 'I know everything is very new to you here, Nicky, but please be patient.' He began to brush her hair, one lock at a time, but she had the impression that his thoughts were elsewhere. He said at last, 'I have not been to Rotham since my quarrel with Father last December. For me to turn up now and with a wife whom I married without his knowledge or his blessing—'

Her tension melted as the rhythmic brushing had its effect.

'It is very hard for you both, I am sure.' She glanced up at his image in the mirror, but his eyes were fixed upon her hair. 'Does he know the truth about us?'

'Yes. I told him the whole at the outset—not that any blame attaches to *you*,' he said as she put her hands up to her burning cheeks. 'I explained to him that I was in a raging fury because Martlesham and that little actress tricked me into marriage. It was all the fault of my wretched temper, which he understands only too well.' He gave a small, twisted smile. 'He is more likely to pity you than blame you.'

'Which is as bad,' she exclaimed. 'I would not for the world have him feel sorry for me.'

Gideon looked at the reflection in the mirror, observing the anguish in those enormous eyes, the flushed cheeks. His skin still tingled from the feel of her lustrous dark hair between his fingers. Putting down the brush, he placed his hands on her shoulders.

'Was I wrong to marry you?' he asked suddenly. 'Was I wrong not to have the marriage annulled?'

Her chin went up.

'Yes. If you will not put the past behind you.'

With a jolt he realised he had not been thinking of the past, merely of the mischief he had done to Nicky by holding her to the marriage. She put one hand on her stomach as she continued.

'It is a little late to discuss this now.' Her tone was prosaic. 'You must do as I do and look forward.'

She gave a little toss of her head, sending her silky hair flowing over his hands. A few dark tresses rippled down over her breasts, outlined beneath the thin linen of her nightgown. Desire stirred again. Whether by design or accident she was leaning back towards him and he turned away before she noticed his arousal—more importantly before his need of her became too great to be denied and he carried her over to the bed and made love to her. He had to get away from her disturbing presence before he took advantage of her innocence. Before he put her at even more risk.

He crossed to the adjoining door and with a curt goodnight he left her.

For a long time Dominique did not move. She had seen that now-familiar look in his eyes, reflected in the glass. At times she could almost think he desired her.

Almost.

When she had sent her hair tumbling down her back it had not been by accident, she had hoped it might evoke a response. His hands had tightened on her shoulders even as the desire leaped in his eyes. He was standing so close behind her that she only had to lean back a little to press herself against him and she had begun to do just that, only to have him rapidly move away. She smiled a little sadly. There was surely an attraction between them. It was not love, but it was a start.

Stifling a sigh, she climbed into her lonely bed and pulled the covers over her. She would be a good wife and mother, she would make him proud of her and then, perhaps he might love her, just a little bit. Snuggling her cheek in her hand, she began to make her plans.

The first weeks at Rotham passed quickly enough. The viscount spent the greater part of each day locked in his study, reading or playing chess with Sir Edward Moorhouse, an elderly widower who lived nearby and called in occasionally. Gideon took his new wife to visit all the local families and the ladies in turn paid their visits to Rotham. When Dominique was not driving out or entertaining her visitors, she observed how the house was run and asked questions of Mrs Ellis, the housekeeper. At the end of the second week she made her first suggestion.

They were sitting in the drawing room after dinner, Dominique at her harp while Gideon and his father played backgammon. When it was time to retire she rose and walked to the door, but before she opened it she turned towards them.

'I have asked Colne to set up breakfast in the oak parlour tomorrow morning.' Gideon's brows rose, but she addressed the viscount, saying with a smile, 'My lord, on my first night here you told me I might act as mistress at Rotham, so I hope you do not object?'

'No, if you and Gideon wish to breakfast downstairs you are free to do so.'

Dominique knew Gideon would declare that he was quite happy taking breakfast in his room. Quelling her nerves, she met his frowning gaze with a smile.

'Thank you, my lord, that room is east-facing, ideal for the purpose, and so much easier for the staff than carrying trays up to the bedchambers. I hope you can be persuaded to join us there one morning.'

She whisked herself away and prepared slowly for

bed, half expecting Gideon to storm in and demand just what she was thinking of, changing arrangements that had stood at Rotham since time immemorial. However, she heard his step passing her door, and the sounds of him moving about in his own bedchamber, so she went to bed. She would discover in the morning if she was breakfasting alone.

'I decided I would not trouble Runcorn to bring breakfast up to me when everything is set out down here.'

Colne had just brought the coffee pot into the oak parlour when Gideon appeared in the doorway. Dominique's welcoming smile was tinged with relief.

'Good morning, sir. There is everything you like—cold meat, boiled eggs, hot rolls in the chafing dish and even ale, should you want it.' She added, as Gideon sat down at the table beside her and took a generous helping of ham, 'I shall continue to invite your father to come downstairs to break his fast, too.'

'You will be disappointed,' he said, splitting a hot roll and filling it with butter. 'My father is too set in his ways. He dislikes company in the mornings.'

Dominique merely smiled, content to bide her time.

Soon her efforts were rewarded. She came downstairs one morning to find her father-in-law already at the table. They greeted each other politely, and even when Gideon joined them no reference was made to this change in the viscount's habits.

Gideon was pleased to see his wife and his father getting on so well. His conscience pricked him a little at the thought that he would soon be leaving Nicky alone at Rotham and he was relieved that she was settling in. He told her so as they strolled in the gardens a little later that day.

'You have made a great difference here,' he said. 'My father mentioned it to me last night. The whole place is brighter, somehow.'

'That is because the wainscoting has been polished for the first time in years,' she retorted. 'It is surprising what a little beeswax can do.'

'You are much braver than I,' he replied. 'I should have been afraid to mention it. Mrs Ellis is not one to take criticism kindly.'

She chuckled. 'I won her over with a supply of French barley and Jamaican pepper.'

Gideon stopped and looked down at her, his eyes brimful of laughter.

'So that is why you had to go shopping again before we left Brook Street. You were stocking up with bribes!'

'Not bribes…' she twinkled back at him '…merely a few treats to ease my path—oh!'

She stopped.

'What is it? Nicky? Are you well?'

She looked up at him, a soft light shining in her eyes.

'Yes,' she breathed. 'I felt the baby move.' She took his hand and placed it on her stomach. 'Wait.'

They stood for a moment, surrounded by sunlight and birdsong.

'Yes! Yes, I felt it, too.' Gideon gave a delighted laugh. 'My child.' He cupped her face in his hands and kissed her gently. 'At last it feels real. Is that the first time you have noticed it?'

'I suspected it before, but it was never so certain.'

'It is like a miracle.' He tucked her arm in his again

and they resumed their walk. 'I would like to feel my child kicking every day.'

'Then stay, at least a few more days.'

Seeing her shy, hopeful smile, Gideon was sorely tempted, but he glanced up at that moment and saw the viscount at the drawing-room window. A lonely figure gazing down at them, reminding him of the perils of loving one's wife too much.

'You would soon grow tired of my company,' he said lightly. 'Besides, I promised Gwen I would look in upon her at Brighton. Then I have to set work in motion at Chalcots, if it is to be ready for you and the baby.'

'Yes, of course.'

Was that a sigh in her voice? She had schooled her face into a smile and began to talk on other subjects. It was for the best, he told himself. Time away from Nicky would be a good idea. He was growing far too fond of her.

Dominique knew she had erred. Gideon had withdrawn from her as soon as she had asked him to stay, the moment she had shown a weakness, a desire to cling to him. Pride came to her aid and helped her to hide her disappointment. She was his wife, the mother of his child, but he could not love her and she must not expect it.

Dominique's sunny spirits had revived by the following morning and she stood at the door with the viscount to watch Gideon ride away. When they turned to go back into the house Lord Rotham held out his arm to her.

'How am I to entertain you, my dear? I would not have you suffering from ennui.'

'What with paying morning visits and receiving them, and the house to look after, I am well entertained, my lord.'

'You must not overtire yourself,' he said quickly.

She laughed as she preceded him into the house.

'I promise you I shall not do that. However, there *is* a little change I should like to propose.'

Those hazel eyes, so like Gideon's, held a wary smile. 'Well, madam?'

'I think we should dine in the breakfast room. With just the two of us it seems so silly to use the dining room. The servants have to carry everything twice as far and the table is so very long...'

She thought for a moment he was going to refuse, but after regarding her soberly for a moment he turned and made his way across to his study, saying over his shoulder, 'Whatever you think fit, my dear. Tell Colne to organise it.'

In an effort to keep herself from missing Gideon, Dominique threw herself into the running of the house. Her body was swelling and she was a little apprehensive, especially when she saw the viscount regarding her so anxiously, but she put her faith in Dr Bolton, who had told her she was perfectly healthy. Besides, there was far too much to do for her to take to her bed. She persuaded the viscount to allow the aged gardener to take on another boy, so that the shrubbery could be tidied up and the paths weeded. Inside the house she explored rooms that had been shut up for years, opening windows and ordering chimneys to be swept in readiness for the winter. She found trunks of material in the attics and used some of it to make cushions, which she scattered on the carved wooden chairs in the drawing room.

Gradually, as summer wore on, the old house came alive under her care, and such was her tact that the servants were happy to oblige her, polishing and dusting and cleaning the rooms until Mrs Ellis declared that the old house was looking almost as good as it had done when Lady Rotham was alive. She also confided to Colne that the master was looking better for the company.

'Aye,' returned the butler, 'he has even ordered the carriage tomorrow, to drive out with Mrs Albury. That will be the first time he has been further than the park for years, save to go to church on Sundays. Bringing the master out of himself, she is. She's proving herself to be a godsend, Mrs Ellis, even if Master Gideon was hoaxed into marrying her.'

The housekeeper wagged a finger at him, frowning.

'I hold no truck with that rumour and I'll thank you not to repeat it in front of the servants, Mr Colne.'

'As if I would,' he retorted, affronted. 'But 'tis what Warner told me Master Gideon had written to his father. Tricked, he was, by the lady's cousin, Lord Martlesham, and that wild set the young master used to run around with.'

'That's as may be, but Master Gideon is changed now, anyone can see that.' Mrs Ellis folded her arms, a satisfied twinkle in her kindly eyes. 'He and the new mistress is a match made in heaven, you mark my words.'

With a liveried coachman on the box and a footman standing up behind them, Dominique found her drive out with the viscount a much more stately excursion than when Gideon had taken her out in the phaeton, but she enjoyed it very much, as she told her father-in-

law when he expressed his surprise at finding her in
the drawing room after dinner that night.

'You have had a busy day, my dear. I would not have
you tire yourself by sitting here with me late into the
night.'

She laughed at that.

'A steady drive with you was a tonic, my lord, and
not exhausting at all.'

'Nevertheless, I have sent a note to Dr Bolton to call
tomorrow morning to see you.'

'I saw him two days ago and he declared me perfectly healthy.' Dominique bit her lip, then added in a
milder tone, 'As I explained to Gideon several times, I
always feel better for a little fresh air.'

'My son is anxious for your well-being.'

'A little too anxious,' she replied, smiling. 'Before
we left London Dr Harris told him that we ladies should
not be cosseted and encouraged to think ourselves ill—'
She broke off, flushing, and added haltingly, 'I beg
your pardon. I realise that not everyone is as fortunate
in their health.'

'You are thinking of Gideon's mother.'

'Yes. I am very sorry if my condition brings back
unhappy memories.'

'It does, but your presence at Rotham more than
compensates for that.' He stared into the fire. 'It was
my fault, you see.'

'My lord—'

'I loved her too much, and she—she could deny me
nothing. I wore her out.'

He put a hand across his eyes. They were sitting together on the sofa before the fire and she touched his
arm.

'Lord Rotham, I am sure—'

He shook his head.

'There is no excuse. She was delicate and I was too hot-headed, too passionate.' He put his weight on his stick to get up and walk to the hearth. 'I only realised what I had lost after she had died. But I made sure Gideon knew of it. I would not have him make the same mistake in his own marriage.'

Dominique thought of Gideon's letters. They were cheery, full of the entertainments and diversions he was enjoying. She could not believe he had gone away to avoid temptation.

'I think your case was very different,' she said candidly. 'You were very much in love with your wife.'

'Ah.' He rested one arm on the mantelshelf and gazed down into the empty fireplace. 'That is something else for which you should blame me, my dear. I am the reason Gideon plunged into marriage.

'When James was… After James died, I refused to let Gideon leave Rotham. He was my heir and I needed him to learn about the estate. He was a young man and needed to see more of the world, I should have understood that. When he inherited the Telford fortune it was only natural he should kick over the traces and go off to town. I live very retired here, but I have acquaintances in London and what I heard of Martlesham's set worried me deeply. Even then I could not see that it was my own doing—if only I had been less hard on the boy—!

'Last December, when Gideon came home, I could only criticise his way of life. Is it any wonder that he stormed off back to his friends?' He turned to look at Dominique, the sadness of the world in his eyes. 'It resulted in a marriage neither of you wanted and I beg your pardon, my dear.'

Dominique forced a smile.

'What is done cannot be undone, but I intend to be a good wife to Gideon.' She went over to him, reaching out to take his hands. 'My lord, I am not a delicate flower from the hothouse that wilts at the first chill breeze. My mother always told me I came of sturdy stock. I promise you if I am tired I shall rest, but otherwise let me do my duty here.'

He regarded her silently for a long, long moment, then nodded.

'Very well. I will send again to Bolton in the morning and tell him not to call. You must forgive me, my dear, I am an interfering old fool.'

With great daring she reached up and planted a kiss on his lean cheek.

'No, sir, you are my caring papa-in-law and I am very grateful for your interest in me.'

With that she said goodnight and went up to her room to reflect upon everything she had heard. It explained a great deal, but confirmed her worst fears.

'A marriage neither of you wanted.'

Well, she was not the first unloved bride, and she would not be the last, but she would make the best of her situation.

Chapter Twelve

Gideon was restless. In previous summers he had enjoyed making his way from one house party to another, but this year nothing pleased him. Even in Brighton with Gwen and Anthony his mind constantly wandered to Rotham.

He corresponded regularly with Nicky, but was a little disappointed that she did not appear to be missing him. At the end of August he made his excuses to leave Brighton and went to Chalcots. He had visited the house only once since he had inherited it—after all, the Brook Street house was much more convenient for when he was in town, but now he realised that this pretty little villa would make an ideal family home and he began to draw up plans for its refurbishment.

September slipped by as he threw himself into the work at Chalcots, exchanging letters with Nicky on colour schemes and plans for the gardens. With all the work he had put in hand the house was quite uninhabitable and he resided at Brook Street, but did not even consider going to the clubs, theatres and gambling dens that he had frequented as a bachelor. He spent his evenings writing to Nicky, or reading her letters.

He was sitting in his study, the cheerful fire there driving off the first chill of autumn, when he realised with a shock how much he missed her and, instead of picking up his pen, he gathered up all the drawings and swatches into a pile. He would take them to Rotham and discuss them with her in person. Tomorrow.

Once the decision had been made he was eager to get away and, after making sure that the builders and decorators knew exactly what was expected of them, he set off, arriving late in the afternoon, tired and dusty, to find the house in uproar. Servants scurried about, too absorbed to notice him. Intrigued, he left his horse in the stables and quickly ran into the house, but arriving in the great hall he stopped and stared in amazement at the scene of feverish activity. The gardener's boy was carrying in armfuls of plants and flowers while the maids were busy covering trestle tables with snowy cloths. And in the midst of it all, issuing directions, was Nicky. Her condition was very evident, but there was a bloom about her that he had not seen before. She looked…radiant.

At that moment she saw him and, after a quiet word to the housekeeper, she came towards him, hands held out. His heart lifted at the sight of her welcoming smile. He took her hands, pressing a kiss on to each in turn.

'What is this, madam?' he demanded with mock severity. 'I am away for a few weeks and return to find Rotham in chaos!'

She laughed.

'We are holding a harvest supper tonight. I am so glad you are here, you will be able to join us.'

'We have not celebrated the harvest here since Mama died.'

Long-buried memories returned as he watched the preparations and heard the snatches of song and laughter coming from the servants as they worked. That, too, was something he had not heard for many years.

He brought his gaze back to her face and grinned. 'How did you cajole my father into this?'

'I was reading *Robinson Crusoe* to him—'

'Wait!' He put up his hand. 'You were *reading* to Father?'

'Why, yes. It would be very monotonous if I could only entertain him with my music, so we play at backgammon or cards, and when the tea tray is brought in I read to him. I bought a number of my favourite works to bring with me. Lord Rotham enjoyed *The History of Sir Charles Grandison*, and Sterne's *Tristram Shandy* although I have not suggested I should read him Mrs Radcliffe's *The Mysteries of Udolpho*...'

'No, don't,' said Gideon, his mind reeling at this new vision of his father. 'I beg your pardon, I interrupted you.' He waved his hand towards the hall. 'You were telling me how all this came about.'

'Well, Defoe mentions sowing seeds and I merely *suggested* that he might like to hold a harvest supper.'

'And where is my father now?'

'In his study, keeping out of the way.' She tried to look serious and failed, going off into a peal of laughter.

Gideon found himself laughing, too, but he sobered quickly.

'I am surprised Father allows you to do so much. He was more anxious than I that you should not over-tax yourself.'

'I am *not* overtaxing myself, Gideon. Your father and I agreed that I am the best person to know just what I can do.' He was not convinced, but she merely shook her head at him, her green eyes full of warm amusement. 'Pray do not be anxious for me, sir. My role here is merely to oversee matters. To prove it, I shall leave the rest to Mrs Ellis and take you away for some refreshment.'

As she led him upstairs to the drawing room, he noticed that the house no longer had a sad air of neglect. Fresh flowers adorned side tables, brass wall sconces gleamed and the grand staircase smelled of beeswax and lavender. The drawing room, too, was much more comfortable. Furniture had been moved into a less formal arrangement, curtains were thrown wide and the hard wooden chairs were covered in cushions.

His valet had also noticed the difference, as he told Gideon when he went upstairs to change.

'Warner tells me the viscount is like a new man. When Mrs Albury began changing things he thought there would be hell to pay, but it seems his lordship is content to let her have her way. And none of the staff have left, either, which was a worry, when the mistress began wanting this cleaned, and that moved, but, no, she's charmed 'em all, just like she did at Brook Street.'

'Yes, well...' Gideon buttoned his jacket, a slight frown creasing his brow '...I only hope she does not find it all too much for her.'

'Not Mrs Albury,' opined Runcorn confidently. 'She's as canny as she can hold together and knows what she is about.'

Gideon bent a searching look upon the valet.

'Do you think her scheming, then?'

Runcorn stepped back, a mixture of shock and outrage contorting his features.

'In no wise, sir! I hears nothing but good of the mistress from everyone who's met her. A proper lady she is, and no mistake.'

Gideon was relieved to know that Nicky was so well respected at Rotham, but he was still concerned that she was doing too much.

He found his opinion shared by the viscount. They were sitting together after the harvest supper, watching as the room was cleared for dancing.

Gideon's eyes were on Nicky as she left the minstrels' gallery after talking to the musicians. He heard his father murmur that she had been up since dawn and must be exhausted.

'She took a rest this afternoon,' said Gideon, 'but it was only a short one.' He jumped up to hold her seat for her when she returned to the top table. 'My father was just saying how tired you must be.'

'Not as tired as you,' she countered. 'You only arrived at Rotham today.'

The musicians struck up a lively tune and a number of couples took to the floor.

'You will not dance.' Her brows shot up and he added quickly, 'I beg your pardon, I do not mean to browbeat you, but I am concerned,'

She smiled. 'And I am grateful for it. You are right, this is far too energetic for me, but you must dance, Gideon. I believe it was always the custom for everyone to stand up together, was it not, my lord?'

'Aye, in the old days,' agreed the viscount, 'although I do not dance now.'

'Then your son must do the honours,' she declared, giving Gideon's hand a squeeze. 'Go along, sir, and do your duty.'

Smiling, Gideon went off to find partners for a suc-

cession of energetic country dances. The mood was very
merry and the old rafters echoed with laughter and good
cheer. When he returned to the top table Nicky pushed
back her chair and rose.

'It looks such fun that I must join in.'

'Oh, no, you must not.'

'I have not worked so hard on this party to be denied.'

'Pray consider, madam, it would be most unwise,'
put in the viscount, frowning.

Dominique pointed to a lady moving ponderously
to join the new set that was forming.

'Mrs Plover is even more advanced than I.' She fixed
her eyes upon Gideon. 'I am not so delicate that I must
sit out every dance, sir. I may not be able to dance a
fast jig, but I shall join in this more stately measure.'
A mischievous smile lilted on her lips. 'Which is why
I instructed the musicians to play something slower.
Now, will you partner me?'

She saw the smouldering fire in Gideon's eyes and
wondered if she had gone too far. The viscount laughed.

'Your wife is a very determined lady, Gideon.'

The anger was replaced by a reluctant gleam. And
there was something else in the back of those hazel eyes
that set her spirits soaring. Admiration.

'I am beginning to learn that, sir.' Grinning, Gideon
took her hand and led her off to join the next set.

He felt a curious rush of pride at the spontaneous
applause that greeted them. It was something of a surprise to find how well she had been accepted at Rotham.
The servants called her 'the new mistress' and even his
father had warmed to her, despite her French blood.

The harvest supper was hailed as a success, and although the servants were clearly stifling yawns as they

served breakfast the next morning there was an air of gaiety about the house that Gideon had not known for years. Nicky was already downstairs and looking none the worse for her exertions and the viscount was positively jovial when he greeted his son.

'I thought I should be breaking my fast alone this morning,' Gideon remarked, smiling.

He noted the bloom on Nicky's cheeks. The thin, rather nervous girl he had married was gone, replaced by a cheerful, confident woman. He decided he liked the change. However, when the viscount suggested she should rest for the day, Gideon could only agree.

'You must think of the child you are carrying,' he told her, softening his words with a smile.

'But I had planned to take a carriage ride today with Lord Rotham,' she protested. 'It has become our custom—'

'Out of the question,' replied the viscount firmly. 'I would much rather you took a rest today.' He hesitated. 'I thought perhaps Gideon might ride out with me, to see the improvements that have been made to the estate.'

Dominique quickly perceived that she had been outmanoeuvred. The viscount was extending an olive branch to his son and he knew she would not do anything to prevent Gideon accepting this peace offering.

'Yes, of course, sir,' said Gideon. 'But I have the renovations at Chalcots to discuss with Nicky.'

Smiling, Dominique shook her head.

'We can do that later. I shall spend the morning attending to my correspondence.' She added shyly, 'But perhaps, Gideon, if the weather holds, you would take a turn in the garden with me when you come back?'

The alacrity of his assent was reassuring and she went off to write her letters. The windows of the morning room commanded a good view of the park, and she happened to look up sometime later to see Gideon and his father riding off together. They looked to be conversing and she hoped that this was the beginning of a better understanding between father and son.

The pair did not return until late afternoon and Gideon went immediately in search of his wife.

'If you still wish to stroll in the gardens, I am at your command,' he told her. 'As long as you do not mind me in all my dirt.'

'Not in the least.' She laughed at him and, taking his arm, she accompanied him out to the shrubbery.

It was a beautiful afternoon with just enough breeze to prevent the heat from being uncomfortable.

'The gardens look better than I remember,' remarked Gideon.

'Your father gave permission for another apprentice gardener.'

He slanted a look down at her.

'At your suggestion? Of course it was, you have no need to tell me.' He stopped and smiled at her. 'You have made a great difference to this house, my dear. I have much to thank you for.'

A stray curl fluttered across her face and Gideon gently pushed the tendril behind her ear. His hand hovered for a moment, cupping her cheek, and she gazed up at him, a shy smile in her eyes. He drew back immediately, alarmed at how quickly the slumbering desire deep inside him had awoken. He looked away and they began to walk on.

'Father and I talked, when we rode out this morning,' he said. 'It is a long time since we did anything together save quarrel.'

'I am glad. One should not be at odds with one's family.'

He heard the sadness in her voice and asked quickly, 'Have you had news of your father?'

She shook her head, frowning.

'No, it is not that. It is Max.'

'The earl? What has he been doing now?'

'It is rather what he did *not* do.' She bit her lip. 'When we lived at the Abbey Mama gave nearly all her letters to Max to frank, but since moving to the village she has been going to the posting office. The number of replies she receives now makes me think that my cousin was throwing her letters away.'

'It would be just like Martlesham to discard the letters and say nothing about it, if he thought Jerome Rainault was dead.' He patted her hand, keen to give her thoughts a happier turn. 'My father has suggested you should invite your mother to come here, at least until your confinement.' She stared at him and he added, 'Father knows how much pleasure Mrs Rainault's letters give you and thought you might feel happier with her close at hand.'

Relief shone in her eyes.

'Oh, I would. So…yes, yes, please. I shall write to her this very day. I did not like to ask the viscount—'

'Why not? You have shown no fear in persuading him to do so many other things.'

'Ah, but that was for Rotham.'

He stopped and gave her a quick hug.

'Dear Nicky, so brave about doing what you see as your duty, yet you would not ask for something for yourself.'

The weight of his arm on her shoulders, his body pressed close to her own, roused the now familiar desire inside her. The warmth in his gaze quickened her pulse, heating her blood. Their eyes were locked, saying so much more than could ever be put into words—but perhaps that was only her interpretation. Wishful thinking.

As if to prove her right, a sudden flush mounted Gideon's cheek. He looked away, cleared his throat and began to walk on again,

'Father is anxious for your well-being, my dear. If your mother's presence would be a comfort, then she must come to Rotham.'

'I would be v-very glad to have Mama with me,' she stammered, still shaken by the effect of his careless embrace. 'But I do not want to impose any extra guests upon your father.'

He chuckled. 'Rotham is big enough to accommodate a dozen guests and Father need not see any of them.'

'Then I will write immediately. In fact, I penned a note to her this very morning. I will open it and add a postscript. I know she will be happy to come and I will be delighted to see her.'

'Good. Tell her to come as soon as possible. I will feel happier if you have more company, especially as I shall be leaving for Brook Street tomorrow.'

He led her to the wooden bench set into an arbour at one side of the shrubbery and they sat down.

She said shyly, 'Must you go?'

'I'm afraid so, I have workmen waiting upon my return to Chalcots.' Work he had deliberately set up so that he could not be tempted to remain at Rotham, but Gideon now found he did not want to part from Nicky. 'I wish you could come with me—'

The words came out in a rush, as if he had spoken on impulse. They gave her some comfort, but she knew it was not practical and shook her head.

'I wish I could, but such a journey would be very tiring for me now and, knowing how anxious you and your father are for my health, it would be inadvisable.'

'Then I shall return again as soon as possible,' he told her. 'And I must set Judd to finding staff for us…'

'Mrs Ellis has a daughter who is looking for a position as housekeeper,' said Dominique, not looking at him. 'She has a sweetheart, Thomas, the first footman, who is very anxious to become a butler. They would make an ideal couple to look after Chalcots.'

'What if they should start breeding?'

Gideon took the opportunity to place his hand on the swell of her belly. The life she was carrying there never ceased to amaze him.

Dominique shrugged. 'We can always find extra help for a few months, if we need to. And you told me there is a cottage adjoining the stables at Chalcots. They might like to live there, even if it takes a little work to make it comfortable.'

'You have thought it all out. Very well, I will mention it to Mrs Ellis today. If the couple marry in the New Year, then they can run Chalcots for us.' He stood up and held out his hand for her. 'Come, it is nearly time for dinner and I must change—and I have yet to show you the plans I have drawn up for our new home.'

As Gideon made his way back to London he pondered on the change that had come over Rotham—and his father. He was surprised at the way the viscount had taken to Nicky—after all, his father had as little cause to like the French as Gideon and yet, not only had he welcomed his daughter-in-law, he had even suggested that her mother should join them at Rotham. Of course, it could be merely that he was anxious for the unborn child, which might well be heir to Rotham, but somehow Gideon did not think so. It was Nicky's doing. She had beguiled the viscount, just as she had beguiled him.

He thought back to their time in the gardens yesterday, the way his heart had stopped when he had looked down into her eyes. Not only his heart, but the whole world. He had wanted to catch her up in his arms and cover her face with kisses, to show her how much he…

His hands tightened on the reins, causing his horse to shy nervously. Madness even to think of it. She was the daughter of Jerome Rainault, a member of the hated Girondins who had murdered his brother. To feel anything for her would be to betray James.

Yet she was his wife and he could not deny he cared for her—as a friend, perhaps, and a companion, but it could not, must not ever be, more than that.

Chapter Thirteen

The first flakes of snow were falling from leaden skies when Gideon returned to Rotham. It was Christmas Eve and he had been fretting for days about the delays that had kept him in London. The baby—his baby—was due at any time and he was anxious to be with his wife. Since he had left her at the end of October their letters to each other had become even more frequent. When she wrote to tell him Gwen and Ribblestone were now at Fairlawns and that they visited almost every day, for the first time in his life he found himself envious of his sister.

At last the old house was before him, the windows glowing with candlelight as the short winter's day drew to a close. Leaving Sam to take the curricle to the stables, he jumped down and ran quickly indoors, only to stop in amazement when he reached the great hall. He placed his hands on his hips and gazed about him, a laugh trembling on his lips. After the harvest supper he should have expected something of this sort. The hall glowed with the golden light of the fire blazing in the huge stone fireplace. Swathes of greenery—holly, mistletoe and ivy—decorated the walls and trailed from the minstrels' gallery.

A discreet cough brought his attention to the butler, who was descending the stairs towards him.

'Well, Colne, it has been some years since we last saw the hall like this.'

'Quite so, sir. Mrs Albury was anxious to keep up the tradition.'

He grinned.

'Of course. Where is she, in the drawing room?'

'No, sir. She—'

He was interrupted by a shriek and Gideon saw his sister flying down the stairs towards him.

'Gideon! We did not expect you until tomorrow at the earliest.'

'I cancelled my appointments.' He caught her hands, saying urgently, 'Where is Nicky...the baby?'

Gwen nodded.

'She is in her room and Mrs Rainault is with her. Doctor Bolton has been called.'

Gideon felt a cold hand clutching at his insides.

'Something is wrong?'

'No, no, only it is her first time and that makes one anxious. Go up and see her, if you like, and then you can wait with Papa, who is so nervous he cannot sit still.'

'That is not surprising,' muttered Gideon, 'when you think of Mama—'

Gwen gave him a little shake.

'Dominique is *not* Mama, Gideon. Doctor Bolton has every expectation that all will be well.'

Gideon took the stairs two at a time as he ran up to Nicky's bedchamber, where he found her pacing the floor. Her dark hair tumbled over her shoulders and she was very pale, almost ethereal in her white nightgown, but she smiled when she saw him.

'I was praying you would be here.'

'So the baby is coming?'

She put her hands around her belly and nodded.

'Mama says it may be some time yet.'

He had not noticed Mrs Rainault, sitting by the fire with her embroidery in her lap, and he belatedly made a bow towards her. His first impressions had been of a rather absent-minded woman, pins falling from her hair and quite careless of her appearance, but since coming to Rotham she seemed to have become much more sensible and was now quietly devoted to her daughter's well-being. He was somewhat reassured by her calm tone when she addressed him.

'This first stage might go on for hours.'

'Then I shall stay and keep you company.'

Nicky took his hands. 'I would rather you dined with Lord Rotham. He is so anxious I fear he will not eat anything if he is alone.'

He pulled her into his arms and rested his head against her dusky curls. It felt so natural, so right, that he wondered why he had not done so more often.

'I am more anxious about you.'

'Thank you, but you need not be.' She relaxed against him and he could feel the hard swell of her belly pressing against him until she pushed herself free, saying with a little smile, 'Go now and look after your father. I have Mama here and the doctor is on his way. I shall do very well.'

It took some time to persuade him, but at last Gideon went off, promising to come back as soon as he had dined. He found Gwen and the viscount in the drawing room, sitting on each side of the fire. Lord Rotham looked up as he entered.

'Well?'

He said, as cheerfully as he could, 'I am told there

may be no news for hours, perhaps nothing until the morning. My wife is anxious that we should eat.'

'Of course you should,' said Gwen, rising and drawing on her gloves. 'You may be keeping this vigil all night and it will do you no good to go hungry.'

'You are not staying?'

'I must go back to Fairlawns.' Gideon's brows rose and she added in an airy tone, 'Not that Anthony will be anxious for me, of course, but he will want to know how things go on here. Send word as soon as there is news, or if you have need of me.' She kissed her father's cheek, adjured Gideon not to worry and sailed out just as Colne appeared to announce dinner.

They sat down at the table in the oak parlour, Gideon commenting that the chamber was so much more comfortable in the winter than the cavernous dining room.

'One of your wife's many suggestions.' The viscount gave a little smile. 'She has transformed Rotham, Gideon. She made me see how reclusive I had become.' He looked at his plate. 'I do not like to eat while she is...'

Gideon, too, was anxious, but he helped himself from the dishes before him and pushed one of them towards his father.

'Try a little chicken, sir. It could be a long night.'

With a shrug the viscount took a few slices on to his plate, but he ate sparingly.

'Childbirth is a dangerous time, my son. I cannot help but worry.'

'Doctor Bolton is a good man. He delivered Gwen's children quite safely.' Gideon tried to calm his own fears but Nicky was so small and delicate that it was not easy.

* * *

After dinner Gideon and his father retired to the drawing room. They were informed that Dr Bolton was even now with his patient, so there was nothing they could do but wait. They indulged in a half-hearted game of backgammon and were just setting up the board for another game when the doctor came in.

'Everything looks to be as it should,' he announced cheerfully, accepting a glass of brandy from Gideon. 'Mrs Albury would not have the month nurse here earlier, but I have brought her now. Mrs Moss is very experienced in these matters and Mrs Albury also has her mother to look after her. There is nothing for me to do at present, so I will call again in the morning.' He drained his glass and set it down. 'I suggest that you both get some sleep. The child will come in its own time.'

'May I see her?' asked Gideon.

The doctor shrugged.

'Of course, but do not expect a warm welcome—the birthing chamber is the women's domain.'

Gideon went immediately to his wife's room. She had been persuaded to lie down and, despite the nurse's less-than-friendly look, Nicky held her hand out to him.

'The pains come and go,' she told him. 'It is quite natural, isn't it, Mrs Moss?'

The nurse had retreated to a chair by the fire and was sucking contentedly on her pipe.

'Aye, lass, you've nothing to fret about, particularly with your mother and me to look after you.'

Gideon sat with Nicky until her eyelids began to droop. When he was sure she was asleep he returned to the drawing room, where he found his father sitting in his chair, his eyes on the dancing flames of the fire.

'Father, why do you not go to bed? You can do no good here.'

The viscount raised his eyes to meet Gideon's.

'Are you going to retire?'

'Er, no.'

'Then I shall keep the vigil with you, if I may?'

'Of course.' Gideon took the chair opposite. 'I shall be glad of your company.'

Nodding, the viscount rang for another bottle of brandy to help them through the long night.

'I did not anticipate I should approve your wife, Gideon, given her birth and the circumstances of your marriage, but I do. In fact, I have grown extremely fond of her. She has made herself indispensable here. Not that she ever puts herself forwards,' he added quickly. 'She behaves just as she ought and yet, one cannot ignore her.'

'No, indeed, sir.' A smile tugged at Gideon's mouth.

The viscount said quietly, 'I could not have chosen better for you.' He shrugged. 'So her father was French—are we to hold that against her? Your aunt fell in love with a Frenchman, after all.'

'And paid the price for it.' Gideon shifted uncomfortably. 'And my brother, too—'

Lord Rotham put up a hand.

'It is time we put that behind us. However, what I cannot forget is my wife's demise.' He said earnestly, 'Dominique may be strong, but too many babies will wear her out, Gideon. If you are prey to carnal lusts, then take a mistress, but for God's sake leave your wife alone, or risk losing her, as I lost your mother.'

They fell silent. It was not the first time the viscount had told Gideon that a surfeit of love had killed Lady

Rotham, that he had been unable to control his passion. Well, that would not be a problem in this case: Gideon did not love Nicky.

Even as the thought entered his head Gideon realised it was a lie. There had been plenty of passion on their wedding night, but since then he had tried to deny that he felt anything for his wife save animosity for her French connections. Now, however, as the clock ticked away the minutes and the night slid quietly and coldly into Christmas Day, he realised how much Nicky meant to him. He wondered what he would do if he lost her, if she died before he could tell her how much he loved her.

The cushions that Dominique had added to the drawing-room chairs made it possible for the two men to slumber fitfully until the grey light of a new winter's day filtered through the window. The fire had burned down and Gideon was becoming aware of the uncomfortable chill around his legs when the opening of the drawing-room door brought him fully awake with a jerk.

The butler stood in the doorway, clearly having difficulty in maintaining his impassive countenance.

'Yes, Colne, what is it?'

The elderly butler drew himself up and announced in a voice that shook slightly, 'Sir—my lord, Mrs Albury's maid has just come downstairs and told us that her mistress has been delivered of a healthy baby. A boy, my lord.'

'And Mrs Albury?' Gideon held his breath.

A smile split the old servant's face.

'She is well, sir.'

Without another word Gideon sprang out of his chair and raced up the stairs, reaching the landing just as Mrs

Moss appeared, her arms full of bedsheets. The woman grinned at him.

'You'll be wantin' to see yer new son, I'll be bound.'

'And my wife.'

'Aye, well, she's exhausted, but no doubt she'll be pleased to see you. We've just cleaned her up and the babe, so in you go.'

Quietly Gideon entered the room. Mrs Rainault was standing by the bed, a small snuffling bundle in her arms. She smiled.

'Come and meet your new son, sir.'

Gideon glanced at the red-faced scrap, but quickly turned his attention to the bed where Nicky lay back against the pillows, her eyes closed. He sat on the edge of the bed and reached for her hand. It was limp and cool in his grasp, but she gave his fingers a slight squeeze.

'We have a son, Gideon. Are you pleased?'

'Delighted.' He smiled down at her. 'But even more pleased that you are well, Dominique.'

Through the fog of exhaustion Dominique noted his use of her name—the first time since their wedding night. With a satisfied smile she slipped away into a deep sleep.

Dominique's insistence that old traditions should be revived made Christmas at Rotham more festive than any Gideon could remember since his childhood, but it was the birth of young Master Albury that gave the celebrations an added edge. Mother and baby continued to thrive under the watchful care of Mrs Rainault and the month nurse, and Lord Rotham ordered that Colne should treat the servants to a few bottles of his best claret to toast the health of his new grandson, James Jerome Albury.

With each day the viscount became more cheerful, never more so than on the first evening that Dominique was well enough to come downstairs for dinner. She took her place opposite her mother, while Gideon and his father sat at each end of the small table in the oak parlour. Conversation was desultory, until the covers were removed and Mrs Rainault announced that she should be thinking of returning to Martlesham.

'I have rather neglected my letter writing since being here with you,' she told Dominique, when she protested.

'Surely you can write your letters anywhere,' remarked the viscount.

'Why, yes, my lord, but I have taken advantage of your hospitality long enough.'

The viscount sat back and steepled his long fingers together.

'I wonder, ma'am, if you might consider moving to Rotham? I own a small house in the village that is empty at present.' He cleared his throat. 'I would like to help you in your efforts to find out what has happened to your husband—Gideon has told me of your quest, ma'am, and Lord Martlesham's—er—reluctance to help you.'

Dominique looked up. 'I believe he discarded Mama's letters, rather than frank them.'

The viscount frowned. 'That would not happen at Rotham, I assure you.'

'But we must not raise false hopes,' said Gideon quickly. 'Our lawyer in London has been looking into the case, but we have had no luck at all.'

'Rogers is a good man,' said the viscount. 'I am sure he has gone through all the official channels.'

'I believe so, my lord.' Dominique sighed.

'I, on the other hand,' he murmured, 'will go through rather more—unofficial channels.'

Dominique stared at the viscount. He was sipping his wine, that disturbing twinkle in his eyes.

'Would you do that for me, my lord? For Jerome?' Mrs Rainault gave a tiny shake of her head. 'I beg your pardon, but I know—that is, I am aware—that you have no cause to think kindly of any Girondin.'

'Dominique has told me your husband advocated moderation. I understand he gave up the chance to come to England with you because he wanted to save his king.'

'That is true, my lord, but we have heard nothing for so many years.'

He smiled. 'Let me see what *I* can do for you, Mrs Rainault.'

By the end of the evening it had all been arranged. Mrs Rainault would remain as the viscount's guest until her maid had returned from Martlesham with her belongings.

'I am amazed and so grateful for your father's kindness,' exclaimed Dominique, when Gideon escorted her upstairs later that evening. 'Especially when he has as little cause to like the French as—' She broke off, flushing.

'As I have,' he finished for her. 'I beg your pardon, Dominique. I treated you very badly when we first met.'

His use of her name again brought a flush of pleasure to her cheek.

'But the provocation was very great,' she admitted.

'True, but I should not have reacted as I did.' He stopped on the stairs and turned to her. 'Can you forgive me, my dear?'

Forgive him for marrying her? For making her fall in love with him?

'There is nothing to forgive.'

He kissed her hand.

'You are too good,' he told her, moving on. 'It is no wonder that my father wants to do all he can to help you and your mother.'

'Just to have someone supporting her has made *Maman* so very happy.'

'And what of you?' he asked her.

'I would just like to know the truth. It has been so long and we have heard nothing.'

He put his hand over hers where it rested on his arm.

'If anyone can find the truth it is my father. Although he has lived retired for the past decade, he is not without influence.' They had reached the door of her bedchamber and he stopped, leaning down to kiss her cheek. 'Sleep well, my dear.'

It was the end of March when Gideon took his wife and child to Chalcots. Thomas ran out to open the carriage door, puffing out his chest to show off his new butler's livery.

'Welcome, Mr Albury, ma'am.'

Silently Gideon jumped out and helped Dominique to alight, leaving Thomas to assist the maid who was following with the baby. Just when he thought he could wait no longer for her opinion of their new home, Dominique squeezed his arm.

'Oh, Gideon, it is lovely.'

He grinned and realised how anxious he had been for her to like the house.

'I hope I have followed all the suggestions you sent

me in your letters.' He took her hand. 'Come in out of the cold.'

'Everything is ready for you, sir,' said Thomas when they reached the hall. 'There is a good fire in the drawing room and Mrs Thomas has set out wine and cakes, too.'

'Perhaps you would prefer to rest first,' suggested Gideon as he lifted her travelling cloak from her shoulders and handed it to the waiting footman.

Dominique did not answer immediately, for she was issuing instructions to the maid to take Baby James upstairs. Then, tentatively, she took his hand.

'May we look around first? I am not in the least tired, I assure you. Now that I have a wet nurse to feed little James I no longer have to coddle myself so.'

'It is not only for our son that I wish you to look after yourself.'

Dominique's heart swelled with happiness at his words. She hoped, now they had a home of their own, that he might share her bed again and that his professed affection might blossom into love.

The house was everything Dominique had imagined. The reception rooms were light and elegant, the nursery perfect for a growing family. For *her* family. Word soon spread that the Alburys were at Chalcots and the invitations began to arrive, a trickle at first, but after Mrs Albury's Court presentation they became a flood. She was delighted that Gideon insisted upon accompanying her to all the balls, parties and receptions, especially when they met Max at so many of the assemblies.

'He is furious to see us so content,' remarked Gideon as they drove back to Chalcots after one particularly pleasant evening. He patted her hand. 'I cannot thank him enough for providing me with the perfect wife.'

'Am I?' murmured Dominique. 'Do you really think me so perfect?'

'Why, yes.' Gideon lifted her hand to his lips. 'I could not wish for a better.'

She said daringly, 'You do not d-demonstrate it.'

There was an infinitesimal pause before he said lightly, 'Faith, madam, I spend every day with you, is that not enough?'

No, I want you with me every night, too!

The words were loud enough in her head, but she could not bring herself to say them, afraid to see his warm looks turn to revulsion when she disclosed her wanton desire for him. She tried to convince herself Gideon was afraid for her, that he was trying to protect her, but when she looked in the mirror each morning a tiny demon in her head whispered that she was not the fair English rose he desired.

Dominique kept herself busy, dividing her time between the baby and the round of social calls that fell to her lot. There was no lack of visitors, but she was especially pleased to see her sister-in-law, who called often.

'I can never see enough of my little nephew,' Gwen explained as they enjoyed a glass of ratafia in the morning room after visiting the nursery. 'I sometimes wish that we had more than just the two boys.' She looked a little wistful, but the next moment the shadow was gone and she said brightly, 'And how do you like Chalcots? Is it not too far from all the amusements?'

'Oh, no, it is but a half-hour carriage ride to town and it is far better for the baby to be away from the dirt and smoke of London.'

Gwen's eyes lifted to the mantelpiece.

'I see you have an invitation to Grayson House to-night. Do say you will be there, Lady Grayson's soirées are always delightful.'

'Is Ribblestone going with you?'

Gwen avoided her eyes. 'Oh, he will be at the House,' she said airily. 'Cecil Hatfield is escorting me.'

'Really? I thought Sir Desmond Arndale—'

She was interrupted by Gwen's brittle laugh.

'Heavens, I have no particular gentleman friend. Goodness me, Dominique, that *would* set tongues wagging.'

Dominique was tempted to say that tongues already wagged, but she stayed silent.

'And talking of gentlemen,' Gwen continued, 'where is Gideon today?'

'He has gone to see Mr Rogers, to discuss business.'

'I must say I was pleased to see Gideon and Papa getting on so well at Christmas. I am glad they have put their differences behind them.'

'Yes, we shall be spending more time at Rotham in future, I think. Gideon is taking much more interest in the estate.'

'And so he should,' declared Gwen. 'It is his inheritance—oh, I know he has always felt a little awkward, stepping into his brother's shoes, but nothing can bring James back.'

'Your father has given him several commissions in town to carry out,' said Dominique. She added, unable to keep the slight quaver from her voice, 'Lord Rotham has also written to many of his old friends—in France and in England. Friends who may be able to help us find news of Papa.'

'My dear, that is wonderful,' cried Gwen, reaching out to take her hand.

'It is not just that we might at last find out the truth,' replied Dominique, wiping her eyes. 'It is that Lord Rotham and Gideon should be p-prepared to help.'

'Yes, that is quite extraordinary,' Gwen admitted. 'We were all devastated when James was killed, but Gideon took it very hard indeed. It was as much as we could do to prevent him posting off to France immediately to seek justice—not that there was any justice to be had, as we discovered when *Tante* and the *duc* were executed. Papa was even more determined that Gideon should remain at Rotham after that, and I think he would be there still, if his godmama's legacy had not given him a measure of independence. But poor Papa, I thought he would never recover from the blow of losing his son and his sister to the Terror. He has been a recluse ever since—until you came to Rotham, my dear. Such changes you have wrought there! I truly believe you have helped Gideon and my father to come to terms with the past. Anthony declares you have worked a miracle!'

Dominique accepted the tribute with a smile, but when she thought of lying alone in her bed every night, she knew there was one miracle it was beyond her power to work.

Chapter Fourteen

The Alburys set out in good time for Lady Grayson's soirée, their carriage bowling swiftly through the darkness.

'If you had known how long your business would take, you could have dined in town and met me there,' remarked Dominique.

Gideon pressed a kiss upon her fingers.

'But I prefer to dine at home with my wife.'

A little bolt of pleasure drove its way through Dominique and she leaned closer, hoping for a more intimate embrace. When it did not come she stifled her sigh and asked him in cheerful tones, 'And was your business in town successful?'

'I believe so. I delivered Father's letters and every one of the fellows declared they would do their best to help.' He squeezed her hand, adding gently, 'That is not to say it will be good news, Dominique.'

'No, Mama and I are both aware that Papa could be—that he might not be alive, but just to know the truth would help. We are very grateful, Gideon, to you and Lord Rotham.'

'Yes, well…' He cleared his throat and after an awkward pause he continued in a matter-of-fact tone, 'Rogers and I had a good meeting, too. We decided that the town house should be shut up for the present. I think if Father ever came to town he would prefer to stay with us. What do you think?'

'Lord Rotham would be very welcome at Chalcots, so I agree we do not need the Brook Street house,' she replied, gratified that he should ask her opinion. 'Perhaps it might be let out and the staff retained?'

'Yes, that is an idea. And a good one, too. I shall suggest it to Father when I write next.' He glanced out of the window. 'Ah, we are here. Come along, my dear.'

Grayson House was packed that evening. The hall and stairs were crowded with guests, the ladies' pale gowns a vivid contrast to the gentlemen's dark coats. Dominique took off her fur-lined cloak to display her own low-cut, high-waisted gown of ruby satin, the hem fringed with gold and worn over a white satin petticoat with tiny puff sleeves and a quantity of fine lace covering the low neckline. Now, as she prepared to accompany Gideon up the sweeping staircase, Dominique wondered if such a strong colour was a mistake, but at that moment Gwendoline appeared and put all her doubts to flight.

'My dear, you look positively dazzling in that gown! I knew we were right to put you in bold colours.' Regardless of the watching crowd, Gwen enveloped her in a scented hug, murmuring wickedly, 'And your figure is so much better since having little James. You are positively *voluptuous*, my dear!'

Dominique laughed and blushed at the same time, and when she emerged from Gwen's embrace she found Gideon smiling and holding out his arm to her.

'Time we met our hostess, don't you think?'

Happily she accompanied him up the sweeping staircase.

'I did not see the man escorting Gwen—' She looked back. 'Ah, there he is with her now…Mr Hatfield. Do you know him, Gideon?'

He glanced briefly down into the hall.

'Hatfield? Yes, I know him.'

She was quick to detect the note of reserve in his voice.

'You do not like him?'

'Not particularly. He is a crony of Martlesham's and a womaniser.'

'Oh. Then should Gwen—perhaps we should warn her.'

'My sister knows what she is about and is using Hatfield for her own purposes—I think she is trying to make Ribblestone jealous.'

Dominique looked again into the hall, where Gwendoline was now hanging on the arm of the rather louche figure that was Mr Cecil Hatfield.

'Will it work, do you think?'

Gideon shrugged. 'I have no idea. I have warned Gwen against pushing Anthony too far. He is an easygoing fellow, but he has his limits. As have I. Let me warn you, madam, that I should not tolerate you flirting with such a man.'

'Would you not?' She saw the dangerous gleam in his eyes and suddenly found it difficult to breathe. 'What—what would you do, Gideon?'

She waited, eyes wide with expectation. Would he knock him down? Challenge him to a duel? The intense look faded and Gideon laughed.

'I should lock you up,' he declared, pulling her up

the last few stairs to meet their hostess. 'Ah, Lady Grayson, good evening, ma'am…'

Dominique did not know whether to be flattered or outraged by his comment, but she put it behind her and set about enjoying herself. She was happy for Gideon to go off to the card room and leave her to join her many acquaintances.

It was some time later that she was momentarily alone and heard an unmistakable voice in her ear.

'So, Cousin, you have provided Albury with an heir. I congratulate you.'

She swung around to find the Earl of Martlesham at her shoulder. His insolent gaze swept over her.

'Marriage suits you, Cousin. You have blossomed. But then it is surprising what marriage to a wealthy man can do.'

'We are very happy, I assure you.'

'And how is my dear aunt?'

'Much better now that she is away from Martlesham,' retorted Dominique. 'You tricked her into thinking you were franking her mail.'

'What does that matter? By the time I became earl there had been no news of your father for years. Why should I humour a madwoman?' He leaned closer, hissing, 'And that is what she is, writing her interminable letters, hoping to find Rainault. Any sensible person would have given up long ago and accepted that he was *dead.*'

Hot rage flooded her and she glared at him before turning away with a shrug of indifference,

'It matters not. She is at Rotham now, where she is

respected and valued. Neither of us need concern ourselves with you again.'

He caught her wrist.

'So you think yourself safe now, do you, Mrs Albury? Well, just be careful that this idyllic world you
have created does not come crashing down about your
ears!'

With another fulminating look she wrenched herself free and stormed across the room towards Gwen,
who saw her approaching and immediately sent her
cicisbeo away.

'Whatever has upset you?' she murmured, linking
her arm through Dominique's and carrying her off to
the supper room. Gwen procured two glasses of wine
and a small table in one corner, where they could talk
undisturbed. Gwen listened while Dominique described
her encounter with Max.

'It was not so very bad,' ended Dominique, her anger
fading. 'He treated Mama abominably, but she is out
of his reach now. Yet still he is not satisfied. He cannot bear the thought that Gideon and I could be happy.'

'Then he must learn to live with it,' replied Gwendoline stoutly. 'No one who sees you and my brother
together could doubt your felicity.'

'And yet…' Dominique bowed her head. She leaned
across the table, lowering her voice. 'And yet—oh,
Gwen, he—he avoids my bed.'

'Oh, my poor girl.'

Dominique was obliged to blink away a tear.

'I th-think he still yearns for his actress—'

'No, no, this is my father's doing,' said Gwen. 'He
has convinced Gideon that—how would he phrase it?—
"carnal knowledge" of one's wife is detrimental to her
health.'

Dominique felt her face burning.

'But Dr Bolton sees no harm—'

Gwen squeezed her hand.

'You must remember that Gideon was a witness to Mama's protracted ill health and her early demise. That is a much stronger argument than any the good doctor can put forwards. Papa told Anthony the same thing— I had left the drawing room one evening, soon after we were married, and when I returned Father was giving his new son-in-law the benefit of his advice—*keep your lust for your mistress, my boy.*' Gwen added, a little wistfully, 'Not that Anthony had a mistress, apart from his politics.'

'So, am I not alone?' murmured Dominique, thinking of the poor French Queen and the salacious accusations against her. 'Am I not w-wicked to have such strong feelings?'

'Not wicked at all, love. But I have told you before— sometimes men need a little push to show them just what is under their nose. You should set up a flirt. There are any number of men here who would oblige you.'

'But I do not want a lover!'

'Not a *lover*, Dominique, merely someone to show you some attention and make Gideon realise how desirable you are.'

'There was such a person in town last year,' said Dominique miserably. 'A Frenchman. I nearly made the most terrible mistake, but Gideon f-found me just in time, only he was not the least bit jealous.'

'Well, that was last year. Gideon thinks a lot more of you now.' Gwen looked up. 'Hush now, he is coming.' She cast a mischievous glance at Dominique and beckoned to Gideon. 'So you have found us, Brother.

What do you think of your wife tonight? Is she not exquisitely *ravishable* in that red gown?'

'Gwendoline!' Dominique's protest was no more than an outraged squeak.

'Exquisite, certainly,' returned Gideon. He held out his hand. 'The singing is about to start, my dear, and I think you would enjoy it.'

'Yes, of course.' She rose with alacrity. 'Thank you, Gwen, for your advice.'

'And what advice would that be?' Gideon quizzed her as he bore Dominique away.

'She says I should make you jealous,' she offered, slanting a look up at him.

Gideon laughed.

'I am not the jealous type, so you would be wasting your time, my dear.'

No, thought Dominique as she accompanied Gideon to the music room. Jealousy argued a strong passion and, apart from their wedding night, so very long ago, Gideon had shown no passion for her at all.

By the time the singing had ended the evening was well advanced and Dominique was happy to agree when Gideon suggested they should go home. They sought out Lady Grayson to take their leave of her and found their hostess deep in conversation with Gwendoline.

'My dears, Lady Ribblestone has been telling me of the delightful burletta that is playing at the Theatre Royal,' said Lady Grayson, when they came up to her. 'What is it called, my dear?'

'Midas,' Gwen replied. 'We are all mad to see it, Gideon, and I am putting together a party for Friday night. Will you join us?'

Dominique held her breath, but Gwen met her eyes for a moment before she handed Gideon a leaflet, saying innocently, 'I obtained this playbill. You will see that the cast is quite unexceptionable.'

Gideon unfolded the paper and Dominique peeped across as he read it. She wondered whether he was relieved or disappointed to find that Agnes Bennet's name was not there.

'Why, yes, I suppose we might go,' he said at last. 'Will Ribblestone be there?'

Gwen replied with an elegant shrug, 'No doubt he will be at the House until all hours, so I shall not wait for him. But you must all come and dine in Grosvenor Square first. What do you say?'

'I should be delighted,' responded Lady Grayson. 'What about you, Mr Albury?'

'Very well, unless my wife has any objections?'

'No, sir, none.'

'Then it is settled,' cried Gwen, clapping her hands. 'We shall all go to Drury Lane on Friday!'

The idea of the theatre party occupied Dominique's thoughts all the way back to Chalcots. She was so lost in thought that when they reached the house and Gideon asked her if she wanted to take a glass of wine with him before retiring, he had to repeat his question.

'Oh, I am so sorry, Gideon, my thoughts were otherwhere.'

'And have been so ever since Gwen mentioned that comic opera.' He laughed and put his hand under her arm. 'Well, perhaps it is a little late. Let me escort you to your room, my dear.'

'I have never been to the theatre, you see,' she confided. 'We did have travelling players that called at

Martlesham when my uncle was alive. I thought their performances quite magical, but I was only a child then, of course. In recent years the only theatricals have taken place during private house parties and Mama deemed them unsuitable for me to attend.'

'Yes, I can believe it.'

His dry comment reminded her that he had probably been part of those same house parties and she said no more, anxious not to awaken unwelcome memories.

Gideon glanced down at the silent figure beside him as they made the short journey along the passage to her bedchamber. She had discarded her cloak and the ruby satin was almost black in the dim light of the wall candles, throwing into relief the white trimming of the décolletage and the creamy skin rising from it. She had filled out a little since having the baby and this gown showed her curvaceous figure to advantage.

When they stopped at her door he paused. He wanted to drop his head and kiss her neck, run his mouth along the fragile line of her collarbone until he reached that fascinating indentation at the base of her throat, to touch his lips to the little pulse that beat just beneath her ear. Desire burned within him—it was so long since he had lain with her, tasted the sweet fragrance of her skin, buried his face in her hair.

She was looking up at him now, her eyes inviting, trusting him. Mentally he drew back. She was too precious. He would not risk weakening her with another baby so soon.

It does not need to result in a child.

The thought flashed through his brain, but it was closely followed by his father's warning. A wife was a delicate creature, to be nurtured, protected. Not for them the carnal lusts of the body.

'Gideon?' She spoke softly, putting her hand up to his cheek. 'Gideon, will you not come in…?'

He reached up and caught her hand, planting a kiss in the palm.

'Not tonight, my dear.'

Dominique watched him stride away into the darkness. She was sure she had seen desire in his eyes, certain he had been moments away from sweeping her into his arms. She clasped her hands together. Oh, how she wanted him to carry her to the bed and cover her body with kisses! She went into her bedroom and looked at herself in the mirror. What had Gwen called her? Voluptuous. Yes, it was true and Gideon *had* been tempted, but not enough. Not enough.

In Drury Lane the crowds jostled outside the theatre and inside everything was colourful and noisy and chaotic. Dominique clung to Gideon's arm as they made their way through the press of bodies.

'Wasn't Cecil clever, to get us such an advantageous box?' declared Gwen, when they took their seats. 'No, truly,' she continued, when Mr Hatfield modestly demurred. 'I had thought there was no possibility of finding a ticket for this performance. I am sure we are all very grateful.'

Dominique agreed. They had dined at Grosvenor Square with Gwen and Lord and Lady Grayson and she had been a little apprehensive when Cecil Hatfield arrived, but since Gideon was perfectly polite to him she had soon relaxed. Their box commanded a good view of the stage and while they waited for the performance to begin she gazed around the auditorium, watching with interest as the audience poured in. Fashionable gentlemen and painted ladies jostled with apprentices in the pit, shadowy figures moved around in the upper gallery and the boxes were filling up, the lamplight sparkling and flashing off the jewels displayed by the ladies who were taking their seats. Max was standing at the front of a box opposite, but she ignored his exaggerated bow and took care not to look his way again, determined not to allow him to spoil her enjoyment of the evening.

The lights dimmed ready for the short farce that preceded the main event and Dominique gave herself up to the performance, applauding with enthusiasm when it ended. Lord Grayson took his wife off to spend the interval strolling in the foyer and Gideon slipped into the empty seat beside Dominique.

'Well, what do you think?'

'Oh, Gideon I am enjoying myself immensely,' she told him, reaching impulsively for his hand.

Gwendoline laughed. 'Then you have obviously been starved of entertainment, my dear! That was quite the poorest play I have seen in seasons. I am sure I have heard most of it a hundred times before.' She put her hand on Mr Hatfield's sleeve. 'What thought you, Cecil?'

'I, madam? Why, I saw very little of the farce, my attention was upon something quite different.'

He leaned closer to Gwen, laughing down at her in an intimate fashion that made Dominique uncomfortable. Her eyes quickly went to Gideon and she saw him frown.

He rose from his seat, saying curtly, 'Hatfield, perhaps you and I should—'

Whatever Gideon was going to suggest she would

never know, for at that moment the door of the box opened and the tall, lean figure of Lord Ribblestone appeared.

'Good evening. I hope I am not de trop?'

The way Gwen and Mr Hatfield jumped apart reminded Dominique forcibly of the farce she had just seen, but she did not find it in the least amusing.

'Anthony!' Gwen began to fan herself nervously. 'I—I did not expect—that is…'

'I left a message that I should conclude my business in time to escort you here, did I not, my love? I would you had waited for me.'

As Lord Ribblestone came further into the box, Mr Hatfield edged himself to the door and, muttering something about seeing an acquaintance in the pit, he disappeared. Recovering her composure, Gwen tossed her head.

'You are so notoriously unreliable, Anthony, I did not want to risk our being late and missing the farce. It is Dominique's first visit to the theatre, you see.'

'Ah, of course. Now I understand.' Lord Ribblestone smiled at Dominique, who fidgeted uncomfortably.

She was aware of the tension between Anthony and his wife and was relieved to feel Gideon's hand on her shoulder.

'My love, no visit to the theatre is complete without promenading through the foyer. It will be a crush, but it is something you should do, at least once.'

Gratefully she accompanied Gideon from the box.

'We are best out of the way,' he told her as he shut the door behind them. 'They can talk more freely if they are alone.'

'I do hope they will not fight.'

'I wish they would,' muttered Gideon as he led her away. 'Tony is far too complacent for my liking. He could put an end to Gwen's little flirtations, if he would.'

Dominique frowned.

'Perhaps he does not care for her.'

'Of course he does,' replied Gideon. 'He is as mad as fire, did you not see it?'

'I felt it,' she affirmed. 'But I thought I might be mistaken. And—and does Gwen care for him?'

'Aye. Why else would she set up all these flirts?'

'Perhaps she is lonely. After all, Lord Ribblestone is always busy with his politics.'

'Well, she needs to tell him. A little plain speaking would sort the matter out.'

Dominique was silent. She knew only too well how difficult it was to speak plainly about intimate matters with a man who hid himself behind a wall of politeness.

As Gideon had predicted, the foyer was crowded and with her diminutive height Dominique found the experience suffocating. It was almost impossible to see beyond the bodies immediately around her and she was about to ask Gideon to take her back when she saw Lord Martlesham's fair head approaching. Her grip on Gideon's arm tightened.

'It is my cousin. Must we meet him?'

But Gideon did not reply. He was staring at the dazzling beauty on Max's arm.

'Good evening, Cousin.' The earl bowed, smiling. 'You know Mrs Bennet, of course, Albury. Mrs Agnes Bennet?'

Chapter Fifteen

If Dominique had not been holding on to Gideon's arm she would have collapsed, for her knees suddenly felt very weak. She was at last face-to-face with the woman Gideon had expected to marry.

In those months leading up to the wedding Dominique had avoided the woman pretending to be Max's cousin, but now there was no escape and she forced herself to acknowledge every detail of the beauty who had stolen Gideon's heart. Agnes Bennet was tall, full-figured and as fair as Dominique was dark. Her golden curls clustered around her head and the whiteness of those smooth bare shoulders made Dominique very aware of the olive tint to her own skin. She hoped her face did not give her away, for Max was watching her carefully.

'Ah, I was forgetting,' he said smoothly, 'you did not meet Mrs Bennet, did you, Cousin?'

The actress laughed, a dark, smoky sound that Dominique thought was sinfully seductive.

'Of course I'm not really *Mrs* Bennet, as Mr Albury knows.' Her blue eyes were fixed upon Gideon. 'That is merely a convention for the stage—I am not married.'

Beneath the sleeve, Gideon's arm was hard as steel.

'I believe it is time we returned to our seats.' His voice was icy, and with barely a nod towards the earl he turned and walked away, Dominique almost running to keep up with him.

Damn Max, trying to stir up trouble!

Gideon fought to control his anger as he pushed his way back through the crowd. He should have expected something of the sort. He had spotted Max in the box on the far side of the auditorium, but in the dim light he had not recognised his companions.

'Gideon, please!'

Dominique's urgent entreaty pierced the red mist that enveloped him and he slowed.

'I beg your pardon.' She was looking up at him, her eyes dark with apprehension, and he muttered through clenched teeth, 'How dare he try to introduce that woman to you!'

'Max likes to make mischief. We should ignore him.'

'You are right, of course.' Gideon struggled for composure. 'Come, let us go back to the box. I hope Ribblestone has not murdered Gwen, or Hatfield...or both!'

She rewarded his attempt at levity with a strained smile. When they reached their box Hatfield was standing outside the door.

'Ah, glad you are back, Albury. Didn't like to go in on my own, don't you know.' He grimaced. 'Dashed awkward, Ribblestone turning up like that.'

Gideon raised his brows.

'Why should that be?' He added, with barely disguised menace, 'Unless you were intent upon some impropriety with my sister—'

'Oh, no, no, nothing like that. I am at Lady Ribblestone's service, of course. Pleasure to be her escort, but nothing more than that, I assure you!'

'Well don't act so damned guilty, then.' Gideon opened the door and stood back to let Dominique enter before him. He waved Hatfield in, but as the man passed he caught his arm.

'Just how did you secure this box at such short notice?'

Hatfield was watching Lord Ribblestone, trying to discern his mood, and he answered distractedly, 'Martlesham gave it to me. Said he had booked it months ago, but that now he was engaged to join another party.'

So Max had planned this. Gideon felt the slow burn of his anger as he took his seat for the main performance. From his seat he could see only Dominique's profile, but when Lady Grayson leaned to whisper something in her ear, the smile she gave in return was forced. The incident in the foyer was not forgotten.

The performance ended, but although Dominique applauded heartily she could not recall a single scene. Lord Grayson went off to his club and Lady Grayson, oblivious of the tensions in the box, reminded Gwen that they had planned to go on to the rout at Baverstock House.

'We shall be there in time for supper, is that not what you said, Mr Hatfield?' Lady Grayson fixed the gentleman with an enquiring gaze and he floundered hopelessly, unwilling to commit himself.

Lord Ribblestone took out his snuffbox.

'I have ordered the carriage to be waiting and I intend to return to Grosvenor Square.' He looked towards his wife. 'Will you come with me, madam?'

Dominique held her breath, willing Gwendoline to go home with her husband.

'But I am pledged to go to the rout,' said Gwen, tossing her head.

For a long moment no one stirred. The atmosphere was brittle as glass. Lord Ribblestone put away his snuffbox and Dominique thought she saw the veriest tightening of his mouth.

'As you will, my dear.'

He departed and Mr Hatfield gave an audible sigh of relief. Gwen did not look very happy with her victory and impulsively Dominique touched her arm.

'Let Gideon run after Anthony and tell him that you have changed your mind.'

'But I have not,' protested Gwendoline, shaking off her hand. 'La, that I should forgo a party of pleasure to sit at home! If you are ready, Lady Grayson, Mr Hatfield, let us be off to the rout.'

'Shall we go home, my dear?'

Gideon placed her cloak about her shoulders and Dominique immediately forgot Gwen's troubles as his hands lingered for a moment, their warmth seeping through the silk and into her skin. The meeting with Max and Agnes Bennet had dominated her thoughts since the interval. Gideon's face was a polite mask, but she had no doubt that he, too, was thinking of it. Dominique understood only too clearly why Gideon had wanted to marry the actress. She was everything that Dominique was not—tall, fair and beautiful—and no doubt well versed in the art of pleasing a man.

All through the comic opera Dominique had thought about her. As the musicians played she had heard that dark, smoky laugh, remembered the graceful beauty, the cerulean-blue eyes and painted lips curving into an alluring smile. It was useless to remind herself that she was Gideon's wife, the mother of his child. If his own father advocated taking a mistress, why should he not give in to the temptation?

In the darkness of their carriage as they drove back to Chalcots he reached for her hand.

'You are very quiet.'

'I am fatigued. It has been a long evening.'

'I hope you are not fretting about your cousin. Or Mrs Bennet.'

'No, of course not.' She was glad he could not see her face in the darkness. She added, unable to help herself, 'She is very beautiful.'

'Exquisite.' Her heart sank. 'But you have nothing to fear from her, Dominique. I have no intention of renewing that particular acquaintance.'

Fine words, but would he be able to resist, having seen her again? Only time would tell.

'Dominique?'

'Yes?'

'You do believe me, don't you?

'Yes. I believe you.'

'That is good.' He kissed her hand and squeezed it before letting it go so that he could put his arm about her. 'If there is anything troubling you, anything at all, you must tell me. Do you understand?'

She leaned against his shoulder, breathing in the familiar scent of him, the mixture of soap and clean linen and the faint spicy cologne he wore on his skin.

'I understand.'

But when they reached the house, he kissed her gently and left her at the bedroom door. As he always did.

* * *

Gideon found his wife very quiet the following morning and she did not greet him with her usual sunny smile. He poured himself a coffee and was debating whether to ask her what was the matter when the butler came in to tell him that the carriage had just returned from Brook Street.

'Ah, yes, thank you, Thomas.' Gideon put down his cup and addressed Dominique. 'Rogers told me yesterday that he has a tenant for my father's house, so I asked Mrs Wilkins to clear the rooms of all our personal effects and send them here. There should not be much, but perhaps you would like to tell the servants where you want everything stored?'

'Yes, of course.' She began to fold her napkin.

Gideon raised his brows.

'You do not need to dash off immediately, my dear. The luggage will wait.'

''No, I—um—I have finished here, thank you. I shall deal with it now.'

Gideon watched her go, a faint crease in his brow. There were dark circles beneath her eyes, but surely they were not caused by the events at the theatre, for he had reassured her that she had nothing to fear. Seeing Agnes on Max's arm had been a shock, but Gideon was surprised at how little he now felt for the woman. Perhaps Dominique was fretting over the baby. He decided he would visit the nursery when he had broken his fast, but when he got there Nurse assured him that Baby James was giving no cause for concern. He went off to his study, still frowning.

Was Gwen's behaviour causing Nicky to be anxious? There was no doubt that his sister was playing a dangerous game with her flirts and cicisbeos. Gideon did not believe she had taken a lover, but if she meant to make Ribblestone jealous by her actions then he feared she would find herself far off the mark. They were dining at Grosvenor Square that evening, so perhaps he would take the opportunity to drop a word of warning in Gwen's ear. Anthony was as easy-going as a man could be, but he would only stand her nonsense for so long. Gideon tried to think what he would do if Dominique were to tease him in the same way and was shocked at the anger that shot through him. He was obliged to push the idea away as he sat down at his desk and began to go through the post that Thomas had left there for him. If there was nothing urgent he would find Dominique and invite her to ride out with him. That might help to dispel whatever worries had driven the smile from her eyes.

The pile of letters was small: a few tradesmen's bills, a note from Rogers, confirming the arrangements for letting the house in Brook Street, and a small, sealed note that had been delivered by hand. He broke the seal and unfolded the paper, his jaw tightening as he read through the neatly written lines.

Dominique stood in the hall, looking at the boxes, bags and portmanteaux before her. She consigned them all to the attics, with the exception of the battered and corded trunk that Max had sent from Martlesham. Her eyes dwelled thoughtfully on the door to the oak parlour, where Gideon was finishing his breakfast, then with sudden decision she directed the servants to take the trunk to her bedchamber.

Mindful of the instructions in the letter, Gideon drove to Piccadilly and left Sam in charge of the curricle while he made his way on foot into Green Park.

He strode quickly to the area between the reservoir and the Lodge and as he approached, a cloaked figure turned and he found himself looking into the beautiful face of Agnes Bennet.

'We'd best walk on,' she murmured. 'It will look less suspicious if anyone should see us.'

There was a flatness to her vowels that he had not heard before. She was no longer trying to pretend she was a lady.

'You wanted to see me,' he said, falling into step beside her.

'Lord Martlesham ordered it.' She met his sceptical glance and looked away quickly. 'He threatened to break my arm if I did not do so. He wants me to make mischief between you and your wife.'

'And do you think you can?'

She shrugged. 'I don't even want to try. Making trouble between a man and his wife ain't my style. Martlesham played you both false last year when he contrived your marriage.' She paused. 'I wasn't easy about that, but if I hadn't done it he'd have found someone else. And he was paying me so very well it was impossible to refuse. I thought it would be a little harmless jollity—'

'Harmless!'

She flushed.

'I did not realise he meant to carry it through to a full marriage ceremony. When I heard—' She looked up at him. 'That was a cruel trick to play on you and on the young lady. I apologise.'

'Is that why you wanted to meet, to salve your conscience with an apology?' Gideon could not stop his lip curling in derision. 'Is that the important matter you wanted to discuss?'

'No! No, although I am glad of the opportunity to tell you I regret my part in the whole thing.'

'What, then?'

'I've information for you, about your wife's dowry.'

'My wife has no dowry. You yourself informed me of the fact when you were impersonating her.'

'That is what Martlesham told me and what he wants you to believe.'

'And now he wants you to tell me differently.'

'No.' She sighed. 'I had best explain. When Martlesham returned to town this spring he sought me out. He wanted to make me his mistress.' She gave a humourless little laugh. 'I am aware of my attractions, but I knew that was not the whole of it, because when I refused his advances he still took me to live with him—made it impossible to refuse him, if you want to know the truth. He believes you're still in love with me—no need to tell me that ain't true because I could see as much last night.' She paused and looked up at him, a sudden smile lighting her eyes. 'We enjoyed those weeks together last spring, didn't we? But it was never going to last, I knew that.'

Looking down into her face, she did not seem quite as bewitching as he remembered. She was still beautiful, but somehow the perfect features and intensely blue eyes failed to rouse any desire in Gideon. Her smile grew rueful, as if she could read his mind. With an expressive little shrug she continued.

'Max installed me in his London house, where he parades me in front of his friends as his mistress—he hasn't yet got me into his bed, but he will, in time.' She rubbed her arms and shuddered a little. Gideon had the impression that she was not at all happy with her current situation. 'He made me give up the stage and in-

sists I remain in the house, even when he is out at some
entertainment. The servants ignore me when they can,
which suits me very well. I have spent my time explor-
ing.' She looked up, her blue eyes cold as ice. 'I will
tell you now, Gideon, that I do not like Martlesham.
He is a cruel man.'

'Then why don't you leave him?'

'I intend to, but he is powerful, so I have to be careful. Whenever I am alone in his house I spend my time
looking through his papers, trying to find something
to give me a hold over him.'

'And have you succeeded?'

She shook her head.

'No. He is as careful as he is bad and most of his papers are in a strong-room. However, there is a locked
drawer in his desk—he keeps the key, but it is a simple matter to open it.' She grinned. 'I knew a picklock
once, and he showed me how to do it. At the back of
the drawer I found some letters from France, from Jerome Rainault.'

'My wife's father,' said Gideon. 'But surely they are
in French?'

Agnes nodded and allowed herself another smile.
'They are, but that language is something else I picked
up in my career! The letters were written years ago,
to Max's father. Monsieur Rainault consigns his wife
and daughter to the earl's care, but he is also anxious
that little Dominique should have a dowry. He transferred a large amount of money from a French bank to
Coutts, in the Strand. Martlesham holds it in trust for
Mrs Rainault and her daughter.'

'They certainly have no money now,' said Gideon,
frowning.

'I know,' replied Agnes. 'The earl told me that Mrs Rainault and her daughter were his pensioners.'

'Then it is all spent.'

'That was my thought,' she said slowly. 'Until I saw a letter yesterday morning, from Coutts, concerning the Rainault funds. They have never been touched and Max wants them transferred to his own account.'

'The devil!' exclaimed Gideon. 'I must see these documents.'

'I thought that might be the case.'

'You did not bring them with you?'

'No, it was only after I saw you and your wife at the theatre last night that I decided to tell you, and I have not had a chance to get back into Max's study.'

'Why?' Gideon stopped and turned to face her. 'Why should you want to help me now?'

She spread her hands.

'I told you, I don't hold with the earl's trickery. I'm up for a bit of fun, but he carried it too far, making that poor chit marry you. And you don't need to tell me that he forced her into it, because I know his ways. And besides…' she wrapped her arms around herself again, as if for protection '…I should be glad to see his lordship get a taste of his own medicine.'

'Do you think you can still get those papers?'

'Yes. The earl will be out tomorrow morning, taking his boxing lesson. That will be my chance. He ordered me to see you—to entice you—so he will not be surprised if I want the carriage again.' She stopped and Gideon noticed that they had come full circle. 'Meet me here again tomorrow, at noon.'

He hesitated.

'You realise the risk, if Max should discover what you are about—'

She laughed. 'He won't. Don't you worry about me, dearie. I have funds. He doesn't know my real name, nor that I have a house of my own in Covent Garden that I rent out. I bought it with the money he gave me for my performance as his cousin. I shan't hang around once I have given you the papers. But first, I want to pay him back, just a little.'

With a nod she left him, hurrying away through the trees, never once stopping to look back.

Gideon drove back to Chalcots, barely noticing the route. If what Agnes said was true, then Dominique was not the penniless bride she thought herself and he knew how much it would please her to know that. It was a risk, of course. This could be one more elaborate plot by Martlesham to drive a wedge between them, but instinct told him Agnes was sincere.

Should he tell Dominique? He had promised her he would not renew his acquaintance with Agnes, but surely this was different. And it might all come to nought. As he deftly turned the curricle through the gates and bowled along the drive towards Chalcots he decided he would say nothing until he had the papers and knew them to be genuine. If they were, then Dominique would be delighted and he was beginning to realise just how much her happiness meant to him.

Dominique stood alone in her bedchamber and gazed at the open trunk. She remembered when she and Gwen had sorted through its contents, pulling out shifts and negligees, finely embroidered stockings and gowns of such sheer muslin they could be folded and packed into a pocket book. Highly improper, all of them. The sort of things a mistress might wear. She lifted out a filmy negligee. It was so fine that her hands were visible, even through two layers of muslin. In her mind's eye Dominique could see Agnes Bennet wearing such a gown, standing before Gideon, offering herself to him.

'No! No, she shan't have him.'

'Did you call me, ma'am?'

Dominique quickly dropped the gossamer-thin garment back into the trunk and was closing the lid as her maid came into the room. A shimmering gown rested across her arms.

'I was just looking out your green sarcenet, ma'am, for you to wear this evening, but if you would like something else...'

'I *would* like something else,' declared Dominique. 'Fetch me my ruby satin, if you please.' She glanced at the trunk. 'But before that, bring me a glass of ratafia—a large glass, I think.'

An hour later she went downstairs, a fur-lined cloak over one arm, her free hand gripping the bannister. Perhaps it had not been wise to have a second glass of liqueur, but the idea of seducing her husband was rather alarming, and she felt in need of a little sustenance.

A footman jumped to open the drawing-room door for her and as she entered she had to resist the urge to pull up her low décolletage. Gideon was standing by the sideboard, pouring himself a glass of wine, but the rustle of her skirts alerted him. He glanced up.

Dominique experienced no little satisfaction as his eyes widened and the hand pouring the wine shook, spilling a few drops on to the white tray cloth. Gideon cleared his throat and bent a searching look upon her.

'Is that a new gown?'

'No, sir. I wore it to the Graysons'.'

There was a fine pier glass fixed atop the walnut console table and Dominique stopped before it to consider her appearance. The last time she had donned this gown she had put on a demure white-satin petticoat with puff sleeves and a wide lace edging that had discreetly covered her bosom. Now she wore one of the shifts from the trunk. The effect was quite startling. Instead of tiny white sleeves covering her shoulders the muslin was so fine it was almost transparent and the delicate lace around the neck merely drew the eye to the low neckline and the deep valley between her breasts.

Gideon came to stand behind her and she met his eyes in the mirror.

'The colour suits you,' he said. 'And the way you have of dressing your hair.' He raised his hand to touch the solitary ringlet hanging down and as his fingers grazed her skin she drew in a sharp breath. His hand moved from the curl to her neck. 'Dominique—'

The soft knock on the door made them jump apart.

'Sir, madam. Your carriage is at the door.'

Dominique noted Gideon's blank look and it was a full minute before he could respond.

'Ahem, yes, of course.' Gideon drank down his wine, then picked up her cloak and placed it about her shoulders. 'I could almost wish we were not going out this evening.'

The quiet words sent a delicious thrill running down her spine. So far her plan was working admirably. She peeped up at him through her lashes.

'We need not stay for supper.'

Gideon was silent as he accompanied her to the door and a glance showed her that he was looking quite bemused. He said, when they were seated together in the coach, 'Has anything occurred today, my dear? A visitor, perhaps? You seem…different.'

'No, I have been at home alone all day.' She tucked her hand in his arm. 'That is why I am glad of your company tonight.'

Gideon said nothing, but he did not disengage himself and when they arrived in Grosvenor Square he helped her down and kept his hand firmly over hers as he accompanied her into the house. Lady Ribblestone's brows rose when she saw them, but a number of other guests had already arrived, so there was no opportunity to speak privately then or during dinner. It was not until the ladies retired that Gwen managed to draw Dominique aside.

'My dear, I have not seen that muslin on you before. It is outrageously revealing. What are you planning, you naughty puss?'

'I am fighting for my husband, Gwen.'

'If you are not careful, you will be fighting off everyone else's,' said Gwen frankly. She added, with the ghost of a sigh, 'Even Ribblestone could not take his eyes off you tonight.'

Dominique spread her fan.

'I have no interest in other men. I do not want to make my husband jealous, I just want him to notice me.'

'Well, you will, love, you mark my words,' retorted Gwen. 'Gideon must be made of stone if he doesn't realise that every man is looking at you tonight.'

If he had heard his sister's words, Gideon could have assured her that he was feeling anything but stonelike. The sight of Dominique in that red gown was teasing him to distraction. He found it difficult to converse and even when the ladies had retired he wondered what she was doing in the drawing room, if she was thinking of him. He had frequently found her looking at him during dinner, although every time their eyes met she would blush adorably and glance away. Damnation, he wanted her so badly he could hardly sit still! And he wasn't the only one to notice her. Every man in the room looked her way at some point—even old Mr Severn, who was seventy if he was a day, had raised his quizzing glass and positively ogled her.

And yet it could not be said that Dominique flaunted herself. She behaved with great modesty and charm all evening, but however frequently her eyes alighted on Gideon, he found it was not enough. He wanted to steal her away and keep her to himself.

Chapter Sixteen

'Your wife is looking particularly well this evening,' remarked Anthony, when at last they made their way to the drawing room. 'Motherhood agrees with her.'

Gideon let his eyes rest upon his wife, who was sitting beside Gwen, laughing at something Lord Grayson was saying to her. Was this the same unhappy lady he had seen at breakfast? The sparkle in her eyes, the alluring tilt to her mouth, was captivating. Motherhood had certainly developed her figure, which looked truly delectable. The swell of her breasts rose from the low décolletage and the creamy tones of her skin were complemented by the vivid colour of her gown. But he could not forget the droop of her mouth this morning and her slightly sad, distracted air. A tiny worm of jealousy gnawed at him. He said suddenly, 'Do you think she has a lover?'

To his immense relief, Lord Ribblestone laughed.

'No, I do not. I believe this is all for you.' He clapped his hand on Gideon's shoulder. 'If Gwendoline tried such tactics with me, my friend, I should consider myself a very lucky man. I should certainly not be wasting my time chasing some lightskirt in Green Park.'

Gideon's head came up and Ribblestone nodded. 'I saw you there this morning. You know I often walk in the park when I need to think things out before a difficult cabinet meeting.'

'It was not—that is, it is not what it seems.'

'No?'

'As a matter of fact I was there to learn something to my wife's advantage.'

'I have heard some excuses in my time—'

'It is *not* an excuse,' Gideon muttered furiously. 'The woman has evidence that Martlesham is trying to defraud Dominique of her inheritance.'

'So Dominique knows of this meeting?'

'Well, no.'

'And are you going to tell her?'

'Yes, of course, eventually. I don't want to raise her hopes, in case it all proves a hum.'

For once there was no smile in Anthony's eyes as he regarded him.

'I think you are playing with fire,' he said at last. 'But then, that is the way with the Alburys. They have no notion of how fortunate they are in their partners.'

From the sofa on the far side of the room, Dominique and Gwendoline watched this exchange.

'If I am not mistaken, you are causing my brother considerable consternation this evening,' Gwendoline murmured. 'He does not know what to make of you.' She slanted a glance at Dominique. 'That is what you wanted, is it not?'

'I *think* so.'

Dominique clasped her hands tightly together in her lap. Gwen reached over and gave them a squeeze.

'Do not lose your nerve now, my dear. Gideon is quite besotted with you tonight.'

She went off to mingle with her other guests and Dominique was left alone with her thoughts, but not for long—Mr Severn was making his way towards her. With a sad want of manners Gideon slipped past him and sat down beside her. The old man stopped in his tracks, then turned and moved off, muttering. Dominique felt a smile bubbling up.

'You show scant respect for your elders, Gideon.'

'Would you prefer that elderly roué's company to mine?'

His voice wrapped about her, deep and rich as warm velvet, and the glow in his eyes sent a frisson of excitement through her. Dominique spread her fan and peeped at him over the top.

'It would be most unfashionable of me to agree, sir.'

'And who says we must be slaves to fashion?' He leaned closer. 'Shall we make our excuses now? I want to take you home.'

Her heart leaped at his words. It began to thud erratically against her ribs—surely he must hear it? She could feel the hot blush in her cheeks and kept her fan raised as she tried to answer demurely.

'It *is* a long drive to Chalcots.'

He turned to look at her, resting one arm along the back of the sofa. She could feel his fingers resting lightly on the nape of her neck, a gentle, sensual touch that bewitched her.

'If we stay to supper we shall be damnably late.'

Swallowing, she struggled to match his indifferent tone.

'G-Gwen promised us cards later. Are you sure you do not want to stay and play a hand?'

'There is only one hand I want to play tonight, my dear,' he murmured provocatively. 'Shall we go?'

She could only nod. Her eyes were fixed on his mouth, the finely sculpted lips which curved now into a smile so devastating she thought she might melt. The feeling intensified when he raised her hand to his lips.

'I shall go now and ask Anthony to order our carriage.'

'What excuse will you give him?'

She was suddenly anxious and was only partly relieved by Gideon's wicked grin.

'No excuse will be necessary.'

Gwen saw her husband on the landing and stepped out to join him. He was staring down into the empty hall, a little smile on his lips. She reached out and touched his arm.

'I cannot find Dominique or Gideon.'

'He has taken her home.'

'Really?' She clapped her hands in delight. 'She was looking particularly delightful tonight.'

'Ravishing.'

Her smile slipped a little.

'Yes. All the men were looking at her. Including you.'

He turned towards her, a look she could not interpret in his grey eyes.

'I am surprised you noticed, since you were busy flirting with Arndale.'

'Sir Desmond?' She fluttered her fan. 'I was not—'

'Don't lie to me, Gwen. I am growing weary of your games, my dear.'

'G-games, my lord?'

He caught the fan, his long fingers closing it up and pulling it from her hand.

'It has gone on long enough, madam, your flirtations and intrigues. I do not want to come home and learn that you are out at this party, or that rout. I need you here, supporting me, do I make myself clear?'

There was something implacable about Anthony's stern gaze that made Gwen's heart flip. She gave an uncertain little laugh.

'La, you are very masterful tonight, my lord. If I did not know better, I would think you were jealous.'

He did not smile.

'If you do not mend your ways, madam, you will discover just how masterful I can be.'

He held out the fan, and when she took it he turned on his heel and walked away.

'Oh, that was quite, quite terrible,' cried Dominiqiiue, when she and Gideon were in their carriage and homeward bound. 'Everyone was smiling when we got up to leave! And, and—oh, heavens. They will think that we, that we—'

'And is that not the truth of it?' He caught her fingers and held them in a warm, sustaining clasp. 'I wanted you to myself, to make love to you.'

'Oh, Gideon.' She tried to make out his face in the near darkness. Whatever the outcome, she must be honest now. 'That is what I want, too.'

With a growl he pulled her into his arms, seeking her mouth, teasing her lips apart so that his tongue could plunder and explore. She responded instantly, aware that this was the first time since their wedding night, a full twelve months ago, that they had come together in passion, rather than the restrained couplings of the marriage bed.

He tugged at the strings of her cloak until it fell away

and his mouth moved to that sensitive spot below her
ear, where the touch of his lips made her pulse leap
alarmingly. He touched her jaw with light, butterfly
kisses, continued down the slender column of her neck,
his tongue flickering in the hollow at the base of her
throat and making her moan softly. She leaned into him,
her breasts hot and aching as they pushed against the
restrictions of her gown. His hands smoothed over her
shoulders, pushing aside the muslin sleeves and leaving her skin free for more kisses. Dominique reached
out for him, fumbling with the buttons of his waistcoat
and shirt. She slid her hand under the fine linen and caressed the smooth, hard frame of his chest.

The coach lurched over a particularly uneven sec-
tion of the road and they were thrown apart. Dominique
fell back into the corner while Gideon slipped to the
carriage floor. She expected him to jump up, but instead he remained on his knees, gently pushing aside the
whispering skirts. She caught her breath as his hands
caressed the soft skin of her inner thigh. Where his
fingers explored his mouth followed. He slid his hands
under her bottom and pulled her towards him, holding
her firm while he kissed her even more intimately, his
mouth and tongue caressing her until she was crying
out at the sheer, swooning pleasure of his touch. Time
stopped. The rocking of the carriage merely enhanced
the intolerable delight he was inflicting upon her, carrying her out of her body into the soaring, weightless
heights of ecstasy.

When at last he ceased the relentless pleasuring she
reached out for him, driving her fingers through his
hair, tugging at the shoulders of his coat and pulling
him up so she could kiss him. Excitement welled even

further when she tasted herself on his lips. With a groan he held himself away from her and slid on to the bench.

'By God I cannot hold out much longer.' He quickly unfastened his breeches, pulling her on to his lap. 'Time for you to come to me.'

Eagerly she straddled him. He held her hips firmly and pushed himself into her slick heat. Dominique gasped, putting her hands on his shoulders to steady herself as he thrust again, and this time she was prepared. She pressed down on him, matching his movements, elated by his groans of pleasure as she rode him, exulting in the feel of his hard length inside her. She was almost out of control with the delicious torment, bucking and shuddering, but he held on to her, driving ever deeper into her until the final juddering thrust. She barely heard his shout of triumph for her own head was thrown back, her eyes closed as she tensed and shuddered and her consciousness exploded into a million stars.

Dominique collapsed against him and he held her close, his breathing ragged. Her whole body was glowing, like the hot coals of a fire after the first, hectic blaze has died down.

'Oh, heavens,' she murmured at last, her head on his chest where she could feel the hammering of his heart against her cheek. 'Have I behaved very wantonly? I do beg your pardon.'

His arms tightened.

'You have been quite delightful this evening, if a little surprising.'

Being in his arms was blissful, but she needed to explain so she pushed herself away into the corner.

'I w-wanted you to notice me. I have tried so hard to

be a good wife to you, but you never come to my bed any more. And I—I *miss* you.'

Gideon sat up and straightened his clothes.

'I have kept my distance because I do not want to harm you, Dominique,' he said quietly. 'I cannot forget what my mother went through.'

'Your mama had too many children too quickly.' She clasped her hands together. She had overcome her embarrassment to talk to the kindly doctor about it, now she must talk to her husband. 'I am very healthy, Gideon, Dr Bolton says so, and he also says we need not—need not refrain.' She added, her voice little more than a whisper, 'Unless you do not want me.'

With a shaky laugh he reached for her.

'After what we have just done you will know that is not the case.' He tilted up her chin and kissed her. 'I shall share your bed tonight, Dominique, and every night, if you will allow. And with a little care we can avoid making you with child again too often.' The coach slowed and turned. Gideon lifted his head. 'We are home, my dear.' He replaced her cloak on her shoulders and as the carriage came to a halt he jumped down on to the drive, turning back to hold out his hand to her. 'Shall we go in?'

'I am not sure I can walk,' she confessed as he helped her out of the carriage.

'Then I shall carry you, as I should have done when you first came here.' With that he swept her up into his arms, explaining to the astonished Thomas that Mrs Albury was feeling a little faint.

Dominique slipped her arms about his neck and buried her face in his shoulder as he carried her up the stairs, knowing that if the butler saw the glow on her cheeks it would give the lie to Gideon's words. Somehow he managed to open the door to her bedchamber and dismissed her startled maid.

'There. That will set the household ringing with conjecture! Now, can you stand? I want to look at you.'

He set her on her feet and pushed the cloak from her shoulders before running his hands down her arms and catching her hands. In the glow of candlelight the ruby gown was almost as dark as her glorious hair. A few glossy curls had escaped and now lay in wayward abandon against the creamy skin of her breasts. They were rising and falling rapidly and the fire in his loins began to burn again. He wanted to tell her how beautiful she was, how much he loved her, but when he looked into her eyes and saw the heat of desire in their emerald depths he lost the ability to speak. Silently he pulled her into his arms and kissed her.

Slowly he unlaced her bodice and with a soft sigh the ruby satin fell in a dark pool at her feet. She stood before him in her shift, a gossamer-thin layer that hid nothing, only enhanced the lines of her body and the beautifully rounded breasts, their pink roseate tips delectably visible. He reached out to take the pins from her hair, while she began to undress him.

They did not pause until every last stitch had been shed. They were standing before the fire and he held her away from him, drinking in the perfection of her body, golden in the firelight. She dropped her head, allowing the dark waterfall of her hair to shimmer over her body. Gently he pushed the dusky locks back over her shoulders, then put his fingers under her chin and tilted her face up to look at him.

'My wife,' he murmured and, unable to resist any longer, he swept her up and carried her to the bed.

* * *

When Dominique awoke she was alone. Sunlight filled the room and she stretched luxuriously, feeling the cool sheets against her skin. She had a new awareness of her body and she smiled, thinking it unsurprising, since Gideon had kissed every last inch of it at least twice during the night. When he had first taken her to the bed they had made love slowly and languorously, taking time to explore each other until desire swept them up and carried them to the final consummation. She had fallen asleep in his arms, only to wake at some point in the darkest hours to find they were making love again.

Dominique shivered a little at the delicious memory. She was thinking that she should get up and find her nightgown when the door opened and Gideon came in. He was fully dressed and, feeling suddenly shy, she pulled the blankets up to her chin.

'Good morning, wife!' He sat on the bed, smiling as he wrested the offending bedclothes from her hands to reveal her breasts. He lowered his head and kissed one rosy nub and then the other, sending little shock waves of excitement trembling through her. Reluctantly she pushed him away.

'What is this, tired of me already?' The warm glint in his eyes robbed his words of offence and she smiled back.

'Never,' she said, shyly reaching up to touch his face. 'It is just that your sister is coming to take me shopping this morning.'

'Ah, she will want to know what happened after we quit Grosvenor Square.' He laughed, catching her hand and pressing a kiss into the palm before sliding off the bed. 'Very well, I shall leave you to dress. What time is she coming? Will you break your fast with me before you go?'

'She promised to be here by ten o'clock so, yes, we can eat together first, if I hurry.'

'No need,' he said, walking to the door. 'Gwen was never one for timekeeping. Don't expect to see her until at least eleven!'

But in this instance Gideon was proved wrong, for the clock in the hall was chiming ten when Gwen swept into the breakfast room, the skirts of her bronze-velvet walking dress billowing around her and the ostrich plumes on her matching hat bouncing quite violently.

'No, don't get up, my dear, finish your coffee.' She put a hand briefly on Dominique's shoulder, then walked around the table to kiss Gideon, who had risen to meet her. 'Dear brother!' She shifted her searching gaze to Dominique. 'Well, what am I to make of your leaving my party so early last night?'

'My wife was fatigued,' offered Gideon, his mouth lifting with the beginnings of a smile.

'Indeed?' Gwen's eyes narrowed as she looked from one to the other, then she gave a little trill of laughter. 'Heavens, but you both look very guilty! You have no need, my dears, I do not need to quiz you, since there is such an air of happiness about you both.'

'So you are off to town this morning.' said Gideon, changing the subject. 'Where do you shop?'

'Bond Street, of course.'

'If you have time, perhaps you would call into Irwin's, on Oxford Street,' he suggested. 'He was fixing a new band on my best beaver hat and it should be ready.'

Gwen pulled a face, but Dominique said immediately, 'Of course we can call there, Gideon. It is not too far out of our way, is it, Gwen?'

Lady Ribblestone gave an elegant shrug.

'No-o, we can as well look in the shops there as anywhere else, I suppose. And afterwards I shall take Dominique to Grosvenor Square for a little refreshment before I send her back to you in time for dinner.'

'Excellent.' Dominique pushed back her chair. 'I will fetch my pelisse.'

As Dominique walked past her husband he caught her wrist. 'I have no objection to you spending whatever you need, my dear, as long as it includes at least one shift as outrageous as the one you wore last night.'

Gwen laughed, but Dominique's cheeks flamed and she almost ran out of the room, dragging Gwen with her.

Gideon drove the five miles or so into town at a steady pace, his mind as much on the events of the night as the forthcoming assignation. Dominique had surprised him yesterday. He stifled a laugh. She had said she deliberately set out to lure him and, by God, she had succeeded. From the moment he had seen her in that red gown, looking so delectable, he had been unable to think of anything else. He had even forgotten to warn his sister to cease her flirtatious behaviour or risk Anthony's wrath. Perhaps there would be time to speak to her when she brought Dominique back from her shopping trip. Dominique. He could even call her by her rightful name now. How wrong he had been to treat her like some fragile creature who would break at the slightest chill wind, when in fact she was flesh and blood, as passionate as he. All those months of restraint, of keeping his distance, of believing she was responding to him only out of duty.

He had thought that the passion they had shared on their wedding night had been a mistake, a heady mix of anger and nerves and wine. Since then he had done his duty, keeping his desires and his feelings buried deep, but it was a long time since he had thought of his wife as a burden, an inconvenience—his wife by mistake. When he had awoken this morning and found her asleep in his arms he had been overwhelmed by some deep, primitive emotion that he now recognised as a profound and all-consuming love. It had cost him something to leave her sleeping, when he had wanted to wake her and tell her of his revelation, but there would be time for that later. First he needed to meet Agnes, to look at those papers and see if they really did mean that Dominique and her mother were not penniless. He did not care a jot that his wife had no dowry, but he knew it mattered a great deal to Dominique and he valued her happiness and comfort far above his own.

He took out his watch: eleven-thirty. He was in good time. He skirted Hyde Park and entered Piccadilly from the west, knowing that Gwen and Dominique were un-likely to come so far out of their way, especially now they were collecting his hat for him from Oxford Street. As on the previous day he left Sam with the curricle and went off alone into Green Park. Several couples were strolling there, but the area of trees where he was to meet Agnes was deserted. He was beginning to wonder if something had occurred to prevent her coming when he saw her hurrying towards him, her grey cloak pulled close, despite the warmth of the late May sunshine.

'I beg your pardon, I was delayed.' She pulled a packet of papers from under her cloak. 'They are all there, including the letter from Coutts' Bank. I hope

you can use them to serve the earl a bad turn. Give 'im
a bloody nose from me, Gideon.'

'I shall do my best.' Gideon glanced at the papers.
He would need to study them, but not here. 'Thank you,
for these. What do you do now?'

'I ain't going back to the earl, that's for sure.' She
folded her arms across her chest. 'That's why I was delayed. I sent my things off this morning and I mean to
follow them.'

'Where do you go?'

She shook her head. 'Best you don't know, my dear.
All I will say is that I am to catch the Holyhead mail.'

Gideon frowned. 'That sets off from the Bull and
Mouth, doesn't it?'

'Aye, t'other end of Piccadilly. I left the earl's carriage waiting for me on the south side of the park. By
the time they realises I ain't coming back I shall be
long gone.'

'It is still dangerous,' said Gideon. 'If the earl dis-
covers what you are about, he is bound to search the
coaching inns.' He thought quickly. 'The next stop will
be where, Islington?'

'Aye, the Peacock.'

'Then I'll drive you there. You will be safer out of
town.'

'That's very kind of you.' She shot a glance up at
him. 'Is it for old times' sake?'

He laughed.

'No, but when you tricked me into marriage it was
the best thing that ever happened to me, so you deserve
something for that! Come along. Let us get you away
from here.'

Chapter Seventeen

Dominique spent the carriage ride into town warding off her sister-in-law's questions.

'This is most ungenerous of you,' protested Gwen, laughing. 'You arrive at my party last night, looking so ravishing that no man has eyes for anyone else, then you steal away with Gideon before the tea tray is brought in! What am I to think?'

'Whatever you wish,' replied Dominique twinkling. Then, relenting, she laughed and blushed. 'Oh, Gwen, it was *wonderful*. I really think he cares for me.'

'Did he say so?'

'Not in so many words, but I hope that will follow.'

'Yes, I hope so, too,' replied Gwen sincerely. 'He was certainly very loving towards you this morning.'

Dominique hesitated. 'Perhaps you should try the same thing with your husband.'

'I gave up trying to woo Anthony years ago. He is more interested in his politics than his wife. I have positively flaunted my flirts before him and he does not notice.' Gwen's mouth drooped and for a moment she looked very despondent, then she gave herself a little shake, and her generous smile reappeared. 'But this is

dismal talk when we have shopping to do. Madame Si-
enna's first, I think, and then perhaps we should visit
Bertram's warehouse and find something to make you
another dashy dress!'

Dominique had been quite happy to go along with
Gwen's plans, her head still full of Gideon and the night
they had shared, but she was forced to put aside her
beatific daydreams when they emerged from the mo-
diste's shop.

'Oh, dear,' exclaimed Gwen, 'it is your cousin. Look,
he has just emerged from Clifford Street. And he is
coming this way.'

There was no avoiding him and, judging by the way
his face lit up when he recognised her, Dominique knew
he was going to stop and talk to her.

'There is no avoiding him now, I suppose,' muttered
Gwen, linking her arm though Dominique's for support.
When he raised his hat she said coolly, 'Lord Martle-
sham.'

'Lady Ribblestone, and my dear cousin.'

His oily greeting immediately put Dominique on the
alert. She nodded silently, hoping he would stand aside
to let them pass, but, no. He merely looked pained.

'So haughty, Dominique, after all I have done to pro-
mote your happiness.'

'To destroy it would be more accurate.'

'No, no, Cousin, your welfare has always been my
first consideration. Does your husband know you are
in town?'

Dominique raised her brows, saying coldly, 'Of
course.'

'Perhaps he has arranged to meet you later.'

'No, he is at Chalcots.'

His smile grew.

'I think not.'

'You must allow Mrs Albury to know best, my lord,' put in Gwen. 'We left my brother taking breakfast.'

Max regarded them with such a knowing smile that Dominique longed to box his ears.

'I hate to disagree with you, ladies, but I think you will find—ah, no.' He stopped and sighed. 'If that is what you believe, then so be it.'

A cold hand clutched at Dominique's heart, but she replied stoutly, 'You can tell me nothing that will shake my faith in Gideon. I trust him implicitly.'

'You trust him implicitly,' he repeated slowly. 'What a good little wife you are to him, my dear. And how I pity you.'

'I do not need your pity. Now, if you will excuse us—'

'And if I should tell you that he is seeing Mrs Bennet?'

'Absurd!' exclaimed Gwen hotly.

Dominique clutched her arm, her legs suddenly very weak.

'You lie.' She glared up at Max.

The triumphant gleam in his eyes only deepened.

'He is meeting her in Green Park at noon.' He lifted his head as a distant church bell chimed the hour. 'Which is now. Why not come with me and we shall see who is right?'

Gwendoline said coldly, 'We do not need to go to the Green Park, my lord. My brother's integrity is beyond question.'

Dominique wanted to agree. She wanted to turn away from Max's tormenting, smiling face, but she could not.

'We will go with you,' she stated, her back very straight. 'But only to prove you wrong.'

Ignoring the earl's outstretched arm, she turned and marched along Bond Street until they reached Piccadilly.

'My dear, this is madness,' Gwen muttered, hurrying beside her. 'Let me take you home instead. I am sure…'

Her words trailed away as Dominique stopped, recognising the elegant curricle and pair trotting towards them at a smart pace.

'So Albury's integrity is beyond question, is it?' The earl's sneering voice only added to Dominique's misery.

She watched the curricle fly past, Gideon intent on negotiating the heavy traffic. At his side was a cloaked figure, the breeze making the voluminous hood billow out to display the unmistakable face of Agnes Bennet. Like a devil at her shoulder, she heard Max chuckle.

'Well, well. This has worked out even better than I expected. Cousin, I am so sorry for you.'

'But where are they going?' asked Gwen. 'Where can he be taking her, and in broad daylight?'

'I have no idea,' drawled Max. 'But it makes no odds to me. She has served her purpose well enough.'

'She has—' Gwen broke off, her indignation too great for her to speak for several moments. At last she said, in arctic tones, 'Pray excuse us, Lord Martlesham. I must take my sister-in-law away from here.'

'Of course, ma'am. If there is anything I can do…'

'You have done quite enough!'

Dominique was rooted to the ground, staring after the curricle. Gwen put her arm about her shoulders.

'Come, love, let me take you back to the carriage.'

Dominique tried to focus. Everything seemed very distant. She saw Max walking away, swinging his cane as if he had not a care in the world. And everyone else, too, was carrying on quite as normal.

'I shall take you back to Grosvenor Square,' said Gwen.

Dominique shook her head.

'No,' she managed, her throat so constricted that it was difficult to speak. 'No, I want to go to Chalcots, if you please.'

'Very well, love, if that is what you want.'

'Yes, yes, it is.' She struggled into the waiting carriage and collapsed into the corner, her world in ruins.

Gideon left Agnes at the Peacock Inn and made his way back to the city to the offices of Rogers & Mitchell. However, when he learned that Mr Rogers was gone out of town he drove to the newly refurbished offices of Coutts & Co in the Strand.

An hour later he was on his way home, well satisfied with the day's work and eager to share his news with Dominique. After last night he half expected her to be looking out for him and to come running out into his arms, but when he pulled up at the main door of Chalcots there was no sign of life. No matter, he would probably find her in the nursery. How her face would light up when he told her that she was heiress to a considerable fortune.

Thomas opened the door and Gideon greeted him with a grin.

'By Gad, you look as if you had lost sixpence and found a groat, Thomas. What is it, has Cook given notice?'

'No, sir.'

'Where is Mrs Albury?'

'She—she's gone, sir.'

'Gone? You mean she has not returned from town yet?'

'N-no, sir. I mean she has gone. Left.' Gideon paused in the act of stripping off his gloves and under his frowning gaze the butler stumbled on. 'Mrs Albury *did* come back, sir, with Lady Ribblestone, but she immediately left again, with her maid, and Nurse and Master James.'

'What!'

Gideon dashed up the stairs. Dominique's bedchamber was the first door he came to and he entered without knocking. The room was in a state of disarray, drawers and cupboards open and clothes scattered, as if someone had left in a hurry. He went quickly to the nursery, which was in very much the same state. He was still trying to take it all in when there was a discreet cough behind him and he turned to find his valet standing in the doorway.

'What has gone on here, Runcorn?'

'As to that I couldn't say, sir. Mrs Albury came in with Lady Ribblestone soon after one o'clock and set the household by the ears.'

'I can see that,' muttered Gideon, grimly surveying the empty nursery.

'From the little that I overheard,' continued the valet in a toneless voice, 'I believe they had met Lord Martlesham in Piccadilly...'

'The devil they did!' Suddenly it all made sense. Gideon swung round. 'Any idea where they were going?'

'I am afraid not, sir, but if it is any consolation, they all went off in Lady Ribblestone's carriage.'

Cursing his stupidity, Gideon went back down the stairs, barking orders as he went.

Lord Ribblestone looked up from the letter in his hand when Gideon was shown into his study.

'Is my wife here?'

Gideon wasted no time on pleasantries, but that did not seem to surprise his host.

'No, and neither is mine.' Anthony held out the paper. 'I have only just come in myself and this was waiting for me. It is very garbled, but it appears Gwen has taken Dominique to Rotham.'

'Thank God.'

Gideon sat down abruptly. Anthony walked over to a side table and filled two glasses from the decanter. He handed one to Gideon.

'Trouble?'

'Oh, yes.' Gideon passed his hand across his eyes and quickly explained the events of the past few hours.

'I hate to say I told you so,' murmured Anthony, when he had finished. 'But if you had told Dominique what you were about…'

'I know, but it is too late for that now.'

'Well, I suppose we must go after them.'

'We?'

Anthony's eyes narrowed.

'My wife has gone, too, you know.'

'Very well, but there is some business that needs attention first.'

'Where are we going?' asked Anthony, following him out of the room.

'To White's. I have a score to settle with Martlesham and I will need a second!'

* * *

Despite the early hour the club was busy and they found the earl at one of the card tables. He was surrounded by his cronies, including Carstairs and the foppish Williams. The earl was counting his winnings, but he glanced up as Gideon entered.

'Albury,' he called across the room. 'Have you come to escape your wife's wrath?'

'Not at all,' replied Gideon, stripping off his gloves.

Max cast a smirking glance at his cronies.

'Quite a shock for her, to see you driving through Piccadilly with the delectable Mrs Bennet at your side. After all, 'twas only a year ago you were intent upon making her your bride, eh?' A few stifled laughs were heard, but Gideon said nothing as he walked towards his quarry. Max was still chuckling as he rose from the table and stood before Gideon, his lip curled in a sneer. 'No doubt you have installed the whore in a little love nest of your own.'

'Don't judge everyone by your own standards, Max. Mrs Bennet is now safely out of *your* way, but she did send something for you.'

Without warning Gideon's fist came up and crashed into Max's face, sending him sprawling to the ground.

Uproar ensued. Everyone crowded around and there were some mutters of 'bad form!' but a gesture from Lord Ribblestone prevented anyone laying hands upon Gideon.

'By God, you will meet me for that!' Max scrambled to his feet, his face suffused with rage and one hand pressed to his bleeding nose.

'With pleasure,' retorted Gideon coldly. 'You planned to dupe my wife out of her rightful inheritance and *I* demand satisfaction for *that*. Hampstead Heath. Nine o'clock tonight.'

'Tonight!' The buck-toothed Williams raised his quizzing glass to stare at Gideon. 'Nay, sir, make it tomorrow, at dawn.'

'I have business that cannot wait,' said Gideon shortly. He fixed his eyes on Max. 'Nine o'clock, Martlesham. Be there, or be branded a rogue *and* a coward!'

The sun had set on a cloudless May day when Gideon drove on to Hampstead Heath. He stopped his curricle behind a closed carriage, from which a sober-looking gentleman in a bagwig was emerging, carrying a leather bag.

'So we have a surgeon on hand, in any event,' he remarked cheerfully.

'Are you sure this is wise?' murmured Ribblestone.

'No, but it is necessary. I should have done it a year ago, rather than forcing Dominique to go on with a marriage that was none of her choosing.' He looked up as he heard another carriage approaching. 'Here's Martlesham now, with Carstairs as his second. Let us finish this.'

Gideon talked to the doctor while Ribblestone conferred with Mr Carstairs. They inspected the duelling pistols—a pair provided by Anthony that Gideon had practised with on several occasions—then the combatants took their places. The light was fading fast and a cold wind had blown up. The white handkerchief fluttered and fell. Gideon's arm jerked up and he fired, seeing a simultaneous flash from the other gun. Martlesham collapsed with a yell and Gideon stood for a moment while his brain ascertained that he had taken no hurt himself. Tossing the pistol back to Ribblestone, he strode off towards the curricle.

'Very neatly expedited,' said Anthony, stowing the box containing the pistols beneath the seat and scrambling up. 'And he is not dead, so you needn't flee the country.'

Gideon set the team in motion, glancing back just once as they drove away. Max was being helped into his carriage by Carstairs and the doctor.

'I never intended to kill him. The bullet in his shoulder is nothing to the pain he will suffer tomorrow when the bank informs him that he no longer has any hope of touching Rainault's fortune. Dominique and her mother will soon have control of that.'

'And if he had hit you?'

Gideon gave a grim smile.

'Max has been drinking all day and in this light he had little chance of hitting a house, let alone a man.'

'What now?' asked Ribblestone as they hurtled through the gathering gloom.

'Back to Chalcots for a change of horses and supper, then off to Rotham.'

Anthony sat up. 'Tonight? But it's fifty miles!'

'What of it? The moon will be up and I know the road.'

'So you plan to arrive at the crack of dawn, unwashed and unshaven. That is sure to endear you to your wife.'

The jibe hit home.

'Very well, we will stop on the road for breakfast and a change of neckcloth. Will that suit you? Damn it all, man, do not expect me to wait until the morning to set out, for there is no possibility of my sleeping tonight.'

He glanced at Anthony. 'I want to see Dominique as soon as may be and put things right. What about you?'

What I want,' said Anthony, with unwonted savagery, 'is to wring Gwen's damned neck!'

The Ribblestone carriage arrived at Rotham shortly before ten o'clock, by the light of the rising moon. It had taken some time to pack up everything Dominique thought it necessary to take with them into Buckinghamshire and they had also broken their journey in order for little James to be fed in comfort, rather than in the jolting carriage. The viscount's household was thrown into a panic by the sudden arrival of the two ladies, together with the baby, his nurse and Mrs Albury's maid, but Lord Rotham took one look at Dominque's stricken countenance and immediately gave orders for rooms to be prepared with all haste. Then he carried Dominique and Gwendoline off to the drawing room, where the whole story came pouring out.

'I cannot believe this of Gideon.' Lord Rotham looked a question at Gwen, who shrugged, but it was Dominique who answered him.

'He t-told me, *assured* me, he had no intention of seeing her, after we met by chance at the theatre.' She pulled her damp handkerchief between her fingers. 'And then to discover him driving through town with her—'

The viscount shook his head.

'My son has many faults,' he said heavily, 'but I had not thought this of him.'

'I wanted to wait and see what Gideon had to say for himself,' put in Gwendoline, 'but Dominique was desperate to get away.'

'I c-could not stay in that house,' cried Dominique, jumping up. 'Not there, where we—where we...'

Her voice was suspended. She hid her face in her hands, feeling the hot tears leaking between her fingers. Gwen put an arm around her and gently eased her back on to the sofa.

'Hush now, love. You are overwrought, and tired, too, I shouldn't wonder.'

'Yes, of course. So foolish of me.' Dominique wiped her eyes. 'I beg your pardon. And yours, too, my lord, for descending upon you in this way, b-but I could not think where else to go.'

His smile was kindness itself.

'Where else should you go? You are my son's wife, the mother of his child. My grandson. You may remain here for as long as you wish.'

'And—and Gideon?'

'He will no doubt arrive here shortly, and when he does he may give his version of events. We may yet find there is a reasonable explanation.' Dominique shook her head and he continued, 'Well, let us wait and see what the morning brings. For now I suggest you should take a little supper and go to bed. I have also given orders for your old room to be prepared for you, Gwendoline. It is too late for you to be going to Fairlawns.'

'Thank you, Papa, but I do not want to burden you. Mrs Ellis mentioned another visitor—'

'Yes, Mr Rogers arrived earlier, but that need not concern you tonight.'

Gently but firmly he shepherded them into the care of the kindly housekeeper, who took them off to the oak parlour and plied them with hot soup and bread and butter. Dominique managed to force down a few mouthfuls before retiring to her room. Unhappiness wrapped itself around her like a cloak, but she was so bone-weary that thankfully, almost as soon as she slid between the warmed sheets, she was asleep.

Dominique awoke early the following morning, but was in no mood for company, so she spent an hour with little James before making her way downstairs to the breakfast room. Gwendoline and the viscount were already seated there, together with a gentleman in a brown wig and plain brown coat.

'Mr Rogers.' She greeted him as cheerfully as she could. 'I am very glad to see you, sir.'

'And I you, Mrs Albury,' he returned. 'Especially so, since my business with the viscount concerns you.'

Her worries were momentarily forgotten. 'You have news of my father?'

'Pray do not raise your hopes too high,' Lord Rotham warned her. 'We should discuss this in my study after breakfast.'

'Oh, please tell me now,' she begged him. 'I cannot bear for you to keep me in suspense—and I am sure there can be nothing that Gwendoline should not hear.' She laid a hand on her father-in-law's arm, saying again, 'Pray, my lord, tell me now. Any news will be welcome after all these years.'

'First let me pour you a little coffee,' said Gwen, suiting the action to the words. 'And take some bread and butter, Dominique. You may eat it while Mr Rogers talks.'

The lawyer dabbed at his dry lips with the napkin.

'Well, if Lord Rotham has no objection…?' The viscount signalled to him to continue and the lawyer twisted slightly in his chair to address Dominique. 'I have information about your father, madam, and because it is of such importance I thought it best to come in person to discuss it with Lord Rotham.'

'Monsieur Rainault is alive!' cried Gwen, clapping her hands.

'Exactly, Lady Ribblestone. That is, he was still alive at the time of the last communication,' amended Mr Rogers with typical lawyer's caution. He turned again to Dominique. 'As you know, Lord Rotham took an interest in this affair last year and he put me in touch with certain parties in France, relatives of his late brother-in-law, the Duc du Chailly. We have had to proceed very carefully. France is full of spies ready to expose anyone they think wishes to overturn the new order. However, with patience and perseverance we located your father. He was being held in a remote prison under a false name. We can only surmise that he assumed this identity in an effort to flee the country.'

'That explains why *Maman's* efforts to trace him failed,' said Dominique, adding darkly, 'Those that were not thwarted by my cousin.'

'Quite.' Mr Rogers nodded. 'My last communication from France arrived early Monday morning and I set off directly for Rotham. Our "friends" in France secured your father's release, madam, but even then it was not safe to make this information public. Your father's moderate views were well known and would not be popular with the present government. I was reluctant to apply for papers to bring your father from France as it would alert the authorities.'

'Yes, yes, I quite see that,' said Dominique eagerly. 'So what can we do?'

'We will smuggle him into England,' the viscount told her. 'I shall send a man to France to fetch him home to you.' He smiled. 'How we are to achieve that is best kept a secret. Mr Rogers and I will go away now to thrash out the details and leave you and Gwendoline to finish your breakfast.'

'Well,' declared Gwen, when the men had departed, 'that at least is good news for you, my dear.'

'I can hardly believe it, after all this time.' Dominique shook her head. 'I shall take little James into the village later to tell *Maman*. It will deflect her attention from my own situation.'

'Ah, yes.' Gwen paused, crumbling a piece of bread between her fingers while she chose her words. 'Perhaps Papa is right and Gideon has a good reason for what happened yesterday.'

Dominique put up her hands.

'Do you not think I have gone over and over it in my mind? He told me I had nothing to fear from Agnes Bennet. And then, at breakfast yesterday, do you remember how he asked where we would be shopping and could we call into Irwin's? Why did he not call in himself, if he was going into town? No, it was all a ploy to keep us from Piccadilly.'

'It is all the fault of your horrid cousin,' exclaimed Gwen, getting up from the table.

'Perhaps, but he could not *force* Gideon to meet with her, could he? And he certainly had no hand in Gideon's taking her up in his curricle.' Dominique drew a long, angry breath. 'I thought I could make him l-love me, but no. He might take his p-pleasure with me occasionally, but it is Agnes who owns his heart, and he can never forget that I am the p-penniless daughter of a F-Frenchman. And even if he could,' she said, angry colour returning to her cheeks, '*I* cannot forgive *him* for deceiving me!'

'So what will you say to him, when he comes?'

Dominique's spurt of temper died away.

'I really do not know,' she said despondently.

'Well, you had best think of something now,' said Gwen, looking out of the window. 'Gideon's curricle is at the door. And—oh, heavens, he has Anthony with him!'

Dominique had jumped up as soon as Gwen spoke and now she stood beside her sister-in-law, staring out through the leaded glass. Her throat dried. She had run away from Gideon, taken his child. How angry he would be about that. Her Gallic blood surged furiously through her veins. If anyone had a right to be angry it was she—after all, he had deceived her, lied to her, and that was unforgivable.

There was the low rumble of voices in the hall. She reached for Gwen's hand and together they turned to face the door.

Chapter Eighteen

Dominique flinched as Gideon strode in, Anthony close on his heels. Both men looked tired and grim, but fury blazed in their eyes. Gideon broke the silence.

'Well, ladies. This is a merry dance you have led us.' His voice was hard, his anger barely contained.

Dominique drew herself up.

'Hardly merry, sir. I did not come here out of choice, I assure you.' She stepped back, as if to hide behind Gwen, when Gideon made to approach. 'Lord Rotham says I need not speak to you unless I wish to do so.'

'By God, madam, you are my wife and you will—'

'Yes, I am your wife, sir,' she flashed, 'and you would do well to remember it!'

Turning on her heel, she dashed from the room.

'Dominique, stop.' Gideon ran after her. 'For heaven's sake, woman, hear me out—!'

As his voice died away Anthony shut the door and stood with his back pressed against it.

'So, you are teaching little Dominique your flighty ways.'

'I have taught her nothing, my lord.' Gwen watched him warily. There was something different about An-

thony. A tension, like a predator, ready to spring. The
anger still glowed in his eyes, but she noted also the
dark shadows beneath. She said suddenly, 'Have you
travelled all night?'

'How else do you think we managed to get here so
quickly? And a curricle is *not* built for sleeping, I can
assure you.'

'I suppose you expect me to come back to London
with you.'

'Not immediately. You have not forgotten our last
conversation, I hope?'

'Of course not, and I really did mean to support you.
I appreciate how hard you have been working these
past few weeks, what with the peace breaking down,
and Bonaparte doing all he can to buy more time with
his tricks and stratagems—but you must see that this
was an emergency.'

'I see nothing of the sort. I told you I would stand
for no more of your games, madam.'

'Flirtations, you called them,' she responded, trying
to conceal her unease. 'This was not like that, I was
helping my sister-in-law—'

'Yes, helping her to run away from her husband.
It would have been better for everyone if you had encouraged her to have this out with Gideon at Chalcots.'

'La, I vow you are grown very censorious, my lord.'
She tossed her head. 'I shall not stay—'

'You *will* stay, madam, until I have finished with
you.'

She stepped back, eyes widening with apprehension.
'What are you going to do?'

'Something I should have done a long time ago.'

He turned the key in the lock and advanced towards her.

* * *

Dominique's headlong flight from the breakfast room caused the servants to jump aside to avoid a collision and she had reached the stairs before Gideon caught up with her.

'Dominique, listen to me!'

He grabbed her arm, but the fury blazing in her eyes when she turned to him made him release her again.

'Why should I listen to you, when all you tell me are lies?'

'No, believe me—'

'You told me you would not see Agnes Bennet and within *days* you were meeting her secretly. I *saw* you, Gideon, in Piccadilly.'

'Yes, but that was because she had news, about Max.' She waved her hand, dismissing him, and sped up the stairs so that he was obliged to run after her. '*Will* you listen to me, you hellcat? I did this for you!'

She had reached the landing, but his words made her turn, her lip curling in disbelief.

'Oh, yes, that is very likely! You met with the woman you love, the woman you wanted to wed, for *my* benefit!' She dashed her hand across her eyes. 'You should never have continued with the marriage, Gideon.'

'I had to, after what happened on our wedding night.'

Even as the words left his mouth Gideon realised his mistake. He saw the misery flash across her face and reached out for her.

'Dominique, I did not mean—'

She pushed him away.

'Oh, I know very well what you *mean*. You cannot forget that I am half French, can you? You abhor that part of me, even though you might desire my body. But that is how men are, is it not? They c-cannot resist the temptations of the flesh. Our marriage has never been anything more for you than a shackle, a yoke that you do not want.'

'No!'

'You were too honourable to put me away quietly.' She continued as if he had not spoken. 'But how I wish you *had* done so, for it would have been better than *this*!' She took a deep, steadying breath before saying icily, 'You need have no fear, sir. I know what is expected of me. You will want more children, of course, but pray give me a little time to become a-accustomed to your, your *diversions* before you demand that I resume my role as your wife.' She shuddered. 'And do not expect me to take any joy in it. You have killed that. I cannot love a man who thinks so little of me.'

Stunned, he remained rooted to the spot while she whisked herself away and into her room. He heard the key grate in the lock, and the heart-rending sound of her muffled sobs from the other side of the door.

Her last words lodged in his heart like a knife. He raised his arm to knock on the door, but realised the futility of it. Slowly he made his way back to the empty drawing room, where he sank down in a chair and stared blankly before him.

How long he remained there he had no idea, an hour, maybe two. He heard the door open and looked around as Gwendoline and Anthony entered, hand in hand. He scowled at his sister, who looked unaccountably cheerful. Gideon realised Anthony was regarding him and he raised his head, saying bitterly, 'You were right, Anthony. I should have told her I was meeting Mrs Bennet.'

'You explained to her the circumstances?' said Anthony, holding up a hand to silence Gwen's questions.

'I tried, but she will not listen. All she can see is that I broke my word. She thinks I see our marriage as a burden.'

'And is it?' asked Anthony quietly.

Gideon dropped his head in his hands

'At the beginning it was...difficult. But now—' He took a breath, facing the truth. 'Now, I cannot contemplate living without her.'

'Oh, Gideon—!'

Gwen's sympathetic utterance was cut short as the door opened again and the viscount came in. Lord Rotham nodded to his daughter and son-in-law and addressed Gideon.

'Ah, my boy. I was informed that you had arrived.'

'As you see, Father.' Gideon rose, nodding at the lawyer following his father into the room. 'Mr Rogers. I called at your offices yesterday, but you were already on your way here. Before you go back to town, I would be obliged if you would see Mrs Rainault and ask her to appoint you to act on her behalf, then you must call upon Coutts, the bankers in the Strand. They are holding a considerable sum of money for her, including a dowry for my wife.'

'A dowry!' declared Gwen. 'But why? How—?'

'Martlesham,' said Gideon shortly. 'Jerome Rainault sent letters to the old earl, instructing him to hold his fortune in trust for his family. Max was planning to keep it for himself.'

'Rogers will, of course, carry out your instructions, my son.' The viscount moved to his usual seat beside the fire. 'But first he has some news for *you.*'

* * *

So Jerome Rainault is alive,' said Gideon, when everything had been explained.

'We believe so,' said the lawyer. 'Lord Rotham hopes to get him to England very soon.'

'How?' asked Gideon, frowning. 'Bonaparte will not want to let him go.'

Lord Rotham nodded.

'You are right, it must be done carefully. I am sending a courier tonight.'

'I will go.' Gideon's announcement was met with silence.

'Out of the question,' said the viscount at last. 'It is far too dangerous.'

'Rainault is my father-in-law. Who else should go?'

'Anyone,' cried Gwen, her face pale. 'How can you even think of it, knowing what happened to James—?'

'Precisely *because* of what happened to James,' replied Gideon. 'My brother was heir to Rotham. *I* should have been the one to go to Paris all those years ago.'

'No,' said Lord Rotham. 'I ordered you both to remain in England. James disobeyed me.' He sighed. 'He was as stubborn and hot-headed as the rest of the Alburys, in his own way.'

Gideon met his father's eyes steadily. 'I have to do this, sir, if only to show my wife that I do not have an implacable hatred for all Frenchmen.'

'No, you cannot go.' Gwen jumped up from her seat and ran to Gideon. 'Think, my dear. You are heir to Rotham now.'

His mouth twisted into a wry smile.

'And *my* heir is presently sleeping in his crib upstairs, so the succession is safe.'

Gwen gave a little huff of impatience and turned to her husband.

'Ribblestone, pray tell him he must not do it.'

'I will,' said Anthony. 'Not for the reasons you have given, but because from today the difficulties of getting anyone in or out of France are increased a hundredfold.' He surveyed the company for a moment. 'It can make no odds if I tell you now, for you will learn of it in tomorrow's newspapers. We have today declared war on France.'

After a moment's horrified silence, Gideon shook his head.

'It makes no odds. I am still going.'

The argument raged on, but at length Gideon convinced them all that he would not be moved and suggested to his father they should discuss how it was to be done. Mr Rogers rose.

'My work is finished here, my lord, so if you will excuse me I shall visit Mrs Rainault and advise her of the news.'

Ribblestone took out his watch, 'And we can do no more good here, so we will go to Fairlawns.'

With a bow he ushered his wife to the door.

'Ribblestone!' Gideon's peremptory call stopped Anthony at the door. He looked back, brows raised. 'So you and m'sister have made it up. How did you do it?'

Ribblestone regarded him for a moment, a faint smile touching his lips.

'Well, if you want the truth—and begging your pardon, Lord Rotham—I gave her a damn good spanking!'

With that, and another slight bow, he went out and shut the door.

* * *

By the time Gideon accompanied his father into dinner their plans had been made. Only two places were
set, Colne informing them that Mr Rogers had departed
to catch the night mail and Mrs Albury had requested
a tray to be sent up to her room. As soon as they were
alone, Gideon explained about his meetings with Agnes
Bennet.

'I should have told Dominique about it immediately,
Father. It was a serious misjudgement.'

'We are both guilty of that where your wife is concerned,' replied Lord Rotham, sadly. 'Your mother was
never strong and I should have taken better care of her,
but my mistake was to persuade you that *all* ladies were
so delicate. When you brought Dominique to Rotham,
she quite stole my heart and I became morbidly anxious
for her. If I have somehow caused this estrangement between you, then I am very sorry for it.'

Gideon listened in silence. It was the first time that
his father had ever unbent enough to make an apology
and he realised how much it had cost him. He looked
up and met the old man's eyes.

'You are not at fault, Father. I have been a fool, but I
shall do better in future, when I get back from France.'

If I get back.

The words hung between them, unspoken, but
Gideon knew that they both silently acknowledged the
risks.

They had not quite finished their port when Colne
announced another visitor.

'I have shown him into the study, my lord, as you
instructed.'

'My original courier,' explained the viscount as the

butler withdrew. 'He will accompany you as far as the coast, but after that you will travel alone until you meet up with your contact in Paris. How is your French?'

'A little rusty, but it will suffice. Come, let us get this over.'

An hour later Gideon went to his room to change for his journey. Once he was ready he walked to the connecting door that led to Dominique's bedchamber and after the briefest of knocks he walked in. She was standing before the fire, rocking the baby in her arms and crooning a lullaby.

Gideon glanced at the waiting servant. 'Please leave us.'

The nursemaid hesitated, glancing uncertainly at her mistress. Dominique handed her the baby.

'Take little James back to the nursery, if you please. I shall come to him later.'

Her tone was gentle, but as soon as they were alone she regarded Gideon with a stony glare, anger emanating from every rigid line of her body.

'What do you want?'

'To talk to you.'

'There is nothing to say.' She turned her back on him. 'Please leave me.'

'I *am* leaving. I am going away. Tonight.'

'Good.'

Her hands were clasped around the bedpost, as if to support herself. Gideon continued quietly, 'Agnes found proof that Max was holding your father's fortune. I wanted to make sure it was true, that I could secure the money for you and your mother before I told you. I was wrong to keep it from you. I beg your pardon for that.' There was no reaction, no movement at all from

the silent figure before him. 'I am going to France, to
find your father and bring him back. Perhaps that will
prove to you that I don't hate you, or your French blood.'
He stopped. He raised his eyes to the ceiling, exhaling
slowly. 'No, it is more than that. My anger has been
misdirected for years. I used it to disguise my hatred
of myself. You see, my French was always better than
my brother's. I might have survived.' He rubbed a hand
across his eyes. 'There is not a day goes by that I do
not wish I had disobeyed my father and gone to France
instead of James. I thought Father's keeping me here
was a punishment for allowing James to die—in fact,
it was because he was afraid of losing me, too. I understand that now, because I finally know what it is to
love someone so much that you cannot bear to contemplate life without them. Dominique, you say you cannot
love me. I understand that. I promise you I shall never
force my attentions upon you, if they are unwelcome.
But I hope, when I return, that we may be able to sal-
vage something from this mess.' He paused, his eyes
fixed on her rigid, unyielding back. 'Will you not wish
me God's speed?'

He waited, but when she made no move he turned
on his heel and left the room.

Dominique heard the door click shut behind him.
Her hands were clenched so tightly around the bedpost
that the carvings cut into her skin. She had wanted to
run to him, to cast herself on his chest and beg him to
be careful, but her anger held her silent and immobile.
She could hear his steps in the corridor, that firm, familiar stride, the *tap-tap* of his boots on the boards,
gradually dying away to silence. With a sob she threw
herself across the room and wrenched open the door.

'Gideon, wait!'

She flew along the passage and to the stairs. From the central stairwell she saw only the flapping edge of his greatcoat disappearing into the hall below. Desperately she sped down the remaining stairs. She could hear the rumble of voices and even as she reached the hall she heard the heavy thud of the door being closed.

'Colne, Colne, tell him to wait!' she called out as she ran. The butler opened the door again as she came up and she dashed past him and out on to the drive.

The moonlight showed her one figure already mounted, and Gideon with his foot in the stirrup. When he saw her he stepped away from the horse and without pausing she hurled herself at him.

'Oh, Gideon, I am so sorry, so sorry!' His arms closed around her and she cried into his shoulder. 'I was so j-jealous when I saw you with her and I quite lost my temper. Please don't go without saying you forgive me.'

He gave a shaky laugh.

'There is nothing to forgive, love.' He put his fingers under her chin and forced her to look up at him. With the moon overhead his face was in shadow, but she could discern the glint of his eyes and it tugged up that now familiar ache of desire deep in her belly. 'Wait for me.'

'Must you go?' she murmured between kisses.

'Yes. I have to do this. For you, for *Tante* and the *duc*. For James.'

'Not for my sake! Please, I could not bear to lose you now. And no one can blame you for obeying your father.'

'Only me. At the very least I should have gone with James—I can never forgive myself for letting him go to France alone.'

'Then your father might have lost both sons and I would never have known you.' She cupped his face between her hands and gazed up at him. 'I love you, Gideon. So very, very much. Promise me you will be careful.'

'Of course.' His grin flashed white in the moonlight. 'I have so much to live for.'

He gave her one last, lingering kiss before putting her from him and mounting up. As he and his companion cantered out of the gates, he raised his hand for a final salute.

Dominique stood on the drive and watched until the riders were out of sight, then she made her way slowly to the drawing room to join her father-in-law. When he saw her he went over to the sideboard and poured her a glass of Madeira.

'So you have made up your differences,' he said. 'I am glad.'

'It all seemed so petty, once he had told me where he is going.'

He held out the glass to her. 'Believe me, my dear, I would have stopped him if I could.'

'I know, my lord, but he is determined, even if it should prove dangerous.' Something in the old man's look alerted her and she sank down on a sofa, saying quickly, 'What is it, what should I know?'

'It *will* be dangerous, my dear. Extremely so, because we are now at war with France again.'

Chapter Nineteen

Days turned into weeks. Dominique busied herself around the house and looked after her baby. She scoured the newspapers every day, but the reports only made her more anxious. Bonaparte's fury at being forced into war before he was ready was manifesting itself in attacks and imprisonment of the English who had not managed to leave France in time. If that was the case for innocent travellers, how much worse would it be for Gideon, if he was caught?

Dominique took some comfort from the fact that Gwen and Anthony were now much closer—so much so that Ribbleston soon told Gwen of the duel Gideon had fought with Max and she promptly passed the news on. Dominique's worst fears—that Max should die and Gideon would then be wanted for murder—were soon eased when the social pages reported that the earl had retired to Martlesham Abbey amid rumours that he was seriously in debt. Dominique could only be thankful that she and her mother no longer lived under his aegis.

There was a small diversion at the end of May when she travelled to London with her mother to see Mr Rogers and go with him to Coutts' bank. The dowry her

father had set aside for her was signed over and the remainder of the Rainault fortune was secured for her
mother's use, but the knowledge that Gideon had made
this possible only added to Dominique's unhappiness.
She had not thanked him for his efforts and the fear
deep in her heart was that now she would never have
the chance to do so.

The atmosphere at Rotham became hushed, expect-
ant, as if the house itself was waiting for news. Mrs
Rainault spent so much time there with her daughter
that the viscount suggested she should come and stay
again until Gideon's return.

'And he will return,' he assured Dominique. 'The
family has many friends in France, believe me.'

But as the summer wore on even the viscount's confidence wavered.

'I am sure that if it was not for our being here, and
little James, Lord Rotham would return to his reclusive ways,' Dominique told her mother, when they were
strolling in the walled garden one afternoon. The July
sun was beating down, filling the still air with the scent
of roses.

'He has told me how much you have changed his
life,' said Mrs Rainault. 'Rotham had grown cold and
silent before you came, but he says you brought it back
to life—more than that, you restored his son to him.'

'And I am the reason he has gone away, perhaps
forever.'

'You must not talk like that.' Mrs Rainault gave her
arm a little shake. 'You must not give up hope, Dominique.'

'But it has been ten weeks. It feels like a lifetime.
You have been waiting for news of Papa for ten years—

how, *Maman*? How have you lived with the pain, the uncertainty?'

Mrs Rainault smiled. 'With love, my dear. And faith. I always believed Jerome would come back to me, one day.'

Dominique felt hot tears pricking at her eyes. If only she could be so certain, but she was afraid that she had not earned such happiness.

'Oh, *Maman*, we have been so foolish, Gideon and I! We wasted so much time. If only—' She broke off, her head going up as she heard the faint scrunch of gravel. 'Is that a carriage?' She shook her head. 'No, no, it is the wind rustling the leaves on the trees. I vow, *Maman*, I am becoming quite a nervous being, jumping at shadows...'

But her mother was not listening. She was looking past Dominique towards the house, such a look of wonder on her face that Dominique found her breathing interrupted by the rapid thudding of her heart. Fearing disappointment, she forced her unwilling body to turn. The long windows leading into the house were thrown open and a tall man stood there, his thin frame slightly stooped. His white hair was brushed back from a pale brow and a pair of familiar dark eyes looked out from his gaunt face.

'P-Papa?'

With a stifled cry her mother ran forwards.

'Jerome? Oh, my love, is it really you?'

The old man stepped out on to the terrace, holding out his arms.

'Mais oui, ma chère.'

Whatever else had changed, his voice had not. It was firm and warm and brought a host of memories flooding back. Her mother was already in his arms, weeping softly into his shoulder. Dominique followed more slowly, not sure of her welcome. Over her mother's head Jerome smiled. He freed one hand and reached out for her.

'Dominique. Daughter.'

She took his hand and for the first time in many months allowed the tears to spill over.

'Welcome home, Papa.' She moved closer, hugging both her parents before stepping away. However much she wanted to be part of it she realised this was their time, two lovers reunited. Lord Rotham was standing in the doorway, his head bowed. He had one hand over his face and his shoulders shaking. His image was blurred by her tears, but she was filled with dread. She had managed to keep her fears buried deep, except in the dark reaches of the night when the demons would taunt her with the thought that Gideon would never return. Now those fears leaped free and she found herself comparing her mother's newfound happiness with her own bleak future.

But it was not only her unhappiness. She wiped away her tears and went to the viscount, laying a hand on his arm.

'Oh, my lord—' There was a movement in the shadowy room behind him and her heart stopped. 'G-Gideon?'

'Yes,' said the viscount, his voice a little unsteady. 'He is here. He is safe.'

He stepped aside and with a sob she flew across the room to the figure standing in the shadows. Gideon caught her in a fierce hug that lifted her off her feet. He was dusty from the road and smelled of dirt and horses, but she did not care, for when he sought her mouth and kissed her she lost herself in the taste and scent of her own dear husband.

When at last he released her she clung to him, burying her face in his shoulder.

'Oh, Gideon, I was so frightened you would not come back!'

His arms tightened.

'How could I not, when I knew you were waiting for me?' He put his fingers beneath her chin and tilted her face up towards him again. 'I dreamed of this moment every night.' He kissed her again, gently this time, his lips a soft caress. 'I cannot tell you how much I have missed you.'

'Let us go and sit down, I want to know everything.'

'Later,' he said, laughing. 'I am far too dirty to sully my father's furniture. Let us join the others in the garden.' He looked up at the silent figure standing by the open windows. 'My lord, will you come, too?'

'Thank you, no. I shall find Colne and tell him to delay dinner by at least an hour.' He held out his hand. 'I am glad to have you back, my son.'

'Thank you, Father. I am pleased to be here.' He clasped the proffered hand for a long moment, holding his father's eyes until the viscount gave a little nod and walked away.

Gideon kept his arm about Dominique as he led her out into the garden. Jerome and Mrs Rainault were some distance away, strolling through the roses, arms linked and their heads close together.

'They have a great deal to catch up on,' murmured Dominique, following his glance.

'As have we.'

Dominique held him even tighter.

'We read such terrifying reports—was it very dangerous?'

'A little, of course, but we had many people to help us, including some of the Duc du Chailly's family and friends.' He was silent for a moment and Dominique waited patiently for him to speak again. 'There are many good people in France, Dominique. I was wrong to harbour such hatred for so many years.'

She waved one hand at him.

'That is all in the past, my love. And I haven't yet thanked you, for thwarting Max's plans to take my father's fortune for his own.' She flushed and added quietly, 'Perhaps I should thank Mrs Bennet, too.'

'Yes, only I doubt you could find her. But I owe her quite a debt, too.'

'Oh?' Dominique stiffened as jealousy pricked her.

Gideon's arm tightened and she glanced up. He was smiling, his eyes boring into her, as if he could read her very thoughts.

He said, 'If she had not agreed to Max's plan in the first place I would never have married you and would never have known how happy a man could be.'

'Oh,' she said again, her jealousy melting away to be replaced by a tingling excitement deep in her core.

He leaned closer.

'You must come upstairs with me now. I cannot wait until tonight to make love to you.'

She blushed.

'I would like that, but what about Maman and Papa?'

'They will not miss us, and if they do, they will understand.'

Gently but firmly he led her back into the house. It was all they could do not to run through the rooms and up the stairs to his bedchamber, but as soon as they were inside all restraint disappeared. They came together eagerly, exchanging hot kisses even as they undressed one another, tearing off the layers until they could lie upon the bed together, skin against skin.

Dominique revelled in the kisses Gideon showered upon her body and she returned them with equal fervour. She cupped his proud erection in her hands, worshipped it with her mouth even as he gently parted her thighs to bestow upon her that most intimate of kisses. The sensations he aroused with his tongue and his mouth soon had her falling back upon the bed, surrendering to the delicious torment. She moaned softly, shivering as wave after wave of excitement rippled through her. His tongue played her, circling and lapping at her core. Her body arched as she felt the climax approaching. She was almost out of control, aching with pleasure, wanting him to stop and at the same time wanting him to carry her onwards.

She reached for him, her fingers clutching at the solid muscle of his shoulders as he slid his body over hers, claiming her mouth for a deep, penetrating kiss even as he thrust into her. Her body tightened about him and she cried out with the sheer joy of it. He moved carefully, stroking her, taking her with him to that final shuddering, shattering climax, a blinding explosion of thought and feeling as the world splintered and disintegrated, leaving them shocked, sated and exhausted.

Gideon wrapped himself around her and pulled her close.

'My wife.' His breath was warm on her ear as he murmured the words. 'My own.'

She twisted in his arms so that she could hold him.

'And I am no longer penniless,' she told him, gently pressing kisses on his eyes, his cheeks and down the length of his lean jaw. 'I have a dowry now, thanks to you.'

'So you have. I had forgotten.'

She stopped kissing him and he opened his eyes to find her regarding him solemnly.

'Does it not matter to you? Do you not want to use it? We could improve Chalcots, perhaps buy another property—'

He put his hand on her lips.

'Let us settle it upon our children. I feel sure there are more on the way. Besides,' he added, drawing her back into his arms, 'with you for my wife I am rich beyond my wildest dreams.'

* * * * *

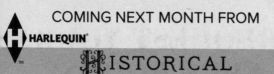

COMING NEXT MONTH FROM

HARLEQUIN®

HISTORICAL

Available February 18, 2014

THE COWBOY'S RELUCTANT BRIDE
by Debra Cowan
(Western)

After receiving menacing threats, Ivy Powell makes a proposition to a ruggedly handsome cowboy. But Ivy's first marriage destroyed her trust, and walking down the aisle again isn't something she'll undertake lightly.

THE FALL OF A SAINT
The Sinner and the Saint • by Christine Merrill
(Regency)

The honorable Duke of St. Aldric has earned his nickname, "The Saint." But when he embarks upon a marriage of convenience with Madeline Cranston, he starts indulging in the most *sinful* of thoughts....

SECRETS AT COURT
Royal Weddings • by Blythe Gifford
(Medieval)

Anne of Stamford's life at court becomes perilous when her mistress marries the king's son. Sir Nicholas Lovayne is determined to uncover hidden secrets, and Anne must do *anything* to throw him off!

AT THE HIGHWAYMAN'S PLEASURE
by Sarah Mallory
(Regency)

Ross Durden leads a double life: farmer by day, highwayman by night. Danger lurks around every corner, not least when he sets eyes on the beautiful daughter of his sworn enemy!

HCNM0214

REQUEST YOUR FREE BOOKS!

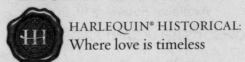

HARLEQUIN® HISTORICAL:
Where love is timeless

2 FREE NOVELS PLUS 2 FREE GIFTS!

3 1133 07259 8115

HH13R